# Staff of Chaos

## Book Three of the Lady of Death

J. F. Posthumus

Three Ravens Publishing
Chickamauga, GA USA

To Susan C.,
 an amazing seamstress and wonderful friend:

Thanks for everything you've done!

## Chapter One

The knock on the door did not awaken the sleeping infant. A good thing, too, because I would have been sorely tempted to turn whoever woke Lenore into a slug before pouring salt on them.

There is something for the adage 'let sleeping dogs lie'. It also applied to babies tenfold.

Opening the door, I took in the man standing on the other side of my threshold. He was the epitome of the 'tall, dark, and handsome' cliche.

His dark hair was curly, his brown eyes twinkled, and he even had a boyish smile. Throw in the fact he looked dashing in the leather bomber's jacket, t-shirt, and snug jeans, and he could have been the poster boy for any romance novel. I suspected even nuns would have drooled over his physique.

"No," I said, shutting the door in his face.

"He could just come in," Maekyl, my undead dragon said.

To be fair, Maekyl was technically a dragon leiche captured within a human's skull. He'd been a gift from my father upon my eighteenth birthday and a source of invaluable knowledge, as well as a never-ending supply of sarcasm and annoyance.

Like now, when the teeth of the skull he was trapped inside chattered in a mockery of laughter. He could show more of his astral form when he desired, but usually did not.

"I swear, if you wake Lenore-" I threatened, my eyes darting to the bassinet where my daughter was snoozing contentedly.

"That child would sleep through a volcano erupting as well as an earthquake," Maekyl said, rolling the small flames that served as his eyes. "Even if it happened at the same time. It doesn't change the fact he could still enter without an invitation."

I glowered at the skull.

Slamming the door had nothing to do with the man, but everything to do with what he brought with him.

"Every single time Raziel shows up it means something bad has happened and I'm going to either be a suspect, threatened by him, or both," I grumbled.

"Since when does the Lady of Death, a woman renowned for not only the terror she causes, but her fairness, worry about being threatened by the puny Angel of Mysteries?" Maekyl retorted. "Weren't you just reminiscing over how you were at liberty to go between this realm, my home realm, and the Fae Realm ruled by your mother? How you are going to rebuild your spy and information network courtesy of your childhood friend, Cildur Laedragryl? Does Raziel have the ability to even go between realms?

Damn it. I hated when he was being logical. Even worse: he was right.

"Fine. But I know I'm going to regret this," I said as I opened the door.

When I reopened the door, Raziel was still standing there, waiting patiently.

"I need your help," he declared immediately.

I slammed the door.

"Not going away," he said from the other side of the wooden obstruction.

I wondered briefly if escaping to my mother's realm, to ask Cildur how the network was coming along, was an option to avoid what was waiting outside my door.

Grumbling, I opened the door once again.

"Thank you," he said. If there was rancor or sarcasm in his demeanor, I couldn't detect it. I've detected those subtleties of his behaviors, and been the source of both, quite often in my three centuries of living, so I had that skill in spades.

"Come in, of your own free will," I invited, while stepping to the side.

"Even when you don't mean to, you bring sarcasm to the table." Raz observed in a weary manner.

That didn't keep him from entering my abode and finding a place to sit. His wings, no longer needing to be hidden, flared out before settling against the plush couch in my front living area.

"You presume it's not intentional," I countered, but added a smile. He responded with a smile of his own.

Poor fellow, he actually looked tired. The glowing aura that always surrounded him was dim, and his face looked like that of a worn and haggard mortal man.

"You've let your disguise slip, Angel of Mysteries." I commented. "You look like a mundane mortal that should be talking to a psychiatrist. Or, at least, a favorite bartender."

"If I could drink to any result, I'd likely be talking to whomever is running the bar at Fellhaven right now," Raz replied.

"It's a Saturday morning. Probably the blond witch they recently hired."

"She's pleasant," Raz observed. "But I am in need of help, not confession or sympathy."

That garnered my attention. Not to mention curiosity about what put him in this condition.

"What can I do to help an angel," I finally asked, after several moments of silence.

"Solve a murder, or, at the least, clear a mutual acquaintance of the mortal crime," Raz said, his voice heavy. His words came in a rapid cadence, which was far from the celestial servant's normal behavior.

"Was that painful to say?" I couldn't resist asking. "If so, was it the need for help or because of the mutual acquaintance?"

"Since I have to respond truthfully, it is both. The... restrictions of my position prevent me from exploring all possible avenues, and I would be distraught if Fi were held accountable for this crime that I am certain she is innocent of."

"Angel Raziel, you shock me," I teased. "I thought any mortal being condemned for crimes they didn't do made you sad."

Then my brain caught up with everything he'd said. Having an infant child, or any child for that matter, is not conducive to repeated nights of peaceful slumber. Or a clear mind working on anything besides the child's well-being.

"Did you say Fi? As in the half-demon female?"

He nodded, just once, keeping his eyes closed.

Glancing at Maekyl, who was remaining oddly silent, I settled into my rocking chair. An antique, it had become my most beloved piece of furniture since my daughter's birth. As I rocked, I considered our 'mutual' acquaintance.

Faith Ingrid Wells was the product of a demonic father and a human mother. Her father was, reportedly, the Right Hand of the Devil himself. Her mother was a librarian and worked at the Waynesboro library. Fi was just over twenty and barely knew how to use magic of any sort.

I'd seen her at Fellhaven on occasion.

I also avoided her every time I saw her.

Not because she was an unpleasant person. I simply had an aversion towards demons. Or rather, they didn't particularly like me. Apparently after you kill one of their most powerful assassins, the news gets around. There may have been more than one instance where I killed or maimed a demon. Or sent it back to whatever level of Hell from which it originated.

Demons tend to take that sort of thing personally. They also seem to have a great deal of animosity towards the person who did it. Perhaps a little fear, as well.

As previously mentioned, I avoided them, if at all possible. So far, I'd managed pretty well, since the only demon of this realm who approached me happened to be an outcast.

"Why would she matter to you?" I said, with more rancor than I intended.

Raziel stood, and some of the glow surrounding him became brighter. His eyes blazed. His voice was louder, more energized, when he spoke.

"Do not presume to understand all the workings of God and those servants entrusted with the Greater Plan!"

Okay, I'd managed to piss off an angel. Again. Not the smartest thing I've done, but neither is it the most foolish.

"I misspoke," I replied instantly. Granted, it was far from the "you dare speak to me, in my place, with such a tone" indignation that I was infamous for, especially during my heyday when I was first known as the Lady of Death.

Blame it on being a parent, or finally acknowledging a wider universe than my own little space.

"Let's try a different path," I said softly. "Why is she so important to you, Raz? Personally?"

The thing about angels is that they cannot lie. Certainly, it's within their ability to withhold information, and they do it better than any other beings. But, if you ask your questions correctly, they have little wiggle room. Usually.

"She just is," he replied. As an answer, it was incredibly lame. "Can that not be enough for you?"

"Nope," I retorted. "If you want my help, you tell me at least how much she means to you. I can figure out the most important facts from there. Or you can tell me why. Your choice."

There has rarely been a time when I've seen someone have so many emotions pass through their eyes. Rarer still have I ever felt guilty for putting someone into a corner. Oddly, I felt pretty guilty for cornering Raziel. Not enough to revoke my words, though.

Lenore shifted in her bed, and my eyes darted to where she slept. I breathed a sigh of relief when she remained silent. There was no missing Maekyl's eye roll, though. Those bright red lights that let everyone know when he was awake were hard to ignore.

The interlude gave Raziel time to come to a decision. He sank into the sofa cushions. His eyes remained fixed on the wall over my right shoulder.

"She is a... friend," he began.

"Aww," Maekyl crooned. "The angel has a crush on the halfling. Is this part of that millennia-old so-called 'fight' between good and evil that the mundanes argue over all the time?" He clacked his teeth together in an overly loud mockery of laughter. "Hoping to steal away a potential avatar? Or is she merely a favorite of Lucifer?"

Raziel jerked around to glare at the skull. Maekyl met the angel's furious gaze with one of pure indifference. I didn't think Raziel could destroy my undead dragon or the skull he resided within, but I didn't want to test that theory. Not when the result could be insanely catastrophic. Ignoring that, my daughter was sleeping not two feet from them.

"I tend to avoid demons and those with demonic blood," I interjected into their possible argument-slash-fight. "That includes those who have barely any inklings on how to use their magic. Faith is one of those beings." Raziel turned to look at me, instead of the skull. I continued speaking, in the hopes of keeping his attention. "So, you really like her and want this resolved so you can continue to court her for your own reasons."

"You avoid demons. The being who likely funds the yearly bonuses at Fellhaven with all the business she gives them," Raz said, and gave a dry chuckle. "Yes, you have the relevant facts of this matter."

"Point to you, sir," I replied with a smile. "Mark, however, is not your normal run-of-the-mill demon. From what I can tell, he doesn't even report to Lucifer. Mark raises many questions, for which I have zero answers."

Shaking my head, I ignored the new questions I had about Mark and Jen. There were already enough questions to do several hours worth of interrogation. If one so desired.

And wanted to pull out all their hair from the lack of answers you'd get from the owners of Fellhaven.

"Tell me everything. The murder, the scene, the name of the person killed." I paused, pursing my lips. "Are you requesting the assistance of a member of the Council? Or is this a personal request between you and me, as the Lady of Death?"

The former would mean I'd have to inform Sterling, my lover and the actual being in charge of the council that policed the magickal community. Since I had become the Speaker of the Council, I'd turned my position into one of actual power. Those within the community would come to me for help or assistance, and I'd recreated my own Court. Complete with a spymaster and Right Hand.

If Raz wanted this to be a personal matter and not a Council one, it meant I wasn't required to inform Sterling. He couldn't complain because I would be doing it as a personal favor between associates. One might even say friends. I'd reclaimed, if not in a formal fashion, my title as Lady of Death. Also, I would use my extensive personal resources. The biggest difference was I couldn't use the Council as leverage on anyone or anything.

Not that I'd need to. Being an infamous necromancer with little remorse worked as wonderful leverage, more often than not.

"I am asking as a personal favor from me to you, without it being a formal request before any Council," Raziel stated. His eyes darted around my living room, refusing to look me in the eyes as he spoke. "If it came out that I came to you, and requested your assistance, the consequences could be great."

"You are so going to owe me for this," I replied. Difficult didn't start to cover what he was requesting. "Let's start with the important information, like the corpse's name."

"Kevin Daniels." Raziel's eyes finally met mine as he spoke. "He was Fi's supervisor. The autopsy hasn't been completed yet, but the body was found with the throat slashed."

"You don't believe that to be the main cause of death?"

Raziel shook his head. "Most people aren't going to stand still for that sort of thing. The scene didn't show any sign of struggle, though there was enough evidence to point towards that being the COD."

It was a good thing I understood police lingo. Otherwise, I'd wonder what a c-o-d had to do with anything, instead of knowing it stood for 'cause of death'.

"So, what do you think the cause of death was?"

"I honestly don't know, Catherine," Raziel replied. "That's part of why I want you to investigate."

"Come now, Angel," Maekyl interjected. "Why not simply ask our Lady to summon the victim's spirit and question it? You'll have the answers you desire and can do your required job."

"Fi is already a suspect, due to having an argument with her former boss. Those in my Community are pressuring me to pin this murder on her. One way or another, due to the sole fact she is half demon."

"I didn't think angels were supposed to be prejudiced." I tried to keep the smugness from my voice. Really, I did.

Raziel gave a heavy sigh, leaned forward, and clasped his hands over his knees like a man with heavy, troubling thoughts.

"Those who spend centuries, sometimes even mere decades, upon the mortal plane, can often end up adopting too many mortal behaviors and characterizations." He paused, his eyes lifting to meet mine. "It is unseemly. We -angels, that is- return to Heaven to cleanse ourselves when we find ourselves becoming too much like the mundanes we're here to protect and help."

That was a pleasant thought. Nice to know angels could be complete assholes, also. Not.

"So, let me make sure I have this correct, so far. Kevin Daniels was Faith's supervisor. Whom she had an argument with, presumably a heated one, prior to his death." I paused and Raziel nodded. I continued. "That really isn't much of a report, Raz. You're going to have to fork over more information if you want me to help. Right now, all I could do is summon the spirit and quiz it and hope I ask the right questions."

He reached into a pocket and removed a small black notebook. Flipping it open, he began reading from it.

"Deceased was found this past Monday at ShenValley Shipping. Preliminary time of death is sometime last Saturday morning or late Friday night. COD is a laceration to the throat, cutting the jugular. Scene doesn't show signs of a struggle." He paused and held the notebook out for me to examine. "That said, ShenValley Shipping was bought out nearly a year ago by a company in Texas. What you may not know is that the company that purchased ShenValley is owned by the demon Abalam. He wanted to broaden his reach, and so left the local office open. His minions are the ones in charge there."

"Why are you being pressured to pin this on Faith?"

Raziel shook his head. "Prejudices, I suppose. Even though she has an alibi, my compatriots don't believe her. They are demanding I dig deeper, because lying and deception is part of her DNA." He lifted his head but remained hunched as he continued. "The demons there want her out. I noticed they weren't fond of the fact that though she was half demon, she didn't embrace that part of her."

"So, she's dealing with the same crap most people of two worlds go through. The demons don't like her because she doesn't embrace that part of her heritage. The angels don't like her because she *has* that heritage."

I gave a slight smile. "And I'll bet the mundanes don't like her because she's unusual and doesn't conform to their perverted view of 'normal'."

"Yes," he said.

"Where was the body found?" I asked.

"In a back room of their IT department. It's a small storage-like room. There's a generator in there, along with some shelves and networking equipment."

"Murder weapon was missing?" I asked. He nodded. "If Faith is a suspect, have you tried searching her residence or vehicle?"

"As far as the mundanes are concerned, her alibi checks out and she would be incapable of committing the murder," he stated. "Our peers aren't so trusting or wishing to believe her alibi. She had a... companion. A gremlin named Gaston who, from all reports, has been with her since infancy. It's believed he could have been ordered to kill Kevin for her."

"So, you can't get a search warrant for the person you're being told to pin this on. There's no other evidence, I presume, to link her to it, aside from an argument."

There was no question about it. I was thoroughly going to regret ever opening that door and letting Raziel into my home. Life. Everything.

The only problem with that was I have a reputation to uphold, and this was one of those requests I would have accepted even during my glory days centuries ago.

"Please tell me you have a personal number I can contact you at," I said with a sigh. He nodded and delved into another pocket to pull out a business card. It had a number written on it in black ink. I lifted a brow. "There is a caveat if I do this for you."

"And that is?"

"You cannot and will not dictate to me any methods I choose to take. I will do whatever it takes. You will not counter or take any actions against me for anything I do. Or don't do."

A frown grew on his face, and his eyes darkened. I remained calm, collected, and kept my gaze even with his.

"You came to me, Raziel, Angel of Mysteries," I said, my tone growing regal as I spoke. "My reign may be over, in the true sense used in bygone days, but I am, and will always be, the Lady of Death. If you don't agree to my terms, then we will part ways and our conversation will not be spoken of again."

"I don't like it," Raziel said slowly. "But I will agree to your terms."

"I will accept your word and not require blood and a signed contract," I teased. He started, but relaxed when he saw my smile. "Our conversations will remain between us." I glanced at Maekyl, and he gave a nod. Or at least what passed for one. "How do I contact Faith?"

"It may be best if you run into her at Fellhaven."

"Will she be there tonight?"

Fellhaven usually held concerts every Saturday night. Local area bands were hired to play, and they drew fairly decent crowds. Frequent patrons knew to either reserve a table or go early and stay late. They also knew to be sure to order plenty of food and beverages, or risk being evicted by their fellow patrons.

Officially, tying up a table or booth for hours was frowned on and disapproved of by the owners. Unofficially, unless the patron had a good reason, it was overlooked during the concerts. I suspected it had more to do with the fact the crowds were too large to truly keep on top of. As long as no fights or arguments broke out, the bouncers stayed at the doors.

It didn't hurt that Fellhaven dropped their prices during the events. Considering they were frequently at full capacity for their restaurant, I doubted they lost any money by dropping their menu prices by a few bucks.

"As far as I know, she will be," Raziel replied.

"Very well. I'll go tonight. My guards have been begging to watch Lenore, so they'll be thrilled at being asked to babysit." I made a face, because I preferred staying in and being a mom these days. "Do you wish to be here when I summon your victim's spirit?"

"I would prefer that, yes," Raziel replied.

"Isn't that sort of thing considered anathema to your type?" Maekyl interrupted. His eyes narrowed on the angel. "Angels typically prefer the souls and spirits to be at rest. Has that changed in the last few centuries? Or even the past year?"

"No, we don't like spirits to be brought back to this realm, or any other." Raziel's frown remained on his face, marring his otherwise handsome features. "However, these are extenuating circumstances. I knew that Catherine would need to bring Kevin Daniels' spirit back to this plane in order to question him. Simply because I do not approve, does not mean I don't see the necessity and accept it."

Maekyl snorted. "Always logical, aren't you?" He paused, then his red eyes twinkled with mischief. "Well, maybe not always. You did fall for a half-demon, after all. Or was that all part of the Greater Plan?"

Color crept along Raziel's cheeks, and his mouth opened and closed a few times. He looked a bit like a fish. It was rather cute, to be honest.

"You know, Maekyl, I've always heard of demons 'spreading their ill begotten seed' upon the mortal plane. Funny that I've never heard anything about angels doing the same," I commented, enjoying the chance to tease the angel sitting on my sofa.

"Didn't you know, darling Catherine? For all their bluster about 'free will', angels have very little of it. They can enjoy the intimate company of another being, of any race or species, but they can't reproduce without explicit permission from their lord and 'savior'." Maekyl's eyes never left Raziel, who was shifting very uncomfortably.

"Wow. That must really suck," I replied, tongue-in-cheek.

Maekyl snickered, and then burst out laughing. Raziel, however, looked decidedly uncomfortable. I took some pity on him. He was, after all, being very polite and hadn't threatened me with bodily harm. Yet.

"Right. No time like the present to garner some answers."

"Especially since Sterling isn't here to object," Maekyl muttered.

"Where is your... beau? If you don't mind my asking?"

"Probably doing Council stuff," I replied with a shrug.

To be honest, I wasn't entirely certain what Sterling did when he left. I didn't ask, because it didn't pertain to me, my job, or my duties as Speaker of the Council. Usually.

He had his businesses, and I had mine. Thankfully, we had finally come to a truce about my necromancy, so we still spent our nights entwined in each other's arms.

"Ah." Raz didn't seem to like my answer, but he didn't have to, either. "Very well. I will defer to your judgment on this."

"Wonderful. Now, let's get on with it before Sterling arrives and begins asking questions none of us want to answer."

# Chapter Two

If you're a social media witch, you're going to think you need a circle with symbols painted in the center to cast any spell. Also, a bunch of crystals or gems. Maybe even some herbs that are better used in a spaghetti sauce.

For the most part, you'd be wrong. Circles are great for certain spells. Such as summoning anything you don't want scampering away after you've called it to you. Namely anything living. Angels and demons? They require more, due to how powerful they are. Circles are not required for every single spell you want to perform.

Summoning a spirit into your living room doesn't require anything other than energy and the right words.

Oh, and the name of the person's spirit you want to summon. Otherwise, you're going to have a houseful of ghosts who want to chat with you. Often, they want you to 'right their wrongs' or send them on to Heaven.

No one ever thinks they're destined for an afterlife in Hell. Reincarnation is never an immediate thing, much to their dismay.

With a few words and a simple gesture, I could feel the magic pooling in the floor between myself and Raziel.

Maekyl snorted. I glanced at him and lifted a brow.

"You're copying Xantos and his movements." He sounded very smug informing me of that fact.

I shrugged. "He's a bad influence."

"Didn't he give you a robe as a birthing gift?" Maekyl asked with a sly twinkle in his undead eyes.

"Shut up," I snapped.

Xantos happened to be a dark-skinned elf, a docelfar, from the same realm that Maekyl's original physical form had come from. A greater necromancer than I, he was also a warlord with millennia of experience behind him. He was also rumored to be a demigod. I'd yet to ask him, despite spending some time in his expansive manor prior to Lenore's birth. He visited frequently, conversing with Maekyl, who had been a former nemesis and sometimes ally, as well as me.

There was also the fact Xantos and I had been lovers during my brief visit to his realm, but that was beside the point. At least in my opinion.

Thankfully, the appearance of Kevin's spirit kept Maekyl from teasing me further. As it was, Raziel was starting to look a bit annoyed.

Kevin Daniels' spirit looked around in confusion. He had frosted blonde hair styled into short spikes in the front, while the rest was swept back. I wasn't certain if he had been attempting some chic look, a beachcomber style, or 90's boy band. He wore a t-shirt under a button-up shirt with a beach design and cargo pants. I judged him to be in his late forties, maybe early fifties and someone who still tried to hit the gym daily.

The spirit of Kevin shimmered and flickered, as though there was a severe interference disrupting the signal. That was impossible, since summoning a spirit was simple and I had the energy to spare for such a spell.

And then the demon within my talisman began giggling. The giggles continued until all I heard was laughter. I reached up and stroked the talisman I constantly wore unless I was sleeping. I knew better than to wear the talisman while I slept. Casting spells while slumbering was not unheard of in the Magickal community, almost always to disastrous results.

Lenore had discovered it made for a wonderful pacifier and sucked on it constantly. Something the demon captured within it hated. He would coil up into the tiniest ball of energy possible and cower while the infant played with my talisman.

Kevin turned to face me, his eyes locking with mine and he smiled.

That's when I knew. Kevin had been a demon. Someone had killed a bloody demon by cutting his throat.

"You asshole," I stated, standing as I spoke. "Why didn't you tell me Kevin had been a demon?"

"Why does that make a difference?" Raziel asked.

"Why does it make a difference?" Maekyl cackled. "As if an angel wasn't aware of The Balance!"

"She isn't leaving it on this plane of existence," Raziel argued, before asking, "Is she? I thought she could send it back."

Maekyl cackled louder.

"Yes, I intend to send *him* back, and there should be no problem doing so," I rejoined. "But it's long been declared that raising dispelled demons from any of the Hells will throw the precious Balance into disarray, even to a cataclysmic level."

"That... is something of an exaggeration. To ward off beings from ever doing so," Raz admitted.

The skull began bouncing and flopping. Maekyl triumphantly cheered, over and over, repeatedly saying, "I knew it!"

"Why am I here?" Kevin's spirit groaned.

"Let's hope you aren't wrong on that, Raziel," I muttered before addressing the spirit. "You are here to answer questions. You cannot refuse me. You will answer truthfully and completely."

"No!" the spirit cried. "Let me go!"

"Ooooo, saucy!" Maekyl observed. "I like this one. Since the Balance thing was lies, can we keep him?"

"Not lies, just exaggeration." Raz insisted, but there was a more serious tone to his voice when he spoke.

"You are not saying a single word to remain on my pleasant side, Raziel," I snapped. "We will deal with this ghost, and then you can either be truthful with me, or I can call off our Deal."

Raziel, to his credit, remained silent.

"You will obey me," I snarled at the ghost, adding energy to my spell. The flickering slowed and then stopped. Kevin glared at me. My talisman was practically purring as I quelled the spirit before me. "You will answer my questions."

Damned if I didn't wish I could summon a pair of demonic canines like those Xantos had used to eat Nick's ghost. That had been an enjoyable evening, to say the least. I had been conversing with the ancient elf, and together we had questioned the ghost of my ex-boyfriend who had tried to kill me.

I really needed to find out how I could do that. It would have been helpful now.

Kevin snarled back but didn't argue this time. He shrugged his shoulders and leathery wings flared out. Maekyl whistled through his teeth.

"Such energy this one had," Maekyl breathed. "Do you think it was harvested when he died?"

"No," I replied thoughtfully. "At least, not by standard means."

"What are you thinking, my lady?" Maekyl replied, instantly alert and watching me.

Instead of answering my skull companion, I addressed the rather angry spirit. "Who killed you?"

"I do not know who killed me, for I didn't recognize them," Kevin replied in a sulking voice.

"Tell me how you were killed," I demanded.

"I had propped the door open to the back room to have a smoke. I saw a figure in dark clothes approaching. They held something up, and then I died." Kevin flexed his wings, his glower firmly in place.

"Why would someone wish you dead?" I asked, trying to get the important questions out of the way before he was jerked back to Hell.

A feral smile curled the ghost's lips. "I am a demon. I have a great many enemies."

"And you're going to have one more if you do not tell me everything," I countered, standing slowly. Magic curled around my hands, as I waited for his response.

"I am a keeper of the Staff of Chaos," Kevin said, anger lacing every word. "As such, I have many who desire what I possess, or the knowledge of where to locate it when not with me."

Oh. Fuck.

This just kept getting better and better. If by better one meant 'cataclysmic time bomb" better.

"Were you the current guardian prior to your death?"

"What do you think?" Kevin retorted, the constant flickering returning.

"I think I want an answer." I growled.

"Yes." Kevin hissed out the word. His smile grew cruel. He glanced over his shoulder before throwing his head back and howling. He looked back at me; the fury gone. "Someone was following me prior to my death. I don't know who, but I suspect it was to accomplish the goal of procuring the Staff." He glanced over his shoulder again and grimaced. "Find the Staff, lady. Keep it safe but be wary of the whispers."

There was another inhuman howl before his ghost vanished in a spray of silver sparks. I watched the last spark fall to the floor and die, without leaving a mark.

"You dare to come to me. To ask for my help. No, no, that isn't correct. You all but demanded my help but did not give all the information. You concealed details of grave importance, and now sit there stoically." I raised my eyes from the floor to meet Raziel's gaze. "You either have a great deal of audacity or are insanely stupid. I'm still trying to decide which it is."

Maekyl's teeth clacked together in his most annoying laugh. "My bet is on the latter. An intelligent being would know to not leave out imperative details with the person from which they're requesting help."

Raziel shook his wings and glared down at Maekyl. "I am operating within the limits of my position, no matter how much it irritates you or myself."

"You deliberately failed to inform her about Kevin being a demon, as well as the fact he was a guardian of the Staff of Chaos," Maekyl argued. "It leaves one to wonder what else you've neglected to mention."

"It's not a matter of neglect," Raziel insisted.

"I know you could have revealed his true identity," I began, piecing everything together as I spoke. "So there has to be a reason for it." I paused, then smiled a little. "Afraid I wouldn't summon him if I knew Kevin had been a demon?"

Guilt flashed through Raz's eyes. Nailed it.

"My, my. You must have it bad," I stated, not hiding my amusement. "Were you aware of Kevin being a guardian of the Staff? And that it has apparently been stolen?"

"The Staff and such articles are usually out of our jurisdiction," Raz replied. "He was but one of the guardians. I was not notified that it was, eh, Kevin's turn, before now."

"How much of the rumors surrounding the Staff are true?" I asked.

With luck, he would say none or very little was true. Unfortunately, I expected him to say 'all of it' was accurate.

"I don't know all the rumors," Raz admitted. "But if you refer to its ability to rend reality into chaos, open all doors, or drain life from its possessors, the answer is yes."

"Those would be the rumors I was referring to," I grumbled. "So, yet another ancient, powerful artifact goes missing, and I've got to find it before an Earth-shattering explosion occurs. That about sum it up?"

"I asked for your help in protecting an innocent," Raz replied.

Maekyl and I exchanged glances before rolling our eyes at the same time. I turned my attention back to Raziel. "I know you can't be this dense, so obviously it's deliberate on your part to remain free from retribution for my 'interfering' with whatever you and your fellow asshole angels have going on. The only way to prove Faith's innocence is by finding the person who killed Kevin."

"At least you won't be bored," Maekyl stated drolly. "I know how much you hate being bored."

"I have a daughter, a nabrasu, and a baby cloud dragon," I replied dryly. "Not to mention frequent requests of audiences by those who wish to have the Lady of Death, Speaker of the Council, resolve their problems. Boredom is not going to be a companion for a very long time."

Nabrasu were felines from Xantos's realm. Though mine was a sweet-tempered cub, it was more mischievous than a house cat. Such creatures fed off negative energy and produced positive. She was also currently curled up at Lenore's head, sleeping peacefully, along with the infant.

Arylla, my hatchling cloud dragon, was outside hunting at the moment. She and Kharzsa, the nabrasu, were best friends and usually kept each other company. It was an unusual friendship, but what in my life had ever been normal?

"I will consider the information you have provided. Certainly, the killer must be found and brought to justice. We will confer and plan again," Raziel declared, just before walking out of my house.

"Plan again, my ass," I grumbled to myself. "The louse planned to set me up from the moment his girlfriend became a part of a murder investigation."

"Are you going to investigate?"

"I can't expect Mister Angel of Mysteries or his cohorts to stop some idiot with the Staff of Chaos, can I?" I snapped back.

"No, no, nor could I anticipate said angel not presuming that to be your attitude," Maekyl countered.

"The fun part will be keeping it from Sterling. Livid won't describe his reaction if he finds out what happened."

"How do you plan on keeping it from lover boy?" Maekyl asked.

"I figure I can talk to Faith at Fellhaven and then start my investigation," I replied. Shrugging, I stood and stretched. "Maybe I'll get lucky, and something will pop up."

"Careful how you word things, my dear. That's usually how bad things tend to show up on your doorstep."

I gave Maekyl a sly smile. "Didn't something bad already show up on my doorstep?"

With that, I winked and walked into my kitchen to fix a snack. Drinking would come later.

Staff of Chaos

## Chapter Three

Not wanting to miss the opportunity, I called Fellhaven and talked to Jen, who ran the tavern with her partner. She assured me that Faith, or Fi, would be there whenever I managed to show up.

That gave me the rest of my day to arrange for Lenore's babysitting, go through the emails requiring my attention, and enjoy being a mother.

Thankfully most of what I did during a typical day could be done fairly easily. By the time the five guards who had protected me during my pregnancy showed up, everything I needed to complete was finished.

"Going to the tavern, Lady?" the lead guard, Zarkull, asked me. As a Magickal being, I saw him and the others in their actual garb. Which was matching sets of lightweight but strong ring and plate mail armor over casual breeches and tunics. Mundanes rarely saw past the glamor spell woven into the armor. Which, for this realm, which made the five beings appear human, decked out in leather pants, jackets, boots, t-shirts, and jeans. They even drove motorcycles.

"Yes, though I doubt I'll be out late," I replied. "Same arrangement as usual?"

"Of course. The fellows and I enjoy our time with the small lady," Zarkull reported. His expression was happy, even a bit eager. A relaxed smile stayed on his lips.

"I certainly couldn't ask for better guardians of her," I replied with an easy smile.

Zarkull and his merry band of guards had been sent by Xantos to protect me from a fae who had been keen on my death. Formerly part of Xantos's personal guards, the five elves had been sent on the ancient docelfar's orders. I had since been allowed to hire them as my own guards, complete with setting them up with their own housing.

He gave a deep bow, which was followed by identical maneuvers from the remaining male guards.

"Have a productive engagement, Lady. Give our regards to the keepers of Fellhaven," Zarkull said.

"I'll be sure to bring something back for you fellows," I replied.

"We would appreciate that, Lady," Krysdos stated, his orange eyes twinkling.

Giving my daughter a kiss on the forehead, I handed her over to Zarkull.

One would think the two women would have remained to care for Lenore, but these elves were docelfar. Such elves have hair and skin usually of the palest colors since they mostly dwelled underground.

The exceptions being the Dahnri, or albino of the Docelfar. Those born dahnri had dark to onyx black skin. Regardless, in their society, the men did all the labor-intensive work, including that of childcare, while the women typically ran everything.

Xantos, from what I'd learned in the past year, was one of the rare exceptions to the rule. Considering how powerful the ancient docelfar was, not to mention his vast holdings and wealth, I wasn't surprised.

One doesn't become an infamous warlord and necromancer by serving the daily meal to the women of the House. He seemed to have taken being born dahnri as a sign that he was born apart from those around him. So rare exceptions really seemed to cling to him.

Keeping with the traditionally cunning and deceptive ways of the docelfar, the dahnri were usually the members of a clan seen by outsiders. The purpose being to keep as much detail of their race hidden from the surface world. My bodyguards, by contrast, were not dahnri.

Alaria and Shyrrik, the female pair of bodyguards, accompanied me when I departed for Fellhaven.

Fellhaven was a restaurant and tavern located in Waynesboro, Virginia. Waynesboro happened to be located in the scenic Shenandoah Valley, where there was a lot of history, mountains, and ghosts from all the wars fought in the past centuries. Staunton, a neighboring city where I rented office space, proudly claimed the title of a historic city. Where Staunton had amazing architecture and touristy-type places, Waynesboro was a pale shadow of its past.

That said, Fellhaven was a popular eatery for those in the Magickal community. A proclaimed neutral territory by the owners, even enemies could go there. Anyone could pull up a seat at the bar, drink or eat, and no one ever worried about harm befalling them.

The owners, Mark and Jen, made certain everyone followed their rules. Those of the Magickal world mingled with mundanes, and none were the wiser.

The employees of the eatery were friendly, welcoming, and made certain the customers were kept fed and hydrated. They supported their community, and whenever they had a fundraiser, they didn't fail to meet their goal.

Oddly enough, each of my guards were on a first name basis with Mark, Jen, and their family. Getting answers of any sort from any of those beings, though, was like pulling teeth from an angry hippo.

A bubbly young mundane woman stood at the podium at the door greeting customers. She wore the usual tan khakis and black polo. The polo had the Fellhaven logo embroidered over her left breast. Her ebony hair was pulled back into a neat ponytail that bounced and swayed as she moved.

Before she could ask for our names, or if we had a reservation, Jen swept up to the door. The female half of the owners smiled brilliantly at me and my "companions".

Despite obviously working, she did not wear the typical uniform. She wore her usual shirt with her name embroidered below the logo, but instead of khakis she wore a black leather mini skirt. Thigh-high heeled boots hugged her legs. Considering the woman was trim, petite, and didn't look her age, let alone like she had birthed five children, I couldn't help but admire her choice of clothing.

"I presume you're torturing your husband tonight?" I joked. "Did he do something special? Or is he in the doghouse?"

"We've been busier than usual," Jen replied, an impish smile curving her lips. "And we're leaving the tavern in Chris's capable hands tomorrow. The younger offspring will be at the grandparents."

"Ahh," I replied, not needing it spelled out.

"Good to know you and your mate haven't changed any over the years," Alaria teased.

"We've merely found new methods of teasing and torturing each other," Jen quipped, dropping a wink.

That brought a laugh from all of us. One day I was going to find out the answers to everything. How were Jen and Mark so close to Xantos? How was Jen so skilled in not only Magick but necromancy? And those were only the top two that remained at the front of my brain whenever I saw them.

Also, how in the heck did an ifrit, which was a vengeance demon, and an elf, produce a son who was a dragon? A fact I'd only recently discovered while Chris assisted me in locating an artifact I'd been hired to retrieve.

There were, to my surprise and delight, seats available at the bar. The rest of the restaurant was filling up quickly. The stage was to the left and the night's band was currently setting everything up.

I didn't recognize the group, but that didn't mean much, since I wasn't heavy into the local music scene. Not to mention Mark and Jen brought in bands from all over Virginia. On rare occasions there would be a band from D.C. or Maryland.

Sliding onto one of the bar stools, my two guards remained near, but not hovering over my shoulders. That might work for some people, but it always annoyed the hell out of me.

"Someone I like told me I had to stay for you. So here I am, and here you are."

The voice wasn't one I recognized, but there weren't many people who would make that proclamation.

Turning around, I found Faith Wells standing behind me with a drink in hand. Judging by the bubbles and color, I suspected she was enjoying a soda. As for the alcoholic content, I couldn't tell. Yet.

Gesturing to the empty bar stool to my right, I invited her to join me. "That same someone, I suspect, also informed you why. Please, sit. The sooner we get this unpleasantness out of the way, the sooner we can enjoy the band."

As the young woman grimaced and did as suggested, I took a moment to study her.

Probably no older than twenty-two or twenty-three, she was slender and curvy with fairly straight auburn hair and blue-gray eyes. Her skin was pale, and I suspected it didn't take long for it to burn in the sunlight.

She wore a simple long black sweater-type dress over seamless leggings and ankle boots. A small purse hung from her right wrist.

Faith could easily be described as 'cute' or even 'pretty'. Despite the fact I knew she was half-demon, she didn't act like any I'd met, and I have met a lot of demons during my centuries of life.

"If you're done assessing my appearance and judging my life, I'd like to get to the questions," she declared.

"Oh, if I wanted to judge your life, I could do it fairly easily," I retorted, though there was laughter in my voice. "I'm going to presume you're aware of who I am and my position in our community."

"Sure, but if you expect me to be intimidated or impressed?" She gave a snort before continuing. "Holiday meals mean my dad's boss is coming to visit. Old 'Scratch' sitting at the table means you learn not to care about anyone on this plane of existence judging anything."

"No wonder he likes you," I replied, amused. "Unless the Laws have changed, I'm guessing you spent many holidays visiting your father on another plane or realm."

"Obviously," she said dryly. She toyed with the straw in her drink, and I caught a whiff of the alcohol in the beverage.

Whoever had made her drink, had made it a double.

Fi stretched her curvy figure and looked at me with a coquettish expression. "So here I am, looking at a pretty lady, and we decide on a pissing contest. Not the best way to spend an evening in lovely company." She gestured to the stage. "There's already entertainment at hand, Ms. Lady of Death, and I'd like my time spent watching or enjoying it instead of being the attraction for those around us. Can we get to your questions?"

Perhaps she was more like the other demons than I'd originally thought. Or maybe I was just cranky because I was here, away from Lenore, on business and not fun.

"Very well. Tell me what happened the Friday before Kevin's corpse was discovered."

"I had a disagreement with Kevin. I wanted to take a week off, but he was giving me a rough time about it." She shrugged and took another pull from her glass. "I had the vacation time, but he was an asshole. Didn't want anyone taking time off if he could prevent it. Unless, of course, you were kissing his ass, or it benefited him in some way."

"What happened?" I nudged.

"He finally gave in," she grumbled. "But it was obvious to my entire department that we'd argued, and he was pissed about it."

"What time did you leave?"

"I left at the same time everyone else on my shift left, which was five o'clock." She glowered at me, adding, "He was alive and fuming in his office when I left, also."

"I know, I know. You've already been asked these questions. But I need to hear the answers from you." I shrugged. "You want to complain to someone, take it up with the one who said to talk to me."

Her features softened slightly, and she stopped bristling. "I may just do that."

"Was Kevin acting odd in the days or weeks leading up to that weekend?"

Faith shook her head. "No. At least, not that I noticed. If anyone else did, they didn't mention it to me."

"Were you part of the gossip vine there?" I asked. She glanced at me, startled. "Every place where beings convene, gossip is spoken and spread. What you hear simply depends on how ingrained you are into the web. Or vine. Or whatever you want to call it."

"I'm pretty into it," Faith replied, thoughtfully. "But nothing was mentioned about Kevin acting odd or weird."

"Did anyone new start there that week or even within the month? Someone who may have asked a lot of questions about him?"

Another shake of Faith's head.

"Did you see any strangers or anyone who seemed out of place around there?"

"Nope. I pretty much did my job, chatted with my coworkers both within my department and outside it, and left. Sometimes I'd go out to lunch with some of the other girls or we'd meet here for drinks. But that's about it."

"What do you know about the Staff of Chaos?" I asked, keeping my voice low.

Faith furrowed her brow and sat on the bar stool sucking soda up through her straw. She remained that way for several long moments.

Finally, she sat the glass on the bar. "Not a lot. Basic knowledge on what it does. Never could figure out why someone would want to make an object that could destroy everything. Rather crazy, isn't it?"

"Ever heard of nuclear weapons? Bio-warfare?" I asked. She opened her mouth and then snapped it shut. "It isn't just a mundane thing. Originally, the Staff wasn't as blood thirsty or devastating to use. A few decades after its creation, the Staff was broken during a battle, and that's when the chaos began."

"So, it really does feed off the life force of the user? Can open doors to all the realms and bring down the Veils?" she asked. I nodded. Her face paled, and she blew out a breath that wasn't quite a whistle. "You'd have to be insane to even want to use something like that."

"Insane by who's definition?" I countered. "Fae are power hungry and vicious beings, yet by a human's definition, they are often 'insane' due to their desires and methods."

"You have a point, there," Fi conceded. "No lack of blind ambition or anger across the realms, or even here."

She cast her eyes toward the people in the restaurant, gathered at the bar, and on their way towards the stage.

"There's probably at least one being here that would give everyone else's life to have that level of power for even one minute," she suggested.

"At least," I agreed.

That look was cast at me again. She'd probably raised the heart rate of many a mundane with that look. It would be easy to get excited, considering her looks and the toxic pheromones that her demon half produced, but I wasn't buying.

"From what I've heard, you might have been that way a few centuries ago," Fi cooed. "Gotta love a babe with the balls to put all the men to shame."

"How do you know I'm still not?"

The longer I talked with Faith, the more I had to wonder if Raziel had succumbed to her pheromones, or if there was some other attraction between them. I needed to ask Maekyl if angels were even susceptible to demonic pheromones. Then again, maybe I could ask Mark or Jen. Provided I could grab one or the other, considering how busy this place was tonight.

Fi let out a satisfied purr and leaned closer.

"I don't. But I want to find out."

"Well, that answers that question," I said, lifting a brow at her attempt at seduction. "Is that your drink talking or are you really this naive?"

"Naive? Maybe I know just what it would mean," she countered, with no hostility or regret. "Not my fault you don't get many who realize all that you are... Lady."

It took my mind a moment to realize she hadn't said that last word in English, American or otherwise. She'd called me "Lady" in the native tongue spoken in the land I had earned my title.

The satisfied smile and twinkle in Fi's eyes let me know I had reacted outwardly enough for her to detect it. I forced down the impulse to change my expression and body language. Instead, I leaned in and gave a smile of my own.

"Thank you for answering any questions I had about you, Fi," I replied. For a bonus, I dropped a wink.

My guards stood at once, as if I'd ordered them to. Of course, I had, gesturing under the table where Fi couldn't have seen me. But it had the desired dramatic effect. She was startled just a bit. Her demeanor shifted as she sat back.

"Enjoy the music," I invited. "Along with anyone else in the crowd. My evening is already booked. There's an angel who needs to hear my opinion of you."

The bewildered look on her face would have to do for satisfaction. At the least, it was the quickest opening to leave. One that I took advantage of and left in search of the tavern owners.

Not seeing either Jen or Mark on the floor or near the bar, I sighed. *Guess talking to them was going to be a bust*, I thought as we neared the front.

"What next, Lady?" Alaria asked quietly.

I shouldn't have been able to hear her, as the band had begun their first song. Yet, I did.

Magick was a lovely thing, and my guards used it with a finesse so few possessed anymore.

"Leaving us so soon?" Jen asked, a smile on her lips. Her eyes traveled over my shoulder to the bar. "Not staying for the band?"

"Actually, I was hoping to talk to you or Mark before deciding on that," I replied.

Her eyes returned to mine, and she tipped her head to the side. "We'll never hear each other in this room. Come with me. Would you like anything to eat or drink?" She paused, a frown pulling at her lips. "Were you even asked while at the bar?"

"No, I was too engaged in conversation for any of the staff to intervene on that count," I said. "Don't hold it against anyone."

"As long as that's the only reason," she replied, moving past the doors to the private rooms. "Would you like a drink, at least?"

She paused in front of the wall at the end of the hallway. I was intrigued and nodded. The hallway had only a handful of doors. Those doors opened into the private rooms, the restrooms, and I suspected an entrance into the kitchen.

"I'm feeling adventurous. Surprise me with whatever delectable beverage you or Mark would suggest tonight."

Jen gave a smirk and turned to the right and traced an intricate design onto the wall. The outline of a narrow door appeared, shimmering atop the wallpaper. Opening the door, an office was revealed.

She gestured for me to enter. My guards took positions in the hallway to look as if they were waiting for someone, or a to-go order.

As I stepped inside, I was reminded somewhat of Xantos's office, when I visited his realm. The paneling was dark wood with a silvery-gray trim. In one corner of the office were filing cabinets, neatly labeled in a shorthand I didn't recognize. A corner office desk made of mahogany sat at the back of the room. There was a desktop, as well as a laptop. A black leather ledger sat between the electronics. Two chairs sat opposite the desk.

There were differences, though. Electricity lit the office, instead of flames and crystals. The desk wasn't as ancient or hand-carved, and of course, the computers.

The walls, though, were decorated with weaponry and two paintings. These paintings, though, were far different from those that graced the walls of the restaurant.

One painting was of a medieval town or city, with buildings made of wood and stone. Elves, humans, and other races filled the streets. They were wearing armor, gowns, or other intricately sewn garments. I could almost hear the people talking, merchants hawking their wares, and the other sounds that went with a medieval life.

It brought back memories, but nothing in this world or my mother's was as intriguing as this painting. That, in itself, was curious, since my mother was a very literal fairy queen, and her realm was separate from that of the mundane.

Realizing I was holding my breath, I let it out slowly and discovered I'd moved closer to the artwork. The painting was signed 'Llaria Dryzmella' and in a delicate script was the word 'Fellhaven'.

The other painting was just as lifelike, although this one was of a tavern in the same setting. Barmaids served tables or took orders from all manner of beings. The tables were wood, stained from food, beverage, and who knew what else. There was also a bar, behind which stood a bald man with tattoos. None of which I recognized. All of those beings wore similar garments as those in the Fellhaven painting.

The central part of that painting had a full table of patrons. An elf with silvery-blonde hair sat between two men with long, dark curly hair. One man, oddly enough, had violet eyes. Considering how rare true violet eyes were in this realm, I wondered if perhaps such was more common in the realm where this trio had been painted. Another woman with auburn hair sat beside the violet-eyed male and the last table mate. That last one also had dark hair, but he wore a solemn expression. Though somehow Llaria, who had also signed this painting, managed to capture a merriment in the man's eyes that wasn't seen on his face.

"Now you know where the name came from," the male owner's voice said from over my left shoulder.

I jumped. I couldn't help it. I'd been mesmerized by the paintings. Turning to him, I smiled and said, "Indeed, and with that, comes even more questions that I'll bet you won't answer."

Mark smiled, an impish twinkle in his eyes. Jen laughed and stepped into the office, closing the door behind her. Oddly enough, the room was silent aside from the sounds from us. So, this room was soundproofed. Yet another similarity between this office and the one Xantos used.

So. Many. Questions.

"Have a seat, enjoy a drink on the house, and tell us what you wanted to discuss," Mark invited. It was then I noticed he was holding glasses in both hands. He held one out to me, which I accepted with a smile.

Taking two steps forward, I paused and suddenly realized that my guards were not in the office with us. Turning, I looked from Mark to Jen with raised brows.

"How in all the realms did you convince Alaria and Shyrrik to remain outside this room?"

"Simple," Jen said, sweeping past me. Sliding onto the edge of the desk, she crossed her legs without flashing anyone. I had to give it to her, she had skills. That was a move most people wouldn't dare while wearing a skin-tight leather miniskirt. "They know we're not going to break our own rules, and you aren't going to break them, either. They'll remain outside unobtrusively, so as to not have people wondering why they're protecting a wall."

"Fair enough," I said, taking a sip of the beverage. Fruity with the perfect combination of sweet and tart, I took a longer pull. There was a reason they kept alcohol on hand when talking to their patrons.

It wasn't just because it loosened tongues.

Mark moved behind the desk and settled into the chair. Jen remained perched on the desk, so I moved the chair on her left back a bit before sitting.

Power plays and more, I thought in amusement.

There was zero doubt that they changed their positions as the need dictated.

"Just out of curiosity, but where do you take the mundanes for private discussions?" I asked.

"The storage room," Jen replied with a grin. "Joking! I'm joking! We actually pull them into the smallest private room for those chats."

Chuckling, I turned to the task at hand. "I was asked to look into the murder at ShenValley Shipping." My gaze drifted to Mark. "I had a question regarding demons and their, ahem, pheromones." Pausing, I waited until Mark gave a nod before continuing. "Are angels susceptible to such? Or is Raziel, the illustrious Angel of Mysteries simply besotted with Faith?"

"Nah, they aren't affected. He's just a sucker for a redhead," Mark answered. He nodded towards Jen's long mane. "Reds have a charm that exceeds realms and planes."

"Poor guy," I muttered. "Has anyone told him how she'll hit on anyone who interests her? I almost feel like he needs to be warned."

"It's likely that her weaknesses attract him as much as her other, more tangible assets," he suggested. "Regardless, you quizzed her. Did it do any good?"

"No, not that I expected it would," I replied honestly. "For a demon, she seems to have been taught only by succubi. They're nothing to sniff at, but they're also at the bottom of the totem pole when it comes to power."

Their lack of power was one reason they were allowed to inhabit this realm so readily and procreate so easily. Sure, it allowed Hell to have a "stronger" foothold on this plane, but compared to the stronger, more powerful demons? They were tiny house cat kittens compared to a three hundred pound pissed off tiger.

Mark shrugged.

"I'm sure she's been around someone's version of worse, I've met her father. But she doesn't seem to be particularly malicious. Far as I can see, she isn't even trying to cause trouble for anyone. She craves being wanted or needed. A trait shared by many races."

"No, she didn't come across as malicious," I admitted. "She needs to pick her targets better, though, since most should know I've never been free with my affections."

"Fi is young and drawn to powerful beings. She's still a baby, despite being an adult in the eyes of the mundanes." Jen paused, and dropped a wink as she added, "But we're getting off topic. Obviously, the girl wouldn't know anything about the Staff of Chaos. What do you want to know?"

My jaw nearly hit the floor. "How...? Is there anything you two don't know?"

Jen giggled, but Mark merely smiled.

"I want your spy network," I grumbled.

"You need to expand your horizons first," Mark replied. "Stop thinking in terms of this place."

"The short version is you can't have it, but you can always ask to use it," Jen teased.

"I would be honored if you would allow me use of your network," I said formally.

I was the Lady of Death. I was *not* a fool. Their network was one worth envying.

"Prettily spoken, and that may occasionally grant you access," Mark replied, "But not this time."

"You can't go to a garden and constantly take without feeding something back in. Otherwise, it grows barren, tough, and useless," added Jen.

Of course. I had fallen into the folly of this century. Expecting always, offering nothing.

"I am pursuing the Staff of Chaos, to prevent the undoing of everything. It was stolen by a demon, who knew of the keeper's charge. I offer any other knowledge garnered in this pursuit, now or in the future, in exchange for use of your network," I said.

"That is a fair exchange," Jen answered, "You may, of course, have use of our network.

"Thank you," I said, bowing my head to them in respect.

"You're welcome," Mark replied cheerfully. "Now, is there anything you want to know about the Staff of Chaos?"

"Has there been any talk about the Staff lately? Kevin Daniels had the Staff prior to his death. He was supposedly being followed prior to his death." Rambling was a horrible thing, but sometimes necessary to figure out the proper questions to ask. "Did he come in here any time leading up to his death?"

"Those are not questions about the Staff itself," Jen observed. She shifted slightly on the desk. "The only talk that I've heard about was between Raz, Gabriel, Michael, and a few others. They were discussing the Staff being missing. Not all of them were content with Fi's alibi."

"Who was content?"

Jen smirked. "It's a good thing we don't keep a tab on all the information we exchange with you. Our bookkeeper would throw a fit."

"You hold out plenty when you feel it's in your better interests," I countered. "This mess concerns us all."

She continued "The three archangels. I don't remember the names of the other idiots who were here. They don't typically show up, preferring the 'ritzier' places."

"Kushiel, Daniel, and Phanuel," Mark stated, leaning back in his chair. "They didn't pay, or tip, so she ignored them."

"Uriel skipped the meeting, but he's a critic of everything," added Jen.

"The general flow of the conversation gave the impression that the Staff is something that is universally respected, if not outright feared. Not many beings could be trusted to use it or confine it. The damage it takes on whomever wields it is ignored because of the overwhelming power that can be manipulated with the

Staff," Mark explained. "One of the old gods made it to spite everyone, especially Lucifer and his almighty parent. Lucifer seems to fear it the most, since he contained it and created the security for its possession. Until it's secure, he's likely going to get more, well, bothersome."

I interjected with "What about 'whispers' that go with it? It was mentioned to be wary of them, should I locate it."

And what in the Hells had Kevin meant by 'keep it safe'? So far, nothing was appearing to be safe from prying fools intent on willful destruction by the use of powerful magickal artifacts.

"The Staff wants to be used, it wants to undo everything," Jen replied. "That's not just a rumor to scare anyone. What isn't well known is that Lucifer put the life draining curse on the Staff. He wanted to make sure anyone crazed enough to use the damned thing would most likely die before real damage could be made."

"I'm expecting an 'unless' in this story," I interrupted.

"There is and it's a doozy," Mark rejoined. "*Unless* a being is knowledgeable enough to undo something, or change something directly, *before* the toll of the Staff is exacted on the user."

"So if a being knows exactly how to, say, cause a planet to implode unexpectedly? They can set it in motion and their death won't stop it," Jen warned. "That death will, in fact, help power the spell to completion."

"Well, that's a lovely thought." Didn't this job just keep improving? I needed a new line of work. "Let's hope whoever has this thing doesn't know how to use it." The pair nodded. "On that same subject, Kevin supposedly thought he was being followed. Did he come here prior to his death?"

"I'm not going to ask how you know all this," Jen said slowly. "I can guess, and if I'm right, you should know speaking to the ghost of a demon isn't really a wise habit to have in this realm. As for Kevin, he came by a few times, but he never acted unusual or as though something was wrong." She swiveled on the desk, turning to look at her husband. "Did you notice anything?"

"Nothing unusual," Mark said thoughtfully. He turned to me. "We'll ask Chris and Curt. If anyone noticed anything, it would be one of those two."

"Thanks. Do you know where he kept the Staff?"

They shook their heads.

"You'll have to ask someone else that one," Mark said, regretfully. "How are you going to keep Sterling from finding out about all this?"

"Of course you can sense when I'm holding back information from anyone. Does it smell different when it's a lover versus a relative?" Mark only replied with a wink and a smirk, so I went on. "I'm sure he'll figure it out. I'll just say I'm helping Faith, which isn't exactly a lie."

"Not exactly the truth either," Jen said with a laugh. "We'll ask around and let you know what we find out."

"You could also check out ShenValley Shipping," Mark suggested thoughtfully. "I'm sure you aren't on the best terms with demons, but there's no denying your skill at retrieving valuable, and dangerous, artifacts. If they want the Staff back, you'll be their best option. Probably why they came to you."

"Thank you," I said, uncertainly. "I'll check out ShenValley Shipping on Monday." I paused, before asking, "Could I request an appetizer plate or two to take home?"

Mark grinned as he stood. "The platters should be waiting for you at the bar. Along with a couple entrees and a traveler for you."

"Always three steps ahead, aren't you?"

The pair laughed.

"Not always," they said simultaneously.

Jen slid from the desk as Mark walked around to meet her. I glanced around the room one last time, my gaze settling on the paintings. As the pair moved to the door,

I followed, envious of the art they kept hidden away in their office.

Outside the hidden room, Mark gave Jen a brief kiss before vanishing through the doors to our right. As I suspected, it led into the kitchen. Jen led me to the front room, where the music was pounding. My guards fell into step behind us. With a wave, Jen vanished into the thick crowd of patrons, slipping through them with ease.

I followed behind her, heading towards the bar, not surprised at how quickly Jen vanished. There was standing room only in the restaurant as the band played classic rock covers. There was a single seat open at the bar due to a small card that said "reserved" on it. I stood beside it, thankful for the available spot.

The bartender, a petite blonde who moved with a graceful ease, slid from patron to patron without missing a beat or spilling a drop from the glasses she served.

"I'm Lena, your bartender for the night," the young woman said as she slid in front of me. A brilliant smile shone on her face and her eyes twinkled with merriment. "Oh, hello, Catherine! What can I get you?"

"Pleasure to see you, again," I replied. "Mark said there should be some platters and entrees for me? A take-out order placed earlier?"

Acknowledgement flashed through Lena's eyes. "I have them right here," she stated, disappearing behind the bar. It wasn't difficult since she was five foot nothing and probably barely taller than the bar itself. When she popped back up, she had several bags in hand. "Here you are."

Five minutes later, my tab had been paid and we were heading out of the eatery.

"We aren't staying for the band?" Alaria asked, looking towards the stage.

Glancing at her, she was staring longingly towards the band. "I'm not, but you can if you wish,' I said.

"No, we will accompany you to your abode," Shyrrik said with a sigh.

Guess she was also wishing to stay. "You two take this whole 'sworn to protect' thing to an unnecessary extreme."

Both women snorted.

"Fine, fine, be that way. At least your consolation prize is their food."

"'Tis a fair trade," Shyrrik declared.

I chuckled as I tucked the food into my car. The ladies still drove motorcycles, so by the time I was pulling out, they were following close behind. Which was perfect because it allowed me to blast my favorite songs on the way home.

## Chapter Four

Docelfar are known for many things. Fierce warriors, cunning minds, devotion to what they hold important. A matriarchal society with spider-loving deities. My guards wear their chain and studded leather armor like most mundanes wear street clothes.

One does not get "babysitters" from their reputations or legends.

Zarkull held my darling child on his lap. He was surrounded by every toy in the house.

Every. Single. Toy. In. The. House.

Before Zarkull and Lenore were nine figurines. My odd collection of comic book heroes, historical figures, and Dia De Los Muertos mariachi band apparently represented six females and three males. All the dragon toys, statuettes, chess pieces, and such, that I had obtained over centuries surrounded the nine.

My actual, living baby dragon, Arylla, faced the nine figures as if she was the main antagonist. Each and every other toy in the household had been used to create a makeshift mountain range and village dwellings.

All except for the small infant xylophone that Lenore had received for a holiday gift. That was being played by Wyrren. Somehow, he was playing an ominous tune on the tiny instrument while looking intently at the toys. Krysdos moved two of the six female figurines closer to Arylla, who sat, Sphinx-like, glaring at the approaching mariachi singer and Cleopatra.

"Merril and Shyndra approached the gold dragon that had gone mad and declared war on all beings who walked on two legs in Nangolthia," Zarkull said in a deep narrative tone. "As they drew closer, Laith raised all of the dead surrounding the mad ruler! The dragon recoiled-" Arylla obediently hissed and arched back, "giving Wolfwood, Paige, and Caliban the opportunity to strike!"

Arylla flopped over, meowing pitifully in her faux death. Krysdos charged at her with three other figurines, wiggling them around her.

The xylophone music became triumphant.

Lenore squealed in delight.

Suddenly, the men noticed we had gotten home.

"Lady!" Zarkull said loudly.

The other two men bolted upright and stood at attention. Lenore reached for the now discarded figures and fussed before she noticed I was in the room. She squealed again and wriggled in Zarkul's lap. Babbling excitedly, she held her hands out, fingers opening and closing. An obvious indication she wanted Mommy.

"Don't stop on my account," I said, carefully tiptoeing around the figures. Reaching down, I took my daughter as Zarkull lifted her up. "I kinda want to know what happens next. Did the adventurers return to the local tavern and celebrate? Or was there another dragon waiting to ambush them on their way out?"

"We will finish the tale another night," Zurkell offered. "Now that you are home, she won't pay attention to the story. She should hear the end as well."

"Most definitely." I gave her a kiss before crossing carefully to the rocker and settling into it.

Arylla hopped up and trotted over to the rocker before flying up to curl around my shoulders. Lenore grabbed her tail and promptly began sucking it.

Shaking my head, I gently tugged the tail from her mouth and replaced it with the pacifier attached to her onesie.

"Did you have a successful trip, milady?" Krysdos asked as the three men began picking up the toys.

"Not as successful as I'd hoped," I replied honestly, before giving them a recap of my trip to Fellhaven. Once finished, I added, "I'll visit ShenValley Shipping on Monday and begin the search there. That will give me tomorrow to find out who is in charge of the local office."

"Inform us of when you plan on visiting there," Zarkull stated, looking up with a serious expression. "We will accompany you."

Big surprise there. "Of course. I do have a question for you and the others, though. Have any of you heard of an artist named Llaria Dryzmella?"

"Dryzmella." Wyrren pronounced it as Drizz-mella, which was different from what I had. "There is an artist from our home realm with that name. She paints amazing portraits."

"Llaria is in 'high demand', as the humans here say," added Krysdos.

"Why do you ask, Lady?" inquired Zarkull.

"There are two breathtaking and captivating portraits in Mark and Jen's office that are signed by an artist with that name. One is labeled 'Fellhaven' and the other 'The Bartered Soul'. Mark said the city is where the name of their restaurant came from." Glancing down at Lenore I smiled at her as she kept trying to catch Arylla's twitching tail. I was thankful the two enjoyed playing with each other. "The paintings were incredibly lifelike. I've never seen anything like them before, and I doubt I will again."

The male guards exchanged a look with the females. The two women smirked.

"I doubt Xantos is unaware that the portrait of the Bartered Soul is in their office," Shyrrik said.

"Yet another test of loyalty," grumbled Zurkell. "As though we had not taken the mantle of the Lady's security."

"The portrait of the Seventeenth District's most notorious tavern belonged to Xantos," explained Alaria. "It was a piece stolen from his favorite competitor. In the final week before you and he came to terms for our employment, he instructed us to be wary for that portrait. It had 'disappeared from the office' and he desired its return."

"Jen and Mark stole it from Xantos?" I asked, stifling laughter as I did.

"We know not," confessed Zurkell. "But considering that he has been in their office many times, no doubt more since we left, then we have to question if he expects one of us to report the painting's current location."

"Despite the fact that he obviously knows where it is," I surmised. "Do you plan to tell him?"

"No," they all said.

"None of us witnessed the portrait," Alaria proclaimed, with a smug expression on her face.

I mulled over that for a bit. "Logical. Do you think it's possible that Mark and Jen are from Fellhaven? How else would they know of the city? It makes little sense to name an establishment about a city you've never visited."

"It is certainly plausible," Zurkell agreed.

"You expect an elf and her demon lover to come from some other realm?" Maekyl cackled.

"There are five such elves, docelfar to be exact, who did just that, in my living room," I replied. "Why couldn't there be others?"

Maekyl snorted. "They were sent here originally by Xantos. Few would come on their own free will when they dwell in a realm where magic is strong and as common as the air you breathe." He paused, clacked his teeth together once, then asked, "Why don't you just ask them?"

"As though they'd actually answer that question," I muttered.

"Is 'pregnancy brain' still affecting you? Do you think you're capable of searching for a Staff capable of destroying the realms, since you obviously aren't putting the clues in front of you together," Maekyl said with not a little snark.

My head snapped up as I glowered at the skull. With the anger, though, came clarity and I realized I really hadn't been thinking about any of it clearly.

Clue one: Jen was very close to Xantos. Mark was close, but more in a son-in-law way. Not only were they close, but Jen adored him in a familial manner.

Clue two: Jen had been given a nabrasu, a creature that originated in Xantos's realm. She was knowledgeable in caring for them, to the point of having a mated pair in her own home.

Clue three: Fellhaven was a city the restaurant was named after.

Clue four: the artist was obviously famous and also from Xantos's realm, and the proprietors of the eatery had not one but two of her paintings from his world.

There was also the fact that my guards were on a first name basis and friendly terms with Mark and Jen. They knew each other too well to simply be guards Xantos brought along on occasion.

"Well, damn," I said after a few silent moments. "I would love to know the story behind why they came here to this realm."

"We only know scarce details," Shyrrik confessed.

"Scarce details are more interesting than none," I suggested.

After all, who didn't like good gossip?

Expressions were exchanged between my guards, and I wondered what unsaid words were being spoken between them. If I hadn't known they were close before, this would have been a dead giveaway. Even to someone with 'pregnancy brain'.

"The names they go by now are ones that fit in with this world," Alaria began. "We saw them while working for Xantos. I'm sure you're aware Jen knows necromancy." I nodded, having seen her command dead faerie dragons just months earlier while still pregnant with Lenore. The docelfar woman smiled and continued. "She was taught by Xantos and was a favored student. There was a lot of discussion among us guards. Not just us, mind you, but all of the personal guards, because Xantos rarely teaches anyone not of his blood."

"Jen was allowed more freedom than most in his employ," Shyrrik added. "Her mother worked for Xantos until her death. It wasn't long after that Jen appeared in his manor, being taught by him. That, alone, was cause for gossip, even if it was spoken in whispers far from his prying ears."

"More like his scrying pool," Zarkull commented. There were nods from all the guards in mutual agreement. "Mark is an ifrit, from one of the planes of hell in our realm. They are vengeance demons. Powerful, cruel creatures, and Mark was one Xantos summoned frequently."

"If you want to know how their initial meeting went, you'll need to talk to them," Wyrren said with a laugh. "Our lady proprietor certainly made an impression with her ifrit, as well as Lord Xantos."

"With all of Fellhaven, to be honest," Alaria added, also laughing. "I don't believe the tongues stopped wagging for a year, which was impressive for a city that thrives upon chaos, deception, and disorder. To say nothing of how there is always someone trying to become the 'talk of the week'. Everyone in the city is always trying to achieve something better, fancier, or more exciting than everyone else."

"I'm definitely going to have to ask them about that," I stated.

"You do that," Krysdos said encouragingly. "The lady discovered how to summon Mark, and they met frequently at our lord's manor. The first time was... interesting. After that, Xantos watched Jen closer and realized there was more than mere infatuation between them."

"Though beings in our world are often open-minded towards inter-racial pairings, demons are not welcomed in any fashion," Shyrrik added. "However it came about, Mark and Jen chose to come to this realm. Fellhaven was backed by Xantos. He is as aware of what they do now, as he was when they lived in his realm."

"So, prejudices are as prevalent there as they are in this realm?" I asked.

"Anywhere there are humans, fear, or envy... prejudice follows," Zurkell declared, his expression dour.

I couldn't argue that, so I nodded somberly.

"Let me guess, you all were assigned to protect Mark, Jen, or both at some point?" I asked, a sly smile on my face.

The guards all laughed heartily. Lenore giggled and cooed, kicking her legs happily.

"We weren't sent to protect them, per say," Alaria said, grinning. "We were sent to keep everyone else safe while Jen was pregnant with her first child."

"She was a bit... wild? We'll go with wild," Shyrrik said, receiving nods from the others as she spoke. "Mark reached out to Xantos, who sent us to help him with his mate. Despite her chaotic tendencies, it was greatly enjoyable."

"There was never a dull moment," Wyrren added, chuckling. "The lady kept us on our toes."

We were still laughing at Wyrren's comment when the door opened, and Sterling stepped in. My heart skipped a beat as I smiled up at him. It might be foolish to love him, but I'd never been known for being logical. Or not making dangerous decisions. And being in love with Merlin - yes, the fabled Merlin of myth and legend- probably wasn't a wise decision. Not when all but one of his children hadn't survived past adulthood let alone died of old age.

But, then again, his other children were born of mundane human women. I was half-fae and anything but mundane.

Our daughter also had role models that included a dragon leiche captured in a skull, a shadow dragon, a hill giant, and a powerful ancient necromancer who also happened to be an infamous warlord in his realm.

Did Xantos count as a role model? Maybe. Probably. Hopefully.

There were also my five guards, who doted upon Lenore. I suspected they would keep her from being too much of a hellion. That also didn't include my parents or other close friends. Something I doubted his other children had in their lives. I knew for a fact that Arthur and Morgana didn't have any of that during their lifetimes.

"I'm afraid to ask," Sterling said, looking around the room.

Smiling at my lover, it took a few seconds to realize he looked troubled and worn. His typically immaculate brown hair was messy. As though he had been running his hands through it in frustration. The usual twinkle in his dark eyes was gone, and he had a five o'clock stubble. Cute, in my opinion, but I knew he didn't agree. Even his polo shirt and khakis, which was 'slumming' in his opinion, were wrinkled and messy.

"What's wrong?" I asked. Glancing at the guards who were once again cleaning up the mess, I added, "They were watching Lenore while I went to Fellhaven for dinner. Which, I might add, is in the kitchen, I believe."

"On the counter," Alaria said. "Ready for whenever these fellows finish with their chore here."

Zarkull glanced at Alaria, and I saw the mischief lurking in his orange eyes.

"I'll remember that," he told her.

"Then why do I distinctly smell trouble and mischief in the air?" Sterling asked, while he looked around at everyone.

Lenore squealed and held her hands out to him. He smiled but looked at me.

"She isn't going to distract me from getting an answer," he warned.

"Oh, we were simply discussing our favorite eatery," I replied cheerfully. Standing, I offered him our daughter. "As for the fellows, they were having fun performing stories for our little one."

"Why were you at Fellhaven in the first place? I could always ask the staff," Sterling replied as he took Lenore.

"I met with a client." Lifting a brow, I added, "I thought we were beyond this? Simply because we have a daughter, doesn't mean I'm going to stop working."

"The existence of our daughter hasn't changed your impulse to charge in where angels fear to tread, either. Or where magick makes a situation worse."

The five docelfar all bristled at the comment. I didn't blame them. I was starting to bristle, also.

"Considering you are the cause for my 'jumping' into situations supposedly on impulse, I don't believe you have a solid footing." I drew a breath and let it out slowly. "As it is, I went to Fellhaven, met the client, spoke with Mark and Jen for clarification on a few points, then returned home. Complete with food. I could have simply called Jade or Trix, or even Roland to watch Lenore while I went out. Instead, I called my guards."

"I will take a page from your story and ignore the implication, just like you're forgetting the centuries of activity before my involvement," Sterling countered, his voice and body relaxed. "The more you try to dodge and deflect, the more likely it seems you're doing exactly what I'm concerned about."

He held up a hand, palm out.

"I am curious about the nature of your client's needs, and little else," Sterling tried to assure us. "Which will, no doubt, explain the presence of chaotic energy here."

The six of us, myself and the guards, all looked at each other, then to Lenore, then to Sterling.

"None of the adults here, that I know of, have been casting any spells. Not in the time I left and returned," I said slowly. "As for the client, I've been requested to search for a missing artifact."

"I didn't presume anyone had cast a spell," replied Sterling. "So there must have been something about the client or beings nearby. The chaotic energy is still clinging to all of you, like smoke to fabric."

Wasn't that interesting? I glanced at Alaria and Shyrrik before turning my attention back to Sterling. The lady guards let themselves out of the room.

"From someone we were near, perhaps?" I asked, my mind whirling. "I know what I'm going to be doing later."

"May I ask the name of the client?" Sterling asked. "If you want to withhold that information, I will respect your choice. There is always chaotic energy at Fellhaven, and if I remember, there is a live performance tonight. So the levels would be higher. It is simply... so much is here, more than ever before."

"I was there to speak to Faith Wells," I replied, tiptoeing around the question. The fae knew how to lie with truths, half-truths, and only a grain of truth. I had mastered the technique while learning at the feet of a fairy queen who also happened to be my mother. "She was doing her best to convince me to bring her home, perhaps *that* is where it's from?"

"The half demon?" Sterling leaned forward, a giveaway that his interest had risen. "She thrives on chaos, produces it, and inflames it wherever she goes. That's more energy than I'd expect to come from her, but, yes, I must agree that would be the probable source. Faith Wells... I must look into her activity."

He finally gave a slight smile as he looked at our daughter. She cooed and grabbed his ears. Lenore's sweet smile spread across her face, which caused Sterling's smile to broaden and soften until it filled his eyes.

"So what has you looking worn out and exhausted? And why do you need to look into her activity?" I asked, deciding it was my turn to interrogate him.

"The unusual level of chaotic energy. I want to see if there is any indication that she's producing or being exposed to such a high amount," my lover explained. "I've spent the day searching for the Staff of Chaos. It was recently stolen from one of the keepers. The worst one, of course. The fool kept it at his mundane place of work."

Well. Shit.

I shouldn't have been surprised. In fact, I should have expected it. A not so small part of me didn't want to acknowledge the fact he would be searching for the Staff, also.

"Then it appears our interests align once again." Tickling Lenore's feet, I watched his expression as I continued. "I've been requested to locate the Staff. The words used were 'keep it safe'. I figured I'd worry about that part of the request after it's been found and retrieved. You know, before complete and utter destruction befalls the world. Possibly even the universe."

Sterling sighed, kissed Lenore, and then kissed me.

"At least we are working together from the beginning, this time. What did you bring home from Fellhaven?"

"Indeed. A pleasant change for once." I grinned and nodded towards the kitchen. "Honestly? I'm not entirely certain. I gave Mark complete freedom on making up the platters and entrees. Shall we go see what's for dinner?"

## Chapter Five

Sundays were just another day for me. Sometimes I took the day off, depending on the jobs I took. Certain businesses weren't open, so Sundays were a day to prep for my week. Or, depending on how chaotic my week had been, I used the day to rest, relax, and enjoy some quiet at home.

Most of my jobs didn't revolve around catastrophic relics being stolen. This was one of those times, though. So this Sunday was spent caring for my daughter while discussing the best approach for locating the Staff.

That particular artifact couldn't be tracked by magical methods, which meant we had to be "Old School" detectives. That wouldn't be difficult, if it weren't for the fact that there were two airports within a short driving distance, hotels, and homes that people can rent for short or long term stays.

Trying to track the Staff if it had been taken cross-country was anything but appealing.

Neither Maekyl nor Sterling believed the Staff had been taken from the area, and I hoped they were right. In the meantime, we had other fish to fry. Starting with summoning one being that could answer the question of if Faith had been involved with the Staff's disappearance: her gremlin.

Because I didn't believe in hiding magick from our daughter, she joined us in my basement as Sterling set the bounds for summoning the gremlin.

"You know his name," I said, settling into a rocker. Since Lenore's birth, I'd begun collecting them so there would be one in every room. Maekyl sat on an end table beside me. Surprisingly, he remained silent as Sterling worked.

Sterling gave me a smile and stepped back from the circle on my floor.

My basement had been built by dwarves shortly after I'd bought my house. In the area I lived, rural Augusta County, full basements were scarce. Ones that weren't damp, cold, or flooded were rarer still. Yet mine remained a constant comfortable temperature, never had mold or algae or anything of the sort, and the main structure could withstand anything short of a volcano erupting.

The dwarves had apologized for not being able to provide such protection, but that sort of thing was beyond their skills for such a small space. Next time, they suggested, live on a mountain.

When you reach a couple centuries old, and have amassed a decent fortune, you quickly learn that sometimes bartering is better than gold. In my case, the dwarves hired me for a job that involved a very displeased undead witch, and in return I received my basement.

Because of their skills, I'd been forced to pour concrete over the original floor to hide a piece of my talisman at one point. After I'd dug it up, I'd returned that area back to normal. Even breaking, then melting, the concrete I had poured didn't damage the original floor of my basement.

I still think I received the better end of that deal.

As Sterling spoke the required words to the summoning, I thought one day I would teach my daughter the benefits of bartering.

My attention was pulled away from the giggling, cooing child in my arms as brilliant hellfire flared to life within the circle. There was no missing the faint scent of brimstone that joined it.

This gremlin wasn't without power, I realized, as his gnome-like form materialized within the circle. No wonder the angels believed he could have killed Kevin.

"Reveal your true form," I instructed the gremlin.

He glowered at me, jaws clenching, but he didn't refuse my order.

Wasn't that interesting?

Yes, it was my circle, but typically the summoned being didn't need to obey anyone other than the summoner. Perhaps it had something to do with the demon purring within my talisman?

The small gnome-like gremlin grew and shifted until he stood before us in his true flaxen-haired form.

Gaston wore typical sixteenth century garments. His black silk and velvet doublet was richly embroidered and tailored to his figure complete with a snug-fitting waist. The full sleeves were loose and paned to reveal the white shirt beneath. His shoes didn't fit with the rest of his clothing. Instead of the usual slipper-style, they were calf-high boots. His thick blonde hair fell straight to just below his shoulder blades and floated in the air. A rapier rested against his left side, and I knew it wasn't for show.

Folding his arms, he remained silent, glowering at us. His eyes fixated upon my talisman.

"You are the companion to Faith Wells," Sterling stated.

Brilliant flame-blue eyes shifted to Sterling. He remained silent but gave a single nod.

"Did you kill her supervisor, Kevin Daniels?" Sterling asked.

"No," he replied stoically.

"We know, you're angry we summoned you. Get over it," I snapped. "We aren't here to send you back to whatever part of Hell you're from or try to pin the murder on Faith."

The gremlin's eyes widened, and he started. "Then… why did you summon me?"

"Because we need to know what happened. You cannot lie while within that circle. Sterling is part of the Council that governs all magickal beings. His word holds at least as much weight as mine when it comes to investigating murders, crimes, and missing artifacts."

"Ah, so you are Lady Catherine," Gaston said, realization flaring in his eyes and showing in his every feature. He bowed low. "Well met, Madam Speaker. Well met, Lady of Death."

Sterling glanced at me; a brow raised. I flicked my own up in a sort of shrug.

"I suppose the gremlins talk," I offered.

"Lady, you are known among more than just we lowly gremlins. You've sent more souls to Hell and Heaven than most other beings." He paused, a sly grin curving his lips. "Mostly Hell, though. It is also known that a demon of great power, one of the best assassins our type ever saw, was killed when it was sent for you. Those involved in that travesty were punished, but there was no question in all the Hells that you killed him."

"Ah." There really wasn't a lot I could say to that.

The demon within my talisman purred louder. He was being such an ass.

"You did not kill Kevin Daniels. Did Faith have anything to do with the murder?" Sterling asked, changing the topic.

"No," Gaston said with a laugh. "She had no reason to kill Kevin."

"Explain that, please," I requested.

Gaston shoved his thumbs into his sword belt and leaned against a non-existent wall. "Kevin was a laughingstock among the demons. Lowest you can be without being a gremlin. Faith's father is Lucifer's Right Hand. Far more powerful than Kevin ever would be. She didn't need to kill the fool. All she had to do was mention her daddy."

"So what happened on the Friday when Kevin was killed?" I asked.

"Fi went into Kevin's office to ask for the week off. He was tripping on his so-called power, since he was a demon in a company owned by his kind. Thought the Big Bosses would make her fear him or some bullshit." He laughed, shaking his head at the comment. "How he managed to get enough souls to throw his name into the raffle, I'll never know. Anyway, Kevin tries to tell Fi she can't take the whole week off because they'd be short-staffed. She says she's taking the time off and he'd better not try to fire her. Dumbass that he is, had the Staff in a drawer. Tried to pull it out but didn't realize the power it leaks out energizes my girl."

Sterling and I glanced at each other before looking back at the gremlin.

"And?" Sterling prompted.

"And she got hopped-up on the power. Energized by it and that led to the full-blown argument. Kevin shoved it back in the drawer, realizing his plan wasn't working the way he planned, and agreed to her demands. She left. The other gremlins and I had a good laugh."

"You mentioned a raffle? Raffle for what?" I prodded.

"Yeah, the Staff of Chaos is protected by seven demons. Each of 'em guards it for seven years. Then, on the seventh day of the seventh month, they trade it off. After the last demon, seven new ones are picked from a raffle. If you meet the right criteria, you get to throw your name in to be one of the Seven."

"What are the criteria?" Sterling asked.

"You gotta have a certain number of Deals made, be a demon for so many years. Not have any reprimands," Gaston said. "There's a few other requirements, but those are the biggest. Especially the Deals thing. Kevin was an idiot. The laughingstock of our kind, as I described earlier, and I don't just mean the gremlins. We're all wondering how he could have made enough Deals to be part of the Raffle."

"Is there anything else you can tell us? Did any of your fellow gremlins see anything the night Kevin was killed?" Sterling asked.

Gaston snorted. "Gremlins do not typically take interest in the affairs of mortals, or even the demons above them."

I raised a brow. "Interesting, since I know many who enjoy creating chaos for the humans and non-humans."

Lowering his eyes, Gaston sighed. "Gremlins enjoy tormenting anyone who owns anything electronic. That is their job on this plane. If they take an interest in their humans, that would be because they are seen. Gremlins are seen as little more than pests in Hell. As such, they don't take a keen interest in their kind. They like Faith, because she treats them with respect." He raised his eyes to meet mine. "So, no. They would be of no help. All the information I have is what I have given you."

"What about the Staff?" I asked.

All amusement fled from his features with the question. "It is suspected, at least among the gremlins and perhaps some demons, that Kevin killed his predecessor to obtain the Staff. He had been using it for over a year. Not constantly, but certainly not infrequently, either. He did have enough sense to know that to use it at its full potency would mean his death."

"Explain that, please," I said.

"The Staff will devour anyone who uses it fully," Gaston stated grimly. "There are very, very few who could possibly wield it without that cost. But even if it doesn't take your life, it will take something else.

Nothing so powerful is ever used without consequence."

"You said it has been used for over a year," I said. Gaston gave a nod. "I wonder…"

"It could be," Maekyl chirped up from the table. "The power the Staff leaks would easily be enough to eat away at the Veils. That is the sort of thing it would do."

Gaston nodded slowly in agreement. His eyes shifted between me, Sterling, and Maekyl, before settling on the infant in my arms. "The young are always the most susceptible to the Chaos created by the Staff, Lady. She has great potential, and babes are easily swayed by Chaos."

I swallowed hard. I knew a warning when I heard one, even if it wasn't spoken directly.

"I appreciate the warning," I said quietly.

Gaston met my eyes, and I saw something akin to compassion shining in their depths. "I have always been the softest towards younglings. It was once my downfall, and then my salvation. Find the Staff, Lady. Protect your youngling. And be wary of the Judas."

"Someone is going to betray Catherine?" Sterling asked, growing tense and alert.

"Betrayal isn't merely a human behavior. Consider all that has happened, and how it could have come to be," Gaston replied ominously. He gave an apologetic shrug. "Sorry, but I'm forbidden to say more."

"What about our daughter?" I asked, my arms tightening on her.

"The child of two powerful beings will always draw attention. More importantly, the Staff of Chaos leaks power, and where it can, it will corrupt." His eyes shifted to Sterling and remained fixed upon him. "Those who are of blood most susceptible to corruption, are beings the power seeks out. The younger the being, the easier it is to corrupt."

"Understood," Sterling said gravely.

"If I learn more, I will contact you," Gaston replied, bowing deeply once more. "Good luck."

Sterling nodded, and with a simple gesture, dismissed the gremlin. As the gremlin faded from view, the power of the circle flared brilliantly before vanishing. A single scorch mark, in the shape of a claw, remained in the middle of the circle.

"I'm getting the feeling someone wants me to find the Staff," I said sarcastically, staring at my floor. "And it isn't someone of minor power."

"You think?" Maekyl asked, with not a little sarcasm. "You recognize the mark."

It wasn't a question.

"Yes," Sterling and I said together.

He met my gaze before we turned back to the circle.

"Do you think Xantos would be willing to care for Lenore?" Sterling asked quietly. "I believe this realm has just become too dangerous for our daughter."

Staff of Chaos

## Chapter Six

Xantos was no stranger to me. Although, to be honest, I'd only known him for just over a year. We had met when the Eye of Amon, an amulet capable of summoning any deity -mythical or otherwise- had been stolen.

A dark elf, with silvery hair and ebony skin, he was a powerful sorcerer, necromancer, skilled warlord, and wealthy beyond belief.

I'd spent some time in his realm, and even more time conversing with him.

Unfortunately, he and Sterling were not what one would call 'friends'. Not exactly, enemies, though. For which I was thankful. Otherwise, I doubt my abode would have survived the two of them being in the same room together, regardless of the reason.

When a portal opened in my living room, I could tell he had created it. Of course, I'd contacted him and asked him to come, so there was that. But when he manipulated energy, cast spells... there was a palpable difference. As if he had a screaming neon fingerprint on everything he did. Maybe, in some ways, he did.

He strode through the portal, dressed in his silkiest black robes with purple and silver accents. His long silver hair flowed gently down his back as he looked around and smiled.

Anyone with an ounce of magickal abilities would have envied his robes. They always reminded me of what wizards in fantasy art wore. Long, flowing, elaborate and luxurious. They spoke of power and mystery. And could have hidden a lot in the voluminous folds of the silken fabric.

"I would wonder at an ambush, but I know you invited me," he observed, oblivious to any of my carefully guarded thoughts. "So, Merlin- or do you still prefer to go by Sterling? - is also here by invitation."

Sterling, best known through the centuries as *the* Merlin of Camelot infamy, rolled his eyes.

"Did we wake you from your nap?" Sterling rejoined. "Perhaps that would explain your lukewarm attempt to rile me."

"Oh, delightful, you have your sense of humor working today," Xantos countered, as he kept his tone pleasant and playful. "So there is no need for greater effort on my part."

He moved to my best couch and sat with the grace of a ballerina ending a dance. His robes billowed around him and seemed to sink against the surface of the couch's material. There was a moment where he worked out a tiny wrinkle in the fabric of his outfit before speaking again.

"So, why did you summon me to this dull realm of yours?"

"As though you would ever answer to an actual summons," I said with a laugh. "Thank you for agreeing to visit."

The dark elf's reply was a single dismissive wave.

"No wonder you found him so charming," observed Sterling.

Xantos, who must have been in a rare mood, dropped a wink at Sterling. Sterling made a dour expression in return.

Warmth flooded my cheeks and swept down my face to my neck. I cleared my throat, while avoiding all eye contact.

Charming? Oh, yes. Xantos was very charming. He was also a gentleman who did not tell a lady 'no'. So I may have spent a couple nights with him while in his realm.

Unlike mundane humans, I did not have the same moral compass that required monogamy. In fact, any being whose lifespan lasted more than a century knew that such an ideal was foolish to attempt.

Some may be able to accomplish such a thing.

I was not one of them.

That did not mean I didn't blush easily, even after a few centuries of life.

"As to why I invited you," I said, changing the topic drastically, much to Xantos' obvious amusement. "Sterling and I have been requested to locate the Staff of Chaos, which has recently been stolen. It is no longer being kept in a place where the magic it bleeds cannot poison the area in which we live."

The mirth from the elf's face and body may have well been smacked away for how quickly it disappeared. He glared at me, then Sterling.

"The Staff has been taken? By what manner of being?"

"I suspect another demon, since they were who were protecting it originally. But I do not currently have any concrete evidence to back up that suspicion," I replied.

There was no way I could fault Xantos for his lack of amusement. I wasn't very thrilled with any of what had happened in the last twenty-four or so hours, either.

The dark elf sat back against the cushions of the couch, keeping eye contact with me.

"So no clue as to the being's intentions, yet. Very troubling," Xantos observed. "I expect you have asked me here to join the hunt."

"No," Sterling interjected.

I knew him quite well, so I was certain he had more than a dash of satisfaction in saying that.

Xantos narrowed his orange eyes at Sterling and waited.

"Cat would like you to care for our daughter until we can secure the Staff," Sterling continued. He wore a mirthful smile and nothing polite twinkled in his dark eyes.

"Yes," Xantos said in a droll tone. "I would be a much better choice to protect the child if the End of All tries to come."

"Oh, shit. Here we go," I whispered. It took all my self-control to not react or intercede between the two most powerful beings I knew.

Sterling flew, literally, across the room, and put his hand around the docelfar's throat. Black energy crackled around his fingers.

Xantos chuckled.

"Tell me, Merlin," Xantos said with a purr, even as the fingers tightened around his neck. "From one talented amateur immortal to the demigod you're trying desperately to choke, did you think this would bother me?"

The black energy doubled, covering Sterling's hand.

"Demigod? Graduated from a lost little servant boy to full delusions of grandeur, have you?" Sterling asked, although his voice was rough with exertion.

"Come now, before my protective wards ruin your soft hand," countered Xantos. "Let's disrobe and compare, so your worst concern may be addressed. Or-"

he looked at me and smirked, "we could just ask the lady of the house."

Sterling growled and tried to squeeze harder. White lightning coursed down from his bicep to the hand enclosed in darkness. There was a loud *crack!* as Sterling was flung back to the recliner chair he'd been in only moments before.

To my further surprise, Xantos did not look pleased.

"You will need a much clearer perspective and thought process to acquire the Staff," Xantos warned. "Allowing petty concerns to enthrall your emotional state is precisely what the Staff of Chaos feeds upon."

The docelfar seemed to realize something, before he turned his attention fully towards me.

"Have either of you been near the Staff or someone who was near enough to feel its effects?" he asked me. His eyes were wider than I'd ever seen them, and he suddenly had the exuberant energy of an excited warrior. I opened my mouth to speak, as he added, "Recently?"

My mind considered the facts before I answered.

"According to a source, I was near someone who was very close to it, prior to the Staff's theft," I replied cautiously. "Why do you ask?"

"It has already started, then," Xantos replied, and gave a heavy sigh.

I lifted a brow in silent question.

"The energy… the chaos produced by the Staff. It festers in most beings, and grows, until rational choice becomes secondary. Or worse." Xantos explained. "This is why demons were assigned to guard it, and only for short periods. They are already used to chaos as a constant, and despite belief to the contrary, are hardly prone to impulse."

He gestured to Sterling.

"A powerful immortal, one who has spent millennia living a path of trying to maintain rational choice and the heavy burden of those consequences. And yet, he, too, has been affected." Xantos sounded a bit sorrowful as he spoke those words.

"Yet, it doesn't seem as though I have been," I stated. I narrowed my eyes at him, suddenly suspicious of what Xantos was and wasn't saying. "Do you have any theories for that? One would believe that as a female, I'd be more prone to the Staff's effects."

The docelfar actually laughed.

"You've been affected, tainted if you prefer. The results have just not borne out as obviously as it has with our dear Sterling. No being, no matter whom or what, may use the Staff without consequence. To be near it is to allow its influence within you." Rising from the couch, Xantos continued. "The influence can be fought or embraced with some success, at least in theory. You enjoy anarchy and chaos as much as the throes of power and control. But never believe you, nor I, nor anyone, could withstand the Staff for long."

I gave a solemn nod, at a loss for what to say to his statement.

He brushed at his robes.

"Very well," he stated, as though he were coming to a decision.

I waited. From everything I knew about the dark elf, I suspected only those of his bloodline, and ones he favored at that, could coerce him into a different decision.

"I shall shelter the child. Protect her until my dying breath, and even then, strive to keep her safe from the Beyond."

I stared at Xantos, taken aback by his proclamation. Yes, I had expected him to agree to watch over Lenore, but the rest? That... that was unexpected. It was an Oath. A declaration that I knew wasn't given lightly. Xantos was entirely serious in his promise to care for Lenore, and it oddly comforted me more than anything else he'd said or done up to this point.

"Thank you," I said quietly, standing. I doubted few beings ever heard that promise.

He nodded, and looked to Sterling, who still appeared a bit dazed.

"The only rivalry between us has been in your mind, Deosop. I know your history better than you know mine. The term 'demigod' has ever been a thorn of irritation to you, no matter to whom it was applied. I had to test you both. I had to prepare for your worse responses and actions. Do not consider this a failure or defeat. I will care for your child, while you endeavor on this grave quest. Better you than I."

Sterling nodded. "You have my gratitude, Zaurahel."

"One final question," I said, meeting his gaze. "Why me? Why is everyone I approach and question saying *I* need to locate the Staff and keep it safe, if it affects everyone adversely?" I gave a half-hearted laugh. "I would think that a demon would be better suited to the task than myself."

"Ask your favorite demon why he isn't volunteering for this jolly adventure," suggested Xantos before adding, "No one else wants to try. There is little fear in you about the task, and others sense that. They are given hope. So they encourage you."

Sterling nodded. "That's accurate. And beings have expected some version of me to clean up every catastrophic mess that's come before this. So we are the ideal team for this, at least to the greater populous."

"So, what cadavers must be met in my part of this?" Xantos said.

Confused by his wording, I looked over to Sterling.

"He's asking what conditions you want while he has our Lenore," Sterling explained.

"Take my guards with her," I stated without thought. My eyes widened a bit, and my face warmed again. "Um, there is no formula in your realm. I sincerely hope you have a method for feeding her, since she isn't capable of eating anything remotely like solid foods yet."

"I know not of this 'formula' you speak of," Xantos answered. "But I have more than enough wet nurses to keep Lenore fed and healthy. As for your guards, they would be better suited here with you, Lady."

That statement I wasn't about to comment on. Nor did I want to know why he would have wet nurses on his staff.

"Thank you, again," I said. Crossing to him, I kissed his cheek, an impish smile on my face. "I have no doubts she will be safe and content with you."

"Try to keep the giant and goblin hybrids from feeding her too much," Sterling said as he walked up beside me. "We don't need our daughter developing tastes or worse that we cannot provide for at home."

Xantos gave each of us a nod.

"Take me to the child," he said.

## Chapter Seven

Monday morning came, and I was feeling anything but excited. I missed my baby girl. I missed rocking her to sleep and waking up to her in the morning.

For that matter, I even missed waking up in the middle of the night to care for her.

My house felt decidedly empty. Too quiet, as well. So when my phone rang while I was trying to figure out if I really wanted to eat something, I was thankful for the distraction.

"Catherine," I said, staring at the chocolate ice cream bars in my freezer.

"That's a pleasant way to answer the phone," Jen's voice said from the other side. "Rough night?"

"No. Actually, it was far too quiet," I grumbled. "Sorry. Is there something I can do for you, Jen?"

"Ah," Jen said, drawing the word out. "You can tell me about it when you come by Fellhaven. It's not too early for a drink, if it's what I suspect. Be sure to leave that dear youngling dragon and your nabrasu at home this time, though."

"I'm sorry?"

"Oh, right. There's someone here who can assist with what you're searching for. And it's going to be a business-only kind of affair, " she replied. "We have a decadent chocolate dessert. You can be a taste-tester before it goes on the menu. It's chocolate on chocolate with whipped cream, pudding... ever heard of chocolate lasagna?"

"No, but I'm sure I'll enjoy it," I replied, a reluctant smile creeping across my face. "I can be there shortly."

"You have a Door there, right?" Jen asked.

My brow furrowed. "Yes, but how did you know?"

Doors, with a capital 'D' were used to travel between realms easily. As long as you knew the right phrase, or key, you could go anywhere. I used mine to go to my mother's realm.

"Oh, please. A child would have a method of visiting her parents, if it were possible. Your mother is a queen. If you didn't have a method to go to her, I'd question your status in her realm," Jen explained.

Something in her voice made me wonder if her parents were still alive. Or maybe it was just me being a morose mother. After all, she and Mark spoke of grandparents often.

"Oh," I replied, simply. What else was there to say?

"Give me a moment and I will give you the Key for the Door here. You'll get here faster. It should also shut Sterling up on anything remotely concerning safety."

There was definitely snark in the lady of Fellhaven's voice. I couldn't help but chuckle at her words.

***

Not ten minutes later, Sterling and I were entering the main room of Fellhaven. The morning crew was cleaning tables, chatting with each other and the few customers, and prepping for the day.

Mark was behind the bar, his dark hair pulled back in his usual ponytail. A pair of glasses perched on his nose, his dark eyes not missing anything happening in the restaurant.

"Morning, lady and lord," he said as a way of greeting. "There's chocolate lasagna and cups of fresh coffee waiting for you, in the small private room."

I raised a brow. Then bit back a laugh when I saw Sterling's sour expression at the title.

"Thank you, dear sir," I said, trying to not laugh.

Turning, I found Jen exiting the room Mark had mentioned. There was a pleasant smile on her face, but it didn't meet her eyes until she noticed Sterling and me.

Without looking back at us, Mark gave an exaggerated bow before scuttling off to tend to some issue at the tables.

"Good morning, Jen," Sterling said, sounding formal even with such a simple and casual greeting.

"Good morning. Good to see you two," Jen said. She nodded towards the room. "The person you want to speak with is in there."

Glancing at Sterling, then looking at Jen, I knew something was going on, but didn't know what. Shrugging mentally, I crossed to her and the door. Sterling kept pace beside me.

Cute. Sweet. But not required.

"I sense you brought your hand scythes," Jen murmured. "Good choice."

Xantos had gifted me a pair of obsidian hand scythes after I completed a deal for him. Obsidian, I'd quickly discovered, deadened magic. So, basically, anything you killed with it, remained dead, beyond even reanimation. Any body part cut off by such a weapon, could not be reattached by magickal means.

I learned through Mark and Jen that Xantos had the market for obsidian weaponry cornered in every realm he dealt in. If you wanted such an item, you could only get them through Xantos.

And the price wasn't cheap.

"Now I feel as though I should be worried," I muttered.

"As long as everyone behaves, none of you will need to worry about anyone," Jen said cheerfully. "Or anything."

With that, she opened the door, and gestured for us to enter. I took three steps inside the room and then stopped in my tracks.

Almost every chair in the room was taken. There were even a few beings standing against a wall. None of them appeared happy. The food on the tables appeared untouched.

Every single pair of eyes turned to face the door. All their eyes fixed on me. I noticed at least half glanced briefly at Sterling, before turning back to me. Or, more specifically, my talisman.

Great. A room full of demons. Just what the bartender ordered.

The unoccupied chair was in a position of power. The back was facing the far wall, and all others could be seen from where it sat empty.

The position wasn't surprising. The fact it was empty was, though.

"Looks like they only planned for a party of one," murmured Sterling. "I will take my coffee and sweets while I stand at the door. Just in case someone gets the idea to leave."

Putting words to action, my partner stepped ahead of me long enough to retrieve the small plate of dessert, a spoon and generously sized mug of hot coffee at the end of the table closest to us. Once obtained, the items were carried back to the single entrance and exit.

Sterling put his back against the door while taking a sip of his beverage. His eyes glittered as he took in every member of the room.

Crossing to the chair, I settled into it. In my glory days, I had my Right Hand to stand over my shoulder. Jade, a hill giant, was not here to take that position. Not that I was concerned.

Anyone who considered violence within the restaurant would have to take on Jen and Mark. An elf and her ifrit. I had come to discover both were powerful and not anyone I'd want to anger.

Dante, one of the few demons I knew by name, sat beside me at the table. A cup of steaming coffee in front of him. The others, I noticed, had beverages, also. Though I wasn't entirely certain all of them were drinking coffee.

"The revered Lady of Death," the demon to my left said. Blonde haired and blue eyed, she wore a crisp business suit, complete with fitted jacket. "Welcome to the table. We are here for peaceful discussion, nothing more."

"How do you come to this table, Dante? I was unaware that demons who had been banished were allowed to converse with old acquaintances," asked Sterling. His tone was not malicious, or taunting.

"There is a beneficial side to being dismissed from The Great Game," Dante replied, and his tone was light, perhaps even pleased. "I don't have to worry about the rules. There is no rule keeping these others from discussing a mutual concern or seeking my council."

I was not in the mood to play games. Then again, I had never been one to play games and talk around a subject. It bored me. I was not a nice person when bored.

"What is it you desire?" I asked bluntly. "You're all aware that we are searching for the Staff of Chaos. All of you should be aware that I do not take kindly to having my time wasted by anything but being to the point."

The demon within my talisman took that moment to growl. It had shifted towards my right, and my eyes moved with it. The demon within my talisman was definitely not a fan of someone at the table.

"We want to know what progress has been made, and how we can assist," Dante replied.

"You may choose to ignore this, but our interests merge at this event," the demon to Dante's left added.

"I believe," the female said, "she is distracted by her talisman's dislike of being so close to Dante."

Stroking the talisman, I glanced at the female demon. "It does seem as though it isn't fond of the fallen one here." Shrugging, I ignored the growling still coming from the necklace. "I do not doubt that our interests coincide. Though I suspect that it is merely my locating the Staff that falls in line with your desires."

"Does it need to be anything else? Is that not significant enough?" she retorted.

"I am interested in if you expect me to return it to your... capable hands," I replied, leaning back in the chair as though I were in charge of the room. I suppose in some ways, I *was* the one in charge.

There was a frightening thought, considering I had, up until this point, done everything within my power to avoid demons.

"If not us, then whomever has been assigned the task of keeping it," the female replied. "We know the selection process will be more stringent from now on."

"I have no doubt," I said in a dry tone. No need to inform them of what I'd been told a couple times already. "What do you know about how it disappeared?"

Dante spoke up again. "The demon known to the mundanes as Kevin Daniels had gotten into the habit of taking the Staff from its hidden space, which he foolishly put at his work office. Speculation has run from he liked to take it out and admire how shiny it gets, to trying to make himself a god of some sort. What is irrefutable is that he became very prideful of having possession of it. There was too much rumor of him 'whipping it out to show it off' to be ignored."

"He showed it to someone with a greater ambition than his own. That being plotted and executed its theft and his doom. We have three suspects, and will provide the means to track them," the female concluded.

"Why only three?" interjected Sterling. "Doubtless there are much more than that number of more ambitious demons, or other beings. Daniels was a demon for the sin of sloth."

"The parameters are who could have been shown the Staff by the fool, more than once, and who had sufficient power and influence to bring about his destruction and the theft."

"A source informed me that Kevin was shot by something, and then his throat slit. Would any of those three be capable of such?" I asked.

"All three. We are not incompetent in the ways of deduction, Lady," the female replied.

"Then why haven't you sought out the three yourselves," countered Sterling.

"You know their limitations, Sterling," Dante rejoined. "They do not trust me to carry through on the task. In truth, I care not but so much about it. I win in so many ways no matter the outcome."

"Why aren't you one of the suspects, then?" I asked. The question was met with chortling laughter.

"He's too lazy, and enjoys his human playthings far too much," one of the other demons said.

"He cannot hold the Staff. It is too powerful for the likes of Dante," stated the female. "He would be lost to it in no time. Had he taken it, the Staff would have claimed him already."

"Is that because he's been banished or is there another reason?" I asked, genuinely curious.

"Banishment takes a cost," Dante replied with a bored tone. "My powers and constitution were lessened considerably. Fortunately, my intelligence, insight, and wit were unaffected."

That comment caused a lot of grumbling from the demon trapped within my talisman. At least he wasn't trying to get out. Yet.

"We can discuss you and my talisman's behavior later," I stated, ignoring Dante's proclamation. No need to start an argument, after all. "For now, let's return to the task at hand and why none of you have tried tracking down the Staff already. I count at least three dark paladins in this room, and none of you are lesser demons. Aside from Dante, that is."

The largest paladin spoke. He was over six feet in height, wearing leather pants, a black silk shirt, and a leather jacket. None of which hid his considerable physique. His hair was short cropped, so the dark skin of his scalp glistened beneath. His goatee and mustache were trimmed to the same length. His shoes were expensive and Italian in origin.

"We have offered. Our lives are a small price for the return of the Staff and its continued safety. Our... bosses do not believe we could accomplish its retrieval, let alone keep it in a box made to prevent anyone nearby from being influenced. The demons cannot leave their designated jurisdictions. If you would prefer, I or either of my comrades would accompany you on this quest. Despite orders to the contrary."

Tipping my head to the side, I considered the dark paladin's offer. He seemed genuine in his statement. His words struck a chord with my own Code.

"And what punishment would you, and your companions, suffer for assisting in the search?"

"Likely an eternity of servitude and torture," the paladin explained. "Which we still find preferable to the End of All or doing nothing."

"Let me make certain I have the facts here. The Staff of Chaos is stolen from a demon. Probably by another demon. And your bosses, who are also demons, would rather it be used than be retrieved by the very beings who are supposed to be guarding it?"

The largest paladin laughed. He didn't sound amused.

"Something like that, yes," he said. "But it is, to those who decide, a matter of not wanting to send those likely to fail on the quest."

"Are these superiors also aware that you may be assisting me in locating the Staff? Someone who has had an... interesting past with your kind?"

The paladin gestured to Dante.

"He is here, and not being dismantled. What was your question, again?"

My turn to laugh. "Fair enough, sir. Fair enough. Would it make a difference if I were to hire you and your fellow paladins? I would prefer to not place anyone into an undeserved life of torture and servitude." I paused, before giving them a sly smile and wink. "Unless it was me doing so."

The paladins looked surprised, although only mildly so. The demons made unhappy noises.

"It would," the largest paladin replied. "It would make all the difference, and outsmart our keepers, er, bosses as well."

I gave them a smug smile. "Give me a price, and I'll pay it. If for no other reason than to outsmart your superiors." I stroked my talisman. "I do have a reputation to keep, after all."

Dante joined in laughing with the paladins. My talisman started to feel a bit warm.

"I will contact you with a price, in the next day or so," the largest paladin promised.

"Is there anything you may want from beings who might actually aid your search?" the female demon said, her tone harsh and aggressive.

"Yes, the names of those you suspect," I replied.

She nodded to Dante. He, in turn, brought up a manilla envelope from beneath the table. The envelope was sealed with black tape and a red wax sigil. In this circumstance, the seal was to prevent anyone but the intended being from accessing the information held within. He placed it beside me.

"You ask, you get," Dante said.

"No time like the present to look these over. That way, I can ask any questions that arise," I said with more confidence than I felt. I broke the seal and emptied the envelope's contents onto the table.

The paladins all walked to the exit. The tallest said "we will await you outside, Lady," before they left the room. Four of the demons walked out without a word. I looked around, before settling my gaze on Dante.

He shrugged.

"They have nothing to offer in the way of information," he explained. "So it is unwarranted for them to be present at this sharing of knowledge. Whatever intel you share with them will have to be sufficient."

I grabbed the dossier that was closest to me and opened it.

"Maxine Olson," I read aloud.

"Demon of Sloth, misery type." Dante rattled off the facts as though he'd written or memorized the dossier. Perhaps both.

"Latched onto a child while she was dying from a seizure and has occupied the body for over forty years." He continued in a matter-of-fact tone. "Managed to eventually fool a paladin-in-training to become her mate. She derailed him from his destiny and all the good he could have accomplished. Has grown fatter and lazier, likely because she ingratiated herself to the paladin male's biological family. She has been dragging her family members down steadily while convincing the elders that she is somehow enhancing their lives. Or- and I love this one- she's their responsibility. I mean, it's brilliant. She hasn't had to bag a soul or work for food for almost 20 years now. Although it's showing in her 'human' guise. Her skin has become far too gray and mottled to appear completely human. Her host body's red hair and light blue eyes are also starting to show wear in the usual ways. The address is listed."

I examined the recent picture and involuntarily grimaced. She looked like a crazy cat lady that started way too early in life. One could only imagine the distress and wear that showed on her victims' physical appearances, let alone their auras or souls.

It didn't take me long to swap to the next dossier.

"Suspect number two: Rick Barker, inhabited for five years, host body in mid-thirties," Dante began.

"He looks like he's in his forties, with that hairline and beer gut," I stated while looking at the photo.

Once was enough. I didn't want to have an even more unpleasant surprise after finding out what the other demons did.

"It's an old picture. He's developed crow's feet that go halfway down his face. Hence why he's always wearing large sunglasses outside," noted the female demon.

"Charming. The ladies must love him."

"You're not far off," Dante rejoined. "His host body was rather popular with the local ladies prior to possession. He was 'properly skinny' to use a phrase, had a well-paying job, and loved to get attention."

"What's his career and what changed," I coaxed.

"Construction and carpentry. He's actually quite good. But life has a habit of reminding the mundane that it's stacked against them and unfair to boot," continued Dante. "So his supervisor, the owner of the business, got a fatal stroke on a job site. Without the benefit of a will being made."

Sterling grunted.

"Was there a widow?"

Dante nodded.

"Oh yes, and she had little to no knowledge about how to run any business, let alone the one her husband had spent his lifetime building up. Also, Rick had refuted her... affections, so she wanted to stick him onto a spit for roasting."

"So no job and suddenly on the outs after being ready to eventually retire from the same job. I smell a deal with a devil in the making, here," I said.

"Oh, it's a deeper cut than that," Dante said with glee in his voice. "He decided to make his own business, figuring his reputation and charm would just carry the whole process forward and into the black in less than a year. Imagine when he's deep in debt, no longer living his extravagant, at least for a 'Southern boy', lifestyle. Drinking himself into middle age and dad-bod territory with the business floundering on a weekly basis. Poor thing. His trophy wife probably had her old flames on speed dial before the first quarter numbers were in."

The demons all laughed at that. For that moment, none of them seemed to be separate entities or even enemies. They all came across like something out of an old Faustian play, chuckling at humanity's folly and foolishness.

"So little Ricky found a devil to make a deal with?"

"An incubus, no less," Dante said. "Who wasn't a newbie at the games or at existence. Our host's second eldest can only hope to be half as clever as that incubus if he decides to embrace his heritage. Regardless, that was five years ago. Rick's body, at least, is staying inhumanly busy with work. Back at his favorite mundane hobbies and interests, such as charming people who have no clue. I think he and that sloth demon the mundane rich got elected to president would find much in common."

"Golf, middle-grade beaches, and NASCAR, oh my," Sterling guessed.

"Just so," agreed Dante. "If you wonder why he is a suspect? He constructed the box that the Staff was kept in at Daniels' work. Installed it and knew what was being put in it."

"Ambition, knowledge of the box's security, easy opportunity?" I surmised.

The female demon said, "The two of them were golf mates, among other common interests."

"Extra attention to that one," I murmured aloud while flipping to the last dossier.

"I would appreciate a moment of everyone's attention," a new voice said. I turned around to find the source.

One of the demons who had stayed at the walls was walking forward, where the light could reveal her features. Going by the near perfect skin and how she oozed sexual energy, I concluded this was a succubus.

Her figure was shapely from the shoulders down, eyes a pristine blue, blond hair gathered around her neck and flowing over her shoulders. Her smile was a comfort and a warning in the same space. My mind took the time to calculate how many proposals she might get in a week and discarded the terrifying conclusions. She stopped next to me and that smile widened. I didn't know if she meant it to be comforting or an attempt to distract me from whatever her intent might be.

"Do not be ready to dismiss the other candidates in favor of the incubus," she advised. "I have dealt with the sloth demon personally, and she is as crafty as a hunter demon in search of big game. It might take an unexpected amount of effort for her to get results, but do not doubt that she is capable."

"The succubus doesn't want us thinking ill of her kind," the first female demon mocked. "Because she prefers to have less work to get results."

"This one never has to work to get her prey. All she needs to do is show up and respond in favor of whomever she decides will be good food for as long as possible," the eldest demon interjected. His tone was not malicious, more amused than anything I could detect.

"I do my job with the ease of one who has put in the time to perfect it," the succubus countered, still smiling.

"You must have taken a century alone to craft your outward appearance for the mundane. I imagine they are rather easy prey at this point," Sterling said.

Was he flirting with her or acknowledging the obvious? I felt a pang of self-doubt before reminding myself that succubi and their male counterparts fed such emotions and ate well from the results. I was no livestock to be fattened for the kill, nor was Sterling.

The succubus laughed for a moment and ran her manicured hands over the silk material of the little black dress she'd squeezed into.

"I have discovered that the so-named nerds of this century make for longer feasts, especially when they need to be brought out from their protective forts of self-doubt. Such a nice break from the scrawny meals gotten from the 'bad boys' that I can gather at a moment's glance," she boasted. "But that is aside from my focus today. My people have no reason to bring the End of Times."

"Someone from every walk of existence has claimed that, even when there are clear examples to the contrary throughout time," Sterling challenged.

To add to his statement, he stood and walked to my other side. One hand was placed on my shoulder. A clear dismissal of her intentions, no matter what they may be.

She took the hint but covered the embarrassment by flipping her hair in a casual manner before walking back to her seat. The succubus made an event out of the journey, slowly swinging her heart-shaped hips in their tight silk prison for all to witness.

"Some things will never change," the elder female demon said.

Her voice did not seem scolding, though. More wistful, perhaps even a bit of longing? I shook my head. The last thing I needed to ponder was demon dating habits.

"If we can move on to the last suspect," Dante rejoined. "I think she is as legitimate a candidate as any of the three."

"Sophie Conner," I said, opening the final dossier. "Seems to have jumped around a great deal before spending the last mortal lifetime in her current vessel."

The pictures included in the folder were of a pleasant looking female human, although the older pics showed a much slimmer and happier version. The current pictures had a body at least sixty pounds past a healthy weight, the smile pasted on ever more with each succeeding year. The hair color and style changed constantly.

I took out what I thought was the oldest of the photographs. The subject looked to be in her mid-teens, slim, glowing, wearing what was referred to in the

1980's as "Goth" attire and makeup. Her hair was its original color but cut in a flattering style. She looked happy and quite pretty.

"This was taken shortly after possession?" I guessed.

"Actually, that was taken a week before. By the body that the envy demon now known as Sophie was occupying at the time," Dante explained. "It is unusual for a keepsake of the former host's existence to remain prominent, but that was copied directly from the pictures she keeps around her abode."

"Rare? A remarkable understatement, even for you," the elder female demon said. "But this is exactly why she is a suspect. Her host was a gifted artist, happy, but with so much doubt and low self-esteem. She was a perfect host for an overactive envy demon. Too perfect, mayhap, since the symbiotic relationship has spiraled so far that it's impossible to tell who controls the body at any given time."

"And the reason that makes her a suspect is-?" Sterling asked.

"A lifetime of exceptionally bad decisions made because one or the other was convinced it would make them feel better for five seconds," Dante replied, and tapped the photos. "I mean, look at the hair choices alone. Staggering."

Even Sterling laughed at that joke.

"It does point towards a 'try anything once because you never know' approach to existence," Sterling admitted. "The 'You Only Live Once' attitude let loose too long and free, with no concept of consequence."

"She could have done much worse. At least she was never in a position of political power," I muttered.

Somewhere in the room, I heard a demon sigh a single word, with reverence and envy.

"Germany."

"If we are steering clear of history lessons, today," Dante interjected, his voice rough with irritation. "You now have the three dossiers reviewed. What questions do you have for us, Lady of Death?"

"What is the woman's connection to the late Kevin Daniels?" I asked, organizing the dossiers until there were three stacks sitting in front of me.

Three faces stared up from photos. Each a suspect. One who possibly had an artifact that would bring about an apocalypse. It wasn't a pleasant thought.

"Oh, this is the fun one. They courted, he played her, she coveted his possession of the Staff," Dante answered.

Oh for Hell's sake.

"He showed it off to an envy demon he was flirting with?"

There were nods all around me. Dante looked like he wanted to dance with glee.

"Are you sure you don't want to handle that one, Dante," I said. "You look like it's the event of the century, and you don't want to miss it."

"I have ulterior motives that make me an unsuitable candidate to defuse the situation," he explained, but his smile became impossibly wider, and his body was vibrating with excitement.

The talisman pulled from my chest and hovered in Dante's direction for a split second. Then, it fell back against my skin.

"Perhaps you should get that out of here," the elder female suggested as she gestured to my talisman.

"Oh, no, no, Keisha! That's no reason to dismiss our honored guests," Dante countered.

I swear, he was trying to not giggle.

The talisman lunged again. I could no longer ignore the demon inside it. He'd been screaming for a while, and I'd just let myself recognize what the noise in the background had been.

"What is the issue here?" I demanded, but I was making the demand to the talisman's demon as much, or more, as to anyone else in the room.

There was some murmuring and chuckles from the demons in the room. Keisha, the elder female demon, gave the others a withering stare while she explained.

"The demon held within your bauble was a competitor against Dante. The methods that Dante took to allow you to capture the demon? Those are what got him banished from all nine levels of home."

"I broke a few paltry rules, and my punishment was being placed in this realm. Here, I serve myself. My competitor has spent the centuries that I've spent accumulating my lovely lifestyle stuck in a small container of metal and stones!" Dante exclaimed before he rocked in his chair, screeching laughter.

The talisman tried for Dante again, managing a longer period of hovering before it ran out of energy. I telepathically instructed the demon in my talisman to calm down. Perhaps instructed isn't the right term. I threatened with dropping it into an active volcano if it didn't shut up and stop throwing a fit.

Dante continued to laugh and laugh.

"Enough." The commanding tone was accompanied by a wave of bright energy that washed over the whole room and the occupants.

The demons, every one of them, flinched and visibly drew back.

I looked back at Sterling. Yep, it had been him. The magickal energy he'd used was still dripping off of him. His face was a stoic mask. Eyes as flat and emotionless as a predator before the kill is made.

"Now that you've brought down the mood, darling, I consider that our cue to leave," I said while getting to my feet. Once I collected the dossiers, I gave Dante, Keisha, and the rest a single nod.

Sterling and I left the room.

Jen intercepted us in the hallway, before we could enter the main chamber where the bar and most of the dining tables could be found. She looked past us, nodded at the lack of others.

"Do we need to send a cleaning crew in there?"

I chuckled at her serious question.

"No, not unless the demons decide to smash their drink and food containers because Sterling made them behave," I replied.

"Sorry I missed that," Jen admitted. "I'm sure it's less of a mess than if they'd provoked enough to find out you're carrying those scythes, though. Figured the weapons were going to come out at some point. Damn, lost a bet with the hubby. Anything I can get you two?"

"I think we could use some lobster stuffed mushrooms and kimchi spring rolls," Sterling replied.

"Funny, Mark just finished making a batch of those," Jen replied and gave us a smile. "I'll have them boxed and bagged for you in less than five minutes."

With a prompt spin on her three-inch heels, Jen headed toward the kitchen.

We found Mark at the bar, mixing beverages for a small group of dwarves who sat in a cluster at the long wooden serving area. Once he passed around the flaming shots, he made his way over to us.

"Jen will have your order out in a minute. We've already charged your account, as usual," the other half of the tavern's ownership declared when he had closed the distance.

"That's great, but we wanted to ask you a couple of questions about recent activity and patrons," I said.

Mark nodded but held up one hand.

"Wait for Jen to get here, so you can ask us both at the same time."

Sterling and I nodded. My significant other gestured at the dwarves.

"Don't see many around here, let alone a group of them," Sterling observed.

"Mostly half-dwarves around the Valley, and most of the state," Mark agreed. "This group comes around four times a year from West Virginia. They come to celebrate the changing seasons, as is tradition in their homelands."

"The celebration includes ignited shots of, what, Blanco tequila or is that vodka?" I asked.

"Oh, the flaming dragon shots, as they are called, involve a pale mead topped with liquor. The liquor is distilled from rice that's grown near volcanoes. It's quite tasty, which is why it appeals to the dwarves. For all their ruff and gruff, they have sophisticated palates."

"They play in the dirt and rocks, but never go cheap on the food," Sterling reflected.

"Especially not the drink," Mark finished.

Finally, Jen arrived with a Fellhaven cloth bag, the bottom swollen with our goodies. She placed it on the bar, then realized we weren't leaving just yet.

"What's up?"

"We've got a few leads on our investigation about the Staff. The three demons we are tracking are a sloth demon, an envy demon, and an incubus. Any increased activity from any of those kinds? Perhaps some bizarre event in the area?"

The pair took a silent minute to consider the questions.

"That incident with the chicken over at Walmart would count," Jen suggested.

"Where the frozen birds started twitching?" Mark replied. "Yeah, that qualifies as bizarre, no question."

"The what started to what?" I blurted.

"We were in Walmart, picking up some charcoal and grilling sticks," Jen explained, leaning against the bar. "As we were walking past the frozen food aisles, someone screamed. Of course we were curious, so we approached. There was a woman with her two children. The pre-teen girl was horror-struck, as was the mother. The youngest girl was amused. 'I didn't know frozen chicken could flap!' the youngest said. We moved in behind them and looked into the window they were staring at. Turned out to be rows of whole frozen chickens. The wings were twitching, the bodies were rolling side to side. Not a great deal, but enough to see. The woman ran away, taking the kids with her. By the time store management arrived, the fowl had ceased to move. We told them we didn't witness anything out of the ordinary. Bought two of the birds to show we weren't concerned. Checked both of them at our home. We couldn't detect anything that explained what we saw. We did incinerate the chickens to be safe and we haven't heard of anyone getting sick or acting weird. That was this past weekend."

"As for the incubus, we've had one coming around a lot. He's been trying to hook up with anyone he can," Mark said. "And I do mean anyone. He's gotten one warning about trying to seduce anyone underage. If it happens again, well, he won't exist for long after."

"That might be better for us to intervene," Sterling said, glancing briefly at me. "Is the incubus a new possession, or one that has grown comfortable in the host's skin?"

"He's comfortable, and before the past two months, a regular customer," Jen answered.

"Meaning no problems, no debts," I surmised.

"With the house rules, yes, and he followed them until recently," said Mark. "But he's gotten... I dunno, desperate or far too cocky, or both. Anyone he even slightly fancies, he approaches. Aggressively. The attempt on an underage lycanthrope was the one that got him kicked out for the weekend."

"His name wouldn't happen to be Rick Barker?" I asked.

"Yep," the pair said in chorus.

I knew the first address we'd be trying. Sterling and I thanked the pair for their help and departed the restaurant, food in hand and a goal in mind for later in the day.

But the unpleasant surprises weren't done for the day. Once we were next to his car, Sterling pulled a small, folded piece of paper from his jacket and handed it to me.

The paper was headed "Last Will and Testament".

"Just in case," he said, not looking at me. "You may want to update your own, presuming you've ever had one."

"Taking this whole thing a bit too seriously, aren't you?"

"This isn't something that can only end in a minor mess, Catherine. It's win or lose, for everything. There is very little gray area. Either of us could end up in Oblivion trying to keep this from ending everything. That's your copy. You're the first executor."

I couldn't think of any way to answer other than a single nod.

## Chapter Eight

Investigations are boring. Don't believe me? Ask any police officer or private detective who's done more than a dozen. Yes, there's the added element of danger and the unknown, especially if you're walking up to a situation, wearing garb that identifies you as someone there for a serious purpose. Worse yet, as someone who can take a being into custody. If you're not dressed in a suit or uniform, the element can change slightly, because the being you're checking out has different expectations or presumptions in play.

Usually.

If you're guilty of one of the seven deadly sins, chances are you're always expecting someone to come after you. For revenge, to stop you, to mess up the fun thing you've got going.

Still, when you knock on a door to a residence, especially one that's modest but definitely not worried about how many bills they have, you also have expectations. Such as the person wearing some manner of clothing.

Yes, the incubus answered the door in the nude. No, I wasn't expecting it. At worst, I would have expected a speedo, maybe even the middle-aged host attempting to look good in a silk teddy. Not stark naked.

Probably because I didn't want to see anything like that today, or any day. But that's how Rick answered the door. Beer gut making an appearance well ahead of the other obviously male part of his anatomy and all. He could have at least worn slippers or have gotten a pedicure.

Sometimes I really hate my work.

Sterling was nearby, and likely laughing. He stayed in the car for the initial contact, since the two of us coming to a door would be more conspicuous. Or we'd be mistaken for people trying to spread a religious message in a mildly concealed attempt at recruitment. I suddenly wished I had a pamphlet to throw up in front of my eyes.

"If this is how you greet visitors, it's no wonder you've been hitting the bars looking for action," I said in absence of a proper introduction or salutation.

"Yes, but your timing is excellent, since I took that magic blue pill less than an hour ago," he replied, seemingly unfazed.

"Just makes it easier to find if I need to hack it off for daring to come too close to me," I retorted.

*That* made him back up and tuck slightly. I was glad.

"Throw on something so I don't have to look at so much of you," I declared, letting myself in.

"Necromancer," the incubus spat the word out. "Had I taken a female host or a rich male, you'd favor me." He was grabbing a robe or jacket from a nearby coat closet, thankfully.

"You've spent too much time in that host's brain, demon. You've taken on the mundane trait of presumed entitlement. That just because you want something, you're supposed to have it. An incubus would remember it's all about the seduction," I answered. "Neither of your proposed alternatives would have changed this situation."

He came back into view, wearing a long black robe. Still no footwear, unfortunately.

"You're wasting my time. I have under four hours to make the most of my... condition, and it's not being taken advantage of by you. Your loss," he stated.

I let the talisman blow off some of its pent-up frustration. The metal grew warm against my skin as energy was manipulated. The incubus shrieked, thighs drawing inward until the knees knocked together. He choked a cry out before his teeth snapped together in pain and effort. The host body fell to its knees.

"Since you didn't take warning the first time, let's up the ante," I suggested, looking down at him. "How about we tear those troublesome bits clean off, then fry them. In front of you for lasting effect? It might take you a week or more to feel up to trolling young girls on Twitter. And everything else will be off the menu until you jump hosts. Oh, wait, we can lock you into this body, can't we?"

I let that all sink in, until a thought occurred to me.

"Or has someone already locked you into this body? I can't imagine you letting your host grow this rotten and unappealing by choice," I said.

Rick, or the incubus he hosted in said body, didn't respond verbally. He twitched and grunted, sweat starting to trail down his face. It took a few moments for me to recognize his inability to respond in his predicament. I covered the talisman with a hand to cut the flow of energy.

The host body collapsed. The incubus turned the head to face me and converse. He didn't sound happy.

"Arrogant witch. You will suffer for that!"

"How? Are you going to nag my social media pages?" I asked, my tone snide. "Or were you planning to drop that robe, hoping my eyes would explode to save the rest of my body from constant vomiting?"

He lunged for the coat closet. I could have acted, but I had been working him up to try to take me down by the strongest means he could. The door opened, he fumbled inside for a moment. I readied my shield spell and the few counter spells that might give me a chance to flee when he brought out the Staff.

The door swung back, and the top portion of his body vanished from sight. I could see movement, but that was all.

When he reappeared, I blinked. Stunned at what he held in his hand.

He had grabbed a wand. A handmade, barely powered up stick with crystals hot-glued to it.

By all the Heavens and Hells. Talk about pathetic.

The lightning bolt that flew out of it and struck my shield spell. Not so pathetic. It actually knocked me back a little. Far more kick than I would have ever expected from it or its wielder.

But not nearly enough.

When Sterling came through the front door a short time later, he didn't seem at all surprised to find me sitting on the one good chair to be found in the front living area. His regard for the incubus, who was face down on the floor, hindquarters up, with the wand jutting from his back side, was equally brief and unsurprised.

The host and incubus were very unconscious.

"It's not him," Sterling stated.

"Obviously," I replied dryly.

Sterling gave me a slight smile before examining the room and nearby spaces. He paused after opening the closet door and peered inside. He continued until he seemed satisfied with his findings.

"Let me guess, you sensed the Staff wasn't out or being used from your position outside, so you checked all around the house to see if there were traces."

Sterling nodded. "Once I was confident he didn't have it, and it hadn't been anywhere on this property, I knew you could handle whatever he might try to do. So I widened my search to be certain he hadn't simply hidden it nearby."

I nodded in turn. Logical and sound reasoning.

"Since you don't have it in hand, the junior detective in me says that means he never had it. He's only been near it once or twice."

"More than twice, I think," Sterling said, and pointed to the visible part of the wand. "That has not been charged by anything from this realm. The Staff was used to either charge it or bring something from another realm to do so."

"Great. Guess it was a bad idea to clonk the demon along with the host."

"Not as much of a problem as you think," Sterling replied, kneeling beside the body.

Energy gathered in an unfamiliar way. I watched fascinated as it coalesced around Sterling's hand. He then smacked the back of Rick's head with said hand. As Sterling pulled his hand back, a shimmering tether fell between his palm and the body's head. Sterling pulled his hand up sharply, and the hazy image of an incubus's face appeared above the human head.

The demon shrieked, the sound seeming to come from some distance away.

"Plznyr, you will answer me," Sterling declared. "Where did the wand come from?"

The demon made some hissing and spitting sounds, which made no sense to me. Sterling did not have the same problem. He nodded and continued to converse with Plznyr.

"When and why was this presented to you?" he asked.

More of whatever language the demon was speaking in came from his mouth. Sterling nodded again and ended the conversation by forcing the image back down into the human head.

As Sterling stood, I asked, "Well?"

"It was a gift from Sophie. Not long after the Staff was taken. He apparently used it once before now, which is why he has a strong trace of the Chaos upon him. It's been driving him mad. Made his lust a thousand times worse."

"Kill him if you want to do the world a favor," I advised. "I'm going after Sophie."

## Chapter Nine

Not so much later, the two of us were traveling to the other side of Staunton in Sterling's car. A 1965 Corvette Stingray doesn't offer much beyond a pair of seats and excessive horsepower, but it does do so in style. Once Sterling had shifted gears to get to a cruising speed, he asked "Are we going to Sophie's house or another address?"

"Her house," I answered, "to start with."

Sophie's house was between the historic downtown, Mary Baldwin College, and several churches that would look more at home in major cities like Chicago or New York. The residence was a curious combination of styles, mixing colonial, Spanish, and somehow a medieval turret was thrown into the mix. Odd but sure enough, it worked. The lawn was so neat and trimmed I took a long moment to make sure the green wasn't artificial turf made to resemble a stretch of golf course.

Sterling approached the porch and knocked on the front door. After a full minute, he announced his name and title, stating we were there to speak to Sophie. He said it in Demonic, no less, so there was no way for Sophie to misinterpret our reason for being there. I became bored. The small communication crystal I had brought along in case someone needed to speak with me became something to fidget with while we waited for any sign of an occupant.

After five minutes, nothing. No noise, no stir of active energy, no one checking out a window, etcetera ad nauseum. Sterling tried the door and found it unlocked.

We stepped into Sophie's house.

And it looked like a museum crossed with a bizarre retail outlet.

"Dragons' whiskers!" Sterling exclaimed. "I haven't seen everything in glass displays like this since the chain of Best Stores went out of business."

The foyer had eight-foot glass displays on either side. Shelves were stocked with a minutia of odd gadgets, decades old tech. In the next visible room, which I supposed was meant to be a living room due to the fireplace and hearth, the show continued.

A large plasma tv was on the left side, an even larger 4K TV on the opposite wall. I lost track of how many different types of TVs were in the large area. All of them were displaying a shopping channel, even the ceiling-mounted projector that I knew was a dinosaur from the early 1990s. The display took up half of a wall all by itself.

Every kind of media device was on display and presumably ready to go around the meager spaces afforded in-between the display screens. From an 80's RCA movie disk player to dual VCR machines, a

Betamax, laserdisc, divx, DVD, blu ray, to every gaming console made.

"I remember that one," Sterling said as he pointed out one of the black boxes. "That was one of the first blu ray players ever offered. Sharper Image, ran about eight hundred dollars."

When I gave him a puzzled and bemused look, he shrugged. "I've spent a great deal of time in commercial airplanes. Read every catalog that company has put out."

"Man of magic, mystery, and frequent flier miles," I quipped.

"I know what's in my wallet," he joked back.

We moved through the house, with no demon, human or otherwise coming to see who was milling about. Every room had a ridiculous amount of gadgets. The kitchen was so piled with devices that there was only two square feet of space to prep any actual food. Of course, that couple of feet had an extra fancy cutting board and knife set in place. The bathroom smelled like a Christmas shop and had enough hair care products to supply a well budgeted movie production.

Upstairs, we glanced into a guest bedroom, another full bath, study, sunroom, stereo room, and finally the master bedroom. Each and every one bursting to the seams with superfluous items.

When we walked into the final room, the master bedroom, Sterling declared, "I believe she has at least one of every item from each catalog Sharper Image has ever printed."

I wasn't about to debate that. It seemed an envy demon's primary way to spend time was acquiring every flashy, commercially enviable prop and device possible. I felt for anyone who'd ever come to this residence as an unsuspecting guest. Worse than someone breaking out a power point or old slide projector full of family vacation pictures. Yikes.

However, this room finally yielded some of what we'd been searching for.

The unmistakable resonance of the Staff of Chaos hung in the room. The article had been used in the room, just this one, but it had been used recently. If Xantos has been along, he might have been able to feel the resonance out on the street. For all I knew, Sterling might have and was waiting to see when I could sense it. Regardless, a large amount of energy had been used from the Staff. No way to tell what kind of spell had been used, or why.

There was also no trace of Sophie. That is, no recent trace. She had not been in this house for at least a day, perhaps two. Dust hadn't formed or settled anywhere. The scent and trace of demon was low and dormant.

The energy signature of the Staff was more prevalent than fresh traces of Sophie.

"Let's search this room and then the guest room again," I suggested after not finding anything helpful in the room. "There has to be some clue somewhere."

Only the sound of our footsteps echoed throughout the house as we began the search. The scrape of wood against wood as drawers were pulled out, followed by paper and objects being shifted around were loud in my ears. Not for any other reason than the silence was starting to grate on my nerves. I brushed it away, placing the blame on the energy the Staff created.

After we'd gone through the nightstand, the dresser, and an older wardrobe, we turned to the antique trunk and the closest.

"Last two places to check in here," I stated needlessly. "Which do you want? Trunk or closet?"

"Closet," Sterling answered, moving towards it.

I knelt before the antique trunk at the foot of the bed. It stretched from one post of the foot of the bed to the opposite side and easily three feet wide. I wasn't certain if the trunk had been an heirloom, a unique antique-store find, or if perhaps this thing had been crafted specifically for her. The lock on it, though, was new and took only a touch of magick to unlock.

Within the trunk were vintage Samsonite suitcases. I began pulling them out, one after another, until I had at least half a dozen stacked up. Some even had suitcases within suitcases, and I felt like I was playing with Russian nesting dolls as I opened each suitcase, just to find another.

At the bottom of the trunk, however, was a long silvery-gray wooden case. I recognized it as ghostwood, a type of wood that deadened magic in this realm. Judging it to be about two and a half feet in length, it was a finely crafted, if not simple, box. Maybe Rick hadn't made just one of the 'specially designed boxes' that housed the Staff and he gave this one to Sophie? Or maybe she stole it along with the staff?

Regardless of those unanswerable questions, there was something inside, shifting as I moved the box. There could be no way in all the Heavens and Hells of all the realms our lives could be this simple.

Flipping the latch up, since there was no lock on it, I opened the box. Resting on the black velvet lining was a wand that smelled distinctly like cedar. Delicate scrollwork had been carved into the entire twelve inches of the wood that tapered to a point at one end. Except for the handle, which had been carved into an open serpent's head. Whatever magic had been within the wand had been used up and I couldn't sense anything of the 'fingerprint' that all magick left behind.

Another lovely side effect of the Staff of Chaos.

Standing in one smooth motion, I turned to Sterling, who was shoving clothing from one side to the other of the closet. Shoes on a three-tiered rack filled the bottom portion of the closet while clothes ranging from goth-chic to boardroom-powerhouse filled the top. There were multiple boxes on the very top shelf, each labeled 'pictures' followed by a year.

"Looks like I might have found something useful," I stated, holding out the box. "Can you figure out what the spell was for this wand?"

Taking the box, Sterling studied the wand and its container.

"Looks like ghostwood," he stated. "Though it isn't just that. Something else was used, also."

"Maybe silver?" I suggested. Sterling pursed his lips and gave a slight shrug. "We can ask the dark paladins what the original box was made of. Or..." I trailed off, a sly smile pulling at my lips. "Do you think Raziel would know?"

"Possibly. Why?" Sterling asked as he picked up the wand.

"Because I'm thinking I should return his favor and bring his attention to one Miss Sophie Conner."

Sterling gave me a questioning look. I did not have the decency to give him anything remotely akin to a chagrined expression. Or even a guilty look. "Raziel is the one who asked me to help Faith."

Sterling sighed. "Anything else you haven't told me?"

"Plenty," I replied sweetly. "But we do not have the months it would take for me to tell you everything I have done that you aren't aware of."

"Right," he retorted, none too happily. "Let's see what answers we can glean from here before we call in the Angel of Mysteries."

Placing the wand on the bed, he held his hand above it at shoulder height. Once again, he spoke in a tongue I didn't recognize. I repeated the words silently, hoping to eventually be able to repeat the spell he used successfully. If he didn't teach it to me later.

A glowing golden replica of the wand formed in the air above it. The replica turned in a circle as Sterling concentrated on the spell. Everyone knew you didn't interrupt a caster in the midst of a spell, so I remained silent, watching Sterling and the glowing wand.

After the wand completed its third circle, it rose until the narrowed end was pointing towards Sterling's hand. Blue sparks shot from the end and fizzled out just before they reached his palm.

I recognized that type of spell, but I didn't say anything, preferring for Sterling to give confirmation to my theory.

Clenching his fingers into a fist, the glowing duplicate vanished, leaving only the empty wand on the bed.

He looked at me. "It was a wand of stunning brilliance. At even five hundred yards, Kevin would have been incapacitated or knocked unconscious."

"Do you think it was charged by the Staff?" I asked.

Sterling shook his head. "No. It doesn't have the right signature to have been charged by the Staff."

He ran his fingers along the velvet lining and found a loose area. Pulling the fabric back, it revealed a shining dark metal.

"That doesn't look like obsidian," I stated, peering at it. "Any ideas?"

"Silver mixed with iridium," Sterling replied as he turned the box over in his hands. "Think Rick made this?"

"It would fit. He made the original box, after all," I replied, turning to look around the room. "Do you think she was helpful enough to leave a diary?"

"We can look, but I doubt you'll get lucky twice in a row," he replied, a slight smile on his face.

"Did you finish searching the closet?" I asked, giving a shrug.

He shook his head. "Not yet. There are still boxes on the shelf to look through. And there's a suitcase on the floor."

"Right," I said, moving towards the closet. "Shall we?"

"We shall," Sterling replied with a smile.

Together we pulled down the photo boxes and began systematically going through them. That is to say, he started with the ones on the left and I started with the ones on the far right. As we rummaged through the boxes, I couldn't help but cringe. There were more copies and photos similar to the ones in the portfolio the demons had given me.

The years passed by my eyes in reverse, in photo form, as I moved from one box to the other. Sterling was doing the same. We had nearly met in the middle when he stilled. The sudden lack of movement caused me to pause in my search through the photos.

"Find something interesting?" I asked, looking into the box he was leaning over.

He nodded. In one hand was a photo of our suspect with Rick Barker. Hovering beneath his other hand was a knife. The blade was dark with dried blood. Looking into the box, I noticed other knickknacks inside it. Though the outside of the box was labeled 'pictures' the inside definitely was not photos.

"Looks like you found the murder weapon," I said before looking in the box.

There were the usual trinkets one collected over the years. Little bottles of sand labeled with names of beaches, postcards, a few birthday cards, jewelry, and a set of tarot cards. A little velvet bag was nestled beside the tarot cards. I grabbed the bag and poured the contents into my hand.

Polished rocks with runes carved into them fell into my hand along with half a dozen goth-type enamel lapel pins. There was even a small quartz crystal in amongst the runes and pins. I dumped it all back into the velvet bag and closed it up. There was no magic to any of it that I could feel. My guess was they were trinkets from her 'goth days' prior to her possession.

Dropping the bag back into the box, I said, "Guess we should definitely give Raz a call, huh?"

"I would say so," Sterling replied solemnly as he replaced the items in the box. "While we wait for him to show up, you can explain when he came to you and what he wanted."

"As you wish," I replied, dropping him a wink.

Sterling smiled and chuckled. "And I love you. Now give the angel a call so we can get this over with, hmmm?"

Smirking, I pulled my phone out and dialed the angel's personal number.

"Hello, Raziel," I said when he answered. "Sterling and I have some important information regarding the death of Kevin Daniels. We're at Sophie Conner's house and have discovered a rather bloody knife."

"I'll be right there," Raziel replied. Followed by silence.

I looked at my phone and made a face. Looking at Sterling, I said, "He hung up on me."

"They do that sometimes."

"He really needs to learn some manners," I retorted.

"You going to teach him?" Sterling asked, amused.

Giving Sterling a sly smile, I replied, "Not today. Today we need to finish searching that guest room before Raz shows up and kicks us out."

## Chapter Ten

Twenty-three minutes later Raziel entered Sophie Conner's home. Not that I was counting. We knew when he entered for a few reasons. The most obvious reason being we heard his footsteps. A second reason being his whistle at what he found when he walked in. The third reason was he called our names.

Okay, maybe the third reason was the most obvious one.

Sterling and I greeted the illustrious angel from the top of the stairs.

"Come on up and see what you've won!" I said in my best show host voice.

"Must you always make light of a crime scene?" Raziel replied, but he did smile after he said it.

"Just be glad there's no corpse this time," I joked as we led him into the bedroom. "In fact, that's kinda part of the problem."

"A body does tend to cause more problems than solve them, at least in my line of work," the angel countered. "Now, why am I here and forgetting that you are?"

"Oh, we found the murder weapon, but no Sophie Conner," I replied cheerfully. "So unless your girlfriend knows the lady in question, our Deal is done."

Raziel's eyebrows went up, but he nodded. He began to pace around, checking details while he spoke aloud.

"Very well, you have helped resolve accusations against an innocent. I came to this residence to conduct a safety check that was requested by associates of the occupant of said residence. The door was ajar, and no one responded to requests of status. You were never here."

Sterling grunted in acknowledgement.

Raziel continued. "Tell me what brought you here, what you have found, and what you think has happened."

"We have three probable suspects. All demons. Rick Barker had a wand charged by the Staff, but nothing useful other than that bit. Sophie Conner is the second of those suspects. She's not here, but there's plenty of energy left from the Staff's use." I nodded towards the box. "What can you tell us about that box and the original used to contain the Staff?"

"The original had thirteen curses etched into the ghostwood. And the interior had plates of obsidian. The objective being to avoid it being opened and eventually the obsidian would dissipate the spell energy within the staff. Yes, it would take centuries, even millennia, but eventually that would make the Staff nothing more than a decoration."

I wondered, briefly, when Xantos had been approached for the obsidian plates. Considering Mark and Jen had been here since Arthurian times, something I kept forgetting, that meant Xantos had been poking around for just as long. Probably longer.

Raziel continued, oblivious to my internal thoughts. "This is one of Rick's 'hideaway' boxes, which he does on a regular basis. The interior panels are dense metals that dampen energy, something like lead, tungsten, or various hybrids. The purpose is to make an item or items difficult or even impossible to detect magickally."

"I had a sword in one of those for a couple of centuries," Sterling added. "They work remarkably well. No one could find that particular, ah, artifact until I took it out of the hideaway box."

I had to interject a question.

"The curses become inert once the item is removed from the, for lack of a better term, storage box, right? I've had some experience with variations of both kinds of boxes, but it's been a while."

"Correct," Raziel confirmed. "When the 'kill boxes'- that's Rick's term for them- are empty, the curses are not active. The idea is to keep an item in, not prevent everyone from opening and closing the box by itself."

"Do you think you'll be lucky enough to get prints off the knife?" I asked. Demons didn't always leave clean fingerprints, but it was worth asking.

"Unless someone else handled the item, I doubt it," he confessed. "But I will have a full analysis done regardless."

He gently placed the knife and box in separate evidence bags. Since there were no mundane beings around, he didn't have to bother with the formality of gloves. Angels didn't have fingerprints, either.

"We still plan on talking to our third suspect to be thorough," I stated, watching Raziel. "But while the three of us are here, I'd like your thoughts on something."

"Please, ask," Raz invited.

"We have been warned of a 'Judas'," I began, trying to choose my words carefully. "I suspect it is meant towards me and someone I know, personally, but I thought I would ask for your opinion. Have you heard anything about me or Sterling being betrayed? Know of any other warnings we should be told?"

"Warned? By one of my people?" he asked.

"Opposite side, actually," I replied. "I presume your side has no such warnings for me?"

"Warnings as such have to be sanctioned, so that all of us know and can respond appropriately," he answered in that maddening, vague manner that both sides favor. "I have not been privy to such concerning you... but I will look into it."

"Then if the being who informed us said they weren't allowed to say more, then they were specifically told to tell me," I said, trying to work out the who and why of the warning. I really did not like where that train of thought was leading me. "I really hate it when you 'higher beings' give vague warnings and refuse to give clues so us 'lower beings' can figure out what the hell ya'll mean."

He gave an exasperated shrug.

"We don't make the rules, Catherine."

"You just follow them to a fault," added Sterling.

"So it has been said. Nevertheless, thank you for bringing this evidence to my attention."

Which was our cue to leave the premises. We didn't attempt any further chat.

"At least he's going to look into the whole Judas thing," I grumbled as we settled into Sterling's Stingray. "Not that I'm going to hold my breath on him telling us anything useful."

"It's how they have to maintain the Balance. I cannot think of a single material being that enjoys it. I doubt some of the celestial ones do," Sterling said while he piloted the Stingray down the roads leading to Interstate 81.

"They're definitely not getting any fruit baskets from me," I quipped as I watched the scenery go by as he drove. "I can say without doubt that this 'Judas' is not you, Jade, Maekyl, or my parents. We can strike out Mark, Jen, and their family. Considering Xantos has our daughter, I can't see him betraying us." At Sterling's frown, I smiled. "He's a lot of things, and I'm certain he would do a great many things, but be that level of betrayer? No. Stab you while looking in your eyes, yes."

"It's not Xantos. The Judas has to be someone from this realm or your mother's," Sterling said with more confidence than I certainly felt about any of this situation.

"The list of people I trust in any form is very short," I stated, refusing to look at him. "If you haven't noticed, my list of friends is rather short. I suspect if it was someone easily ferreted out, I would have done so by now. That leaves trying to locate a powerful artifact before it can be used."

"Which is why we are traveling to the ass end of this valley. Where this car will stick out like a new Benz or Bentley. To question our third suspect."

"Let's just hope Maxine doesn't live on some deer-path of a road off one of the paved one-car roads," I said with not a little trepidation.

Some of the roads in the county were barely big enough for one car with usually a ditch deep enough to eat a car. Your only hope was that no one was coming along those stretches, or they were kind enough to go off the road on their side. That doesn't include the one-car-only mountain roads where one side was a steep bank, and the other side was a cliff. If you encountered someone on those stretches, someone was backing up until you could pull to one side or the other.

The joys of living in a mountainous area.

But, of course, she lived down a pig-path road with ruts, potholes, and the usual hell for any car. Especially one low to the ground. We didn't make a quarter mile before Sterling applied a levitation spell to his ride and floated up to her front porch.

The house was a modified double-wide modular home. Nothing wrong with that. I recognized the design immediately, even if it had been placed into a foundation, had an awning, enclosed back porch and was fitted with the latest satellite hookup for entertainment. The front lawn was immaculate, with two rock gardens and large potted flowers around the house perimeter.

What clued us in as to the actual nature of the occupant was what happened when we opened the car doors.

A stench that seemed more at place in the busiest section of a county dump hit us on the first breeze of wind. The closer we got to the house; the more things fell into place.

The lawn was astroturfed. The plants were all artificial. Dust was on everything. From a distance the whole scene looked pleasant. The closer you got, the more it all looked barely attended to. And that smell just got worse and worse.

Sterling got to the front door first. Before he could knock or otherwise announce our presence, a husky but still feminine voice yelled "Door's open." He looked at me, I cocked an eyebrow, and we went in, wondering how long we could hold our breath.

The interior was much like Sophie's house, if she'd shopped at thrift stores, flea markets, and department chains where the "high-end" merchandise rarely topped the hundred-dollar mark. Also, if the place had been hit by a tornado, or several partying college fraternities, or both at the same time.

While there was some nice stuff to be seen, the mess and filth made everything seem like garbage. Pizza boxes, Asian takeout containers, fast food wrappers, and bags were all over the place.

Most weren't empty. Only a couple looked less than a week old. Nothing was organized, clean, or from what I could see, even put away. The sole living occupant aside from flies and their offspring lay sprawled out on a chesterfield sofa that at one time had to have been one of the best on a showroom floor.

Enough of Maxine's real copper strands remained to give a hint of the fiery mane that existed decades ago. When I say enough, I mean about a fourth of what was still attached to the scalp. The rest was a mashup of fire engine red and the popular imitation shade favored by people who wanted to be redheads but genetically didn't have a prayer.

Skin that may have once been a creamy complexion was now dulled with a greyish tint and too many blood vessels that had burst just below the surface. Eyes of deep blue seemed to have no light in them. They reminded me more of a well-made doll's eyes than anything belonging inside a skull. Her clothes, consisting of black leggings and a Duran Duran sweatshirt, were somehow spotless and looked clean.

She appeared to be somewhere in the ballpark of two hundred fifty pounds. Give or take fifty pounds.

A tv that looked like the piece de resistance at Sophie's house was on a show hosted by a celebrity doctor. Said host was listening to someone complain about how they had to decide between their baby daddy, sugar daddy, and the non-binary partner they'd met a year ago on social media. The tv sat on the hearth above an artificial fireplace, surrounded by more discarded trash and various knick-knacks that hadn't been removed from their original packaging. On the considerable chest and belly of the couch's occupant was a large smartphone, a tablet, and the tv remote.

When the woman shifted to look at us, some of the hair stuck to the couch. The colored strands had sickly white roots.

"What do you want?" she asked, although her delivery sounded more like a bored statement. She kept glancing past us, towards the television.

"Maxine?" Sterling asked.

"Yes, oh high-and-mighty poohbah of the Council, that's me," she replied with the same bored tone. Then she let out a brief cackle, apparently quite amused with her own wit.

"I thought she was living with a former paladin-in-training and his family?" I stage-whispered to Sterling.

"Oh, he went and got himself a little girlfriend!" Maxine erupted. The dulled eyes showed a little fire. "I'm punishing his parents and him by living here in their summer home. Or is it their fishing camp? I don't remember. Doesn't matter."

"They know you are residing here?" Sterling asked, keeping his gaze on her.

"I would hope so since I made them bring me here! Ungrateful snots will just have to deal with their own errands, hygiene, and medications without my kind assistance. Gotta tell you, it's never been a better time to be a sloth demon. Apps to have all kinds of food delivered, and stuff. All my favorite kinds of stuff. Sure the delivery expenses ain't cheap, but that's what they get for not making me feel appreciated! Well, that's what *he* gets. When his parents see their credit card bills for the last six weeks, they'll remind him! They'll all be begging me to come back and make their lives easy and carefree again."

I looked at Sterling, then to Maxine, then back to Sterling. "Can I kill her? I believe it would be considered an act of mercy for the paladin and his family."

"You tell him, sister!" She suddenly bellowed. Her bulk sprang into a sitting position, making the sofa creak uneasily. "That's what I NEED! Why can't I find someone who wants to fight for MY LOVE?!? Let alone more than one to go all battle royale for exclusive rights to me! Yeah!"

I realized she was addressing the tv show. She hadn't heard a word I said.

"She heard you. This is something she does to deflect responding to what she doesn't like," Sterling explained, not bothering to lower his volume or tone. He was probably responding to the nearly painful eye roll I'd just done.

"Why can't people just choose those that give them adoration instead of treating them like shit? Stupid humans! Two centuries ago, this form would have been the envy of queens!" Maxine continued to rage in the direction of the tv.

"Four centuries and two plagues ago, perhaps." Sterling said. That apparently hit her where she um, lived. Her eyes locked on him, and the full lips became a hard, thin line.

"That would be before your pretty little thing's time, sorcerer," Maxine grumbled, giving the barest of nods in my direction. "You sure you can talk like that in front of her? She won't get too lost to feel important?"

"Never mind my question. I'm going to burn the bitch right into that long suffering couch," I replied sweetly. The talisman thumped against my chest, signaling my captured demon's agreement to the idea.

Sterling said, "I think a vengeance demon of our mutual acquaintance would be very displeased. He's been waiting for the chance to do much worse to this one."

"Really? I've got him on speed dial. Well, the tavern, but anyway, let's get him over here and take turns! We can make a day of it."

"Wait, what? Who do you mean?" Maxine interjected.

Sterling acted as though she hadn't spoken.

"The issue becomes if you terminate the mortal form, Cat. That would allow her to jump to another person. It's what she probably wants. Even if it means effort.

Sloth isn't a total lack of effort. Just applying none when not gaining what's wanted."

I frowned.

"I'm reminding you, Cat. Because the satisfaction you get from lashing out on the flesh shell here would not solve the paladin's woes or his family's," Sterling coaxed.

"Yeah, I could jump into his little girlfriend! Ooooooo, that would be great! C'mon you oversized elf, burn me down! You're ugly and your momma dresses you funny!" Maxine finally sounded enthusiastic about something.

"Our vengeance demon friend isn't the only one who knows how to prevent a demon from jumping bodies," I stated, stroking my talisman. "Young I may be, but I have plenty of knowledge to make up for it."

"You obviously haven't dealt with a sloth demon," Sterling replied gently. "That is part of their nature. Violence is their fast track to another possession. Death is the slow way. Vengeance isn't the same. But it has to be sanctioned."

"You mean he can't snuff this shitbag until the paladin gives consent?" I asked. I could feel my teeth grinding together.

"And he won't," Maxine cackled, "because the fool thinks he's the better person for it!"

Sterling gestured with his left hand. A small, very subtle movement, but the effect was immediate. The sloth demon's fleshy mouth kept right on going, but we were spared any noise being produced by her, or the flies, or the tv.

"I don't blame you in the slightest. Our mutual friend has a strong bond of friendship with the former paladin-in-training," Sterling said. "I'm sure if he ever gets consent, he'll at least let you come along for the show."

"We better see if there's any clues here, and fast. If I have to dwell in her presence for long, it won't matter what the consequences are or who I piss off." I confessed.

Sterling looked over at the demon, who had worked her host body into quite a fit. The skin that was visible was red and sweating. The snarl of an expression on the face was bone deep. The eyes were no longer blue, but black. She had apparently stopped talking for the moment and was glaring at us.

"It's fine if we look about, isn't it?" Sterling said in a cheery tone. "Don't bother to get up!"

She inhaled deeply and started to yammer on about I don't know what- the silence spell was still in effect- while flapping one hand in clear dismissal towards us. Sterling nodded and we began looking around.

The silence did not remain blissful. Lack of distracting sounds, even the demon's cackling laugh or complaints, made the mess and filth all around us stand out even more. Piles of items and discarded containers meant plucking through to search for anything of significance.

Flies are more bothersome when you can't hear them coming. Also, no sound seemed to make the stench even more prevalent. I took the time to consider opening windows, but even that took using some magick to avoid touching anything. Then I realized that most of the windows were already open.

Had Sterling already done that? Or gods above and below, did the fresh air just make it all worse? I hoped that the family which the demon had entrenched herself with had the good sense to burn this place to the ground when she vacated it.

Unfortunately, I couldn't sense much in the way of energy here, magickal or otherwise. The only energy was the standard kind used to power household appliances, and the raw darkness pouring off of the sofa-lounging demon.

I looked over to Sterling, who was using spellcraft to levitate one pile of junk after another in a vain attempt to search for, well, anything worthwhile. He looked as fed up and disgusted as I did. Looking over my shoulder, I noted that Maxine was rolling with laughter. She hadn't really moved. Her position was the same from when Sterling had thrown out the silence spell to spare our sanity. I had no idea what she was laughing at, and the more I pondered, the less I wanted to know.

The urge to get out and shower for a week was rising exponentially.

Sterling took a few steps out of the living room or whatever this room was supposed to be. He returned less than a minute later, his face more grim and disgusted than before. He shook his head and nodded to the front door. I nodded back.

Once we were out of the house, the silence spell ended. We didn't run to the car, but it didn't take us long to get there, either. Before we closed the Stingray's doors and drowned out everything else with the roar of the antique eight-cylinder engine, we heard the same thing over and over from Maxine, punctuated by her cackling laughter in between shouts.

"Straight to Hell! Going straight to Hell!"

"That went well," I stated as Sterling levitated the car back to the main road. Sadly, he didn't even glower at me. Only grunted. "Shall we return home and take extensive showers before planning our next course of action?"

"I'm not sure a single shower will make our skin stop crawling, but that's as good a plan as any," he stated, as the tires touched the road. He shifted gears, and the engine purred as he reached the speed limit.

We both rolled down our windows.

Shielding my thoughts from him, I contemplated taking some drastic actions against Maxine. Maybe a nudge or two would convince the paladin to sanction her death.

My musings were interrupted by my phone alerting me to a text.

"Looks like we will have to postpone that shower. The dark paladins are requesting a meeting at Fellhaven," I said after reading the text.

Sterling gave a nod, and I settled against the back of the seat as I replied to the message.

Maybe some good food and drinks would remove the bad taste from my mouth.

## Chapter Eleven

As Sterling navigated his Stingray through the streets towards Fellhaven, I went over what I knew about paladins, their opposites, and those labeled as 'dark paladins'. Paladins typically chose a life of service, usually as a first responder of some sort.

They were the police officers that made the news for buying someone a car seat instead of giving the parents a ticket. Or worse. They were the paramedics who worked 'miracles' and helped their patient survive horrific injuries. The firefighters who managed to walk into burning buildings and rescue humans and animals without losing their life. Usually. They followed a code similar to the angels, doing only good and fighting against evil.

Anti-paladins were their opposites in every way, shape, and form. They preferred the side of evil to the side of good. Their battles against the paladins were epic and gory.

The dark paladins were the ones in the middle. Despite their label, they preferred having a structured organization or government to stand behind. They swore unwavering loyalty to whomever employed them. Never questioning their orders. They chose a side and stuck to it.

The best example I could think of was if a CEO of a company began working against the greater good of the company. An anti-paladin would kill the CEO if they thought they could garner more power or money. A paladin would follow the CEO, never believing the CEO would do wrong. A dark paladin, though, would kill the CEO and place someone in charge who would continue working for the greater good of the company.

Coins always had two sides, but they also had a center. It was the dark paladins that worked towards keeping the Balance in place.

Usually.

Sterling parked his Stingray in the back, well away from the usual traffic. Despite the fact that most attacks came in the back of the restaurant did not deter him. Probably because he also parked beside the SUV belonging to the owners of the establishment.

"Hold a moment," Sterling said. He gestured. A strong breeze pushed around us both, smelling of roses and sage. My sinuses suddenly reminded me they were miraculously alive. My partner tapped the end of his nose.

"The stench still clung to us."

I gave Sterling a grateful nod.

Entering Fellhaven, the hostess gave us a brilliant smile before stating our party was awaiting us in one of the private dining rooms.

We followed one of the many servers to what I was starting to compare to a throne room. The general area where the rulers of a realm conducted their business and settled problems amongst their courtiers. All the room lacked was a dais and the thrones.

The same three dark paladins were sitting at a table in a far corner, away from the others in the room. Silence blanketed the room the moment Sterling and I entered. There was no ridding my mind of the image of rulers entering a room. Minus all the bowing and scraping, that is.

Although the three dark paladins did stand as we made our way to the table. Sounds of murmuring, silverware being used, and glasses being lifted rose slightly as we moved past one table after another.

"Lady and consigliere," the largest of the paladins said. He gestured towards the empty chairs. "Thank you for meeting us."

"Thank you for considering my offer," I replied, taking the chair that placed my back to the wall. Sterling waited until I was seated before taking the chair beside me.

"Allow me to begin by introducing ourselves," the paladin began as the trio settled back into their seats. "I am Elliot Saunders. These are my companions and compatriots. Scott Williams and Michael Black."

The other two men gave a nod as Elliot said their names.

Scott reminded me of someone more at home in the mountains and countryside than in a city. He wore a leather jacket over a dark red polo shirt. The jacket had obviously seen a lot of years and taken some beatings. His copper hair was pulled away from his face before falling down in messy waves. His beard was cut close with a braid on each side. If I didn't know better, I'd have sworn he was part dwarf.

Michael Black was more of what you'd expect of a paladin: broad shouldered, blonde hair cut in the usual military-style, no facial hair, crisp black shirt, and shining leather jacket. Very military in posture and demeanor. I couldn't help but wonder if he ironed his blue jeans.

"A pleasure to meet you all," I said, my eyes returning to Elliot. "Shall we begin with what I'm to pay you and then settle on terms?"

"Sounds good to us," Scott said, speaking up. He lifted the tankard in front of him and took a long pull. "The three of us have been long-time admirers of yours, Lady. The fact you've figured out a method to outwit our bosses and allow us the honor to work for you? It only strengthens our resolve to help with this problem."

Elliot gave a nod. "Your reigning days as the Lady of Death, a queen of power amongst pretenders, placed you above any other ruler known to our kind." He laughed at Sterling's frown. "Ah, that's right! The mighty Council did not approve of our Lady's blatant use of magick during that era. But Sir Consigliere, can you think of any other ruler who didn't strive to broaden her reach yet was forced to do so? Not by her choice, or a force of might, but by the request of those who saw a force to be reckoned with and could give food, shelter, and protection during days when most lived on the narrow knife's edge of starvation?"

"She didn't care if you were demon, angel, paladin, or any other type of living creature," Scott added, leaning back in his chair. "All she cared about was making sure no one tried to ruin her lands, her people, and especially her fun."

Sterling gave me a sidelong look. I shrugged. "They aren't wrong."

"No," Sterling retorted in a pleasant tone. "But they are too young to know of others who ruled in a similar fashion."

"She kept a balance within her kingdom," Michael stated, finally speaking up. He even had that no-nonsense tone I associated with soldiers. "And yes, it was a kingdom. If she killed someone, they deserved it. Either for wasting her time, for attacking her or what she claimed, or for doing something really stupid. Otherwise, she was fair and just. Ruled with an iron fist, sure, but it kept everyone and everything in check. When she left? There was a power vacuum that lasted for over a century.”

“Back to the task at hand,” I said, ignoring the unwavering stare from Sterling. “I appreciate your words and thank you, but for now we should be concentrating on the current problem. Not a life lived centuries ago.”

“Well spoken,” Elliot said, a sly twinkle to his eyes. Though I didn’t trust it, I couldn’t help but smile as he continued. “Our fee will be ten thousand Swiss francs each. Including expenses. Deposited into our accounts. Half now, half after the completion of the job. As is standard.”

“Agreed,” I stated without flinching. “A bit cheap, aren’t you?”

“You didn’t ask what the ‘expenses’ entail,” Scott stated, downing more of his amber beverage, which I suspected was one of Fellhaven’s house beers.

It was my turn to give a sly smile. “You’re right. So what are the expenses?”

“Should any of us die, you will deposit fifty thousand francs into the account of our choosing. If, for any reason, any or all of us have to fake our deaths, you will deposit twenty thousand per person. You will also cover any hospitalization or healing of any sort that is required,” Elliot stated with the tiniest of smiles.

His gaze didn't leave mine and I couldn't tell if he was trying to out-stare me or see if I was going to flinch.

"Done," I stated without flinching. "All of it is reasonable. Now for my terms."

The trio became alert and all three leaned forward ever-so-slightly. Their bodies revealed an intentness that spoke of excitement and apprehension.

"You will follow the rules I set forth," I stated evenly. "If any of you refuse to carry out the order or disobey, which I doubt will happen, the agreement is breached and thus void. You can keep the deposit, but you will not be paid anything more. Even should you die."

The trio all nodded as one. This was going to be so much fun!

"I have my own personal guards. I'm certain they've been seen by you, and your employers. There will be no fighting amongst you; they will receive the same orders. You will work together. If there are disagreements, my guards are the final say." More nods from the paladins. So far, so good. "Your assignment, should you accept it, will be to seek out and track down any clue or tip that is given to locate the Staff. Should any other chaotic instances like the animated poultry at the local grocer occur, you will assist with ending them. Reports will only be given to myself, Sterling, or whomever else I may appoint, without question and they will be in complete detail."

The trio exchanged glances with one another before giving nods. Not a single one appeared phased or bothered by anything I'd said so far. Which was good, because I suspected we were going to need all the help we could get before the end of this mess concluded.

"And finally, should you locate or believe you have located the Staff of Chaos, you will contact myself or Sterling immediately. You will reconnoiter the area, and if possible, keep the being in that vicinity."

"Those are all reasonable terms, and we agree," Elliot stated with firm finality. The other two gave nods, showing their agreement as well. "Do you have any rules or requests in regards to our methods?"

"None," I replied easily. "You may use whatever contacts and sources you have at your disposal, as well as the methods you believe will bring a truthful answer." Sterling cleared his throat, and I lifted my chin in defiance. "Unless you're planning on saying they can forgo any laws in this task, please don't argue."

"I don't have to like it," Sterling grumbled.

"I don't believe liking any of what's going on ever entered the equation," Scott replied. "Our bosses aren't too happy that the Big Boss Down Below is growing crankier and crankier with each passing day. They're all walking around like someone's going to shoot them in the ass with blessed bullets."

"Makes one wonder what the other side is like," I mused thoughtfully.

Michael chuckled. "Probably circling the wagons and preparing for the upcoming Armageddon." At my questioning look, he explained. "The angels can't handle the Staff. They're control freaks to the extreme. There are those who think Lucifer's fall was because he believed humans should have more freedom of choice. The choice to do good, evil, or whatever and then deal with the consequences after the decision is made."

"Big Daddy in the sky didn't agree, and the argument ended with Lucifer being kicked out and those who agreed with him followed. Either by choice or by force, no one really knows," Scott added. "Either way, the angels ended up having less choice and became the ultimate control freaks while the demons enjoyed freedom of will and choice."

"Where do the dark paladins fall?" I asked, intrigued by their tale.

Elliot smirked, his dark eyes glittering with mirth. "There are some dark paladins who fall on the side of the angels, though usually it's the paladins that follow them with unwavering loyalty. Most of our creed prefer the demons. Not only do they pay better, but they have more free will in what they can do. Despite what some people think, they're allowed to do good, if they believe it will further their goals."

"You'd be amazed how often doing something good can further the power and goals of any number of demonic machinations," Michael added.

"I can honestly say that I try to avoid the demons," I stated with a smile. "We don't exactly have a pleasant history."

All three men burst into laughter.

"That's an understatement," Elliot replied, shaking his head.

"If it's any consolation, the demons feel the same," Scott added, still chuckling. "The fact they were willing to parley with you at a place of neutrality says a lot about the current situation."

"Not all demons have a problem with her, though," Sterling stated. "The illustrious owner of this establishment for one."

"Except he isn't beholden to the Boss Down Below," Elliot said with a shrug. "Don't know who *his* boss is, but it isn't Lucifer. As such, the Laws set by Lucifer don't pertain to him."

"Even the banished demon, Dante, isn't without fear of the Lady," Michael added. "He's the one who sent the assassin after you all those centuries ago."

"What is the story with that, anyway?" Sterling asked. "We all know the result, but no one has explained what started it. Or why Dante was banished because of it,"

"Ol' Dante convinced Khatep, your captured demon, that you were a threat. That you were amassing power in an attempt to rule all the lands, heavens, and hells. Or something along those lines. The reason isn't important. Khatep, the idiot, got all worked up by Dante and went storming off after you, determined to take your head," Scott said with a grin. "It was a standard power play. Dante wanted Khatep's assets and Khatep didn't realize he was being set up."

The demon within my talisman was fuming. His wings were unfurled, and I could feel his anger as he paced around in his gem. I stroked my talisman like one would try to calm an angry cat. So far with the same result. That is, none.

"After Khatep's death and the capture within your talisman, Khatep's friends went to a higher power. Dante might have played your demon, but he didn't get to enjoy the fruits of his labor. Somehow, Khatep's friends managed to convince one of the sub-princes of Hell that Dante was out for his position. They used Khatep's death as proof, showing just how canny Dante could be. When Asmodeus looked into your kingdom, he saw you were not a threat, which meant Dante was the one for whom he should be concerned," Michael continued, picking up where Scott left off. "Dante was then banished, losing his place amongst the demons, and unable to take souls or make Deals."

"Before you ask, Dante is not someone any of us would work for," Elliot interjected. "He is only interested in amassing power and wealth, willing to do whatever it takes to achieve the position he once held. Not that he'll ever be accepted back amongst the ranks of the demons, but he tries. Hoping to one day garner the approval of Lucifer or another higher-ranking prince than Asmodeus."

"So more chaotic and a freelancer than most," I stated. The three men nodded. "No wonder he tried to court Faith."

"Fi? Fi Wells?" Elliot asked. I nodded and he laughed. "Yeah, the girl has the hots for the angel. Those two are so stupid for each other it's not even worth joking about."

"Perhaps we can stay on-task?" interjected Sterling.

"He's always the killjoy in the room," Scott replied.

Elliot countered. "He is usually correct, however, and today is no exception. Your terms, Lady, are agreeable. You accepted ours. I believe we have the proverbial deal."

"We have an accord," I stated. "Someone should be in shortly, I hope, to take our orders. While we dine, perhaps we can discuss how best to begin your part of the search?"

Even as I finished the sentence, the second-oldest son to Mark and Jen entered. Hunter was in the middle of his teen years, and just starting to not look like a colt: all arms and legs. The trio gave nods and spoke their agreement. Even Sterling didn't object.

Maybe with some luck, we could stay ahead of the chaos the Staff was leaking. I wasn't going to hold my breath, but I could certainly hope.

# Chapter Twelve

Less than ten minutes later we were all eating. Hunter had delighted us with suggestions for what we wanted to eat. He was developing his father's knack for such instincts. In fact, I suspected the orders had been placed before he entered the room, allowing for some changes just in case we decided differently. But since we all agreed to his choices, the food came in fresh and hot with remarkable speed.

Sterling had just offered Elliot a sample of the truffle and caviar appetizer when the door burst open. A nightmare version of some Saturday morning cartoon flooded the room.

Tiny ponies, in every hue from the color scale, stormed in, trampled onto our tables, and wrecked our plates. Some began projecting energy beams in random directions. My mind had the impression they were trying to violently redecorate. The absurdity of the situation clashed with what was happening, so I suppose that's why my mind went into such an odd place?

Even as all of us moved to stand and fight, three familiar beings charged into the room. Jen was armed with a short sword in her right hand and a dagger in her left. Mark and Chris were right beside her, but neither appeared armed.

"Sorry! Bit of a mess! They started in the kitchen!" Mark called out. Faint images of long horns and enormous wings had sprouted from him. He thrust a hand forward, a ball of dark red and gray energy flew from the palm. The spell vaporized the pony it touched, a light blue one with a rainbow-hued mane.

Jen was shredding through the ones on our left flank, while my mind caught up with a few interesting facts. One was that no matter where she sliced them, there was no blood, but the odd critters seemed to fall lifeless. Secondly, she moved with a practiced ease, indicating that she'd had many hours of practice with the weapons. Third, those said weapons were unmistakably from Xantos' forge. Obsidian blades are rather distinctive, and the craftsmanship was too familiar. I'd watched such being made, after all.

Chris gave the greatest revelations for those who weren't aware of his 'inner' nature. His fingernails and teeth had grown two inches, ending in points. His taloned hands plunged into the pony closest to him, brought the writhing, objecting being to his now unhinged maw full of dragon teeth. Chris chomped down on the pony's face, then tore the head off with a vicious twist of his neck. Fluff or some other stuffing material dropped out of the head and body. Chris spat the head out. He used the limp body to pummel the next living oddity near him.

Another pony, this one bubble gum pink, jumped onto Chris's back. It- I couldn't tell if there were genders- used its hooves to climb over his shoulder. The pony should have stayed away or on his adversary's back. Without pausing in his gleeful pummeling of the other one, Chris hissed, opened his mouth, and let loose a bolt of lightning that fried all but the odd tattoo-like mark on the pink pony's hind quarters. The scorched patch of skin, or cloth, or whatever it was, drifted slowly down to the floor.

Chris moved on; each clawed hand armed with what looked like a large stuffed animal pulled from a war zone. The next pony he found got beatings from both sides.

Dragons. Just don't get them angry. They get nasty.

I looked around. The pony getting beaten by the corpses of its comrades was the last living one in this room. Jen and Mark had finished off the rest in the little time I had been focused on Chris's partial transformation and savage behavior.

Sometimes I have difficulty explaining what I witness, but here it goes.

There was stuffing and toy pony limbs everywhere. Some of the mess was smoldering. Other remnants were frozen, most were torn or sliced apart.

"Dinner is on the house. Next time you're here, free appetizers and first beverage sound fair?" Mark asked us. We all stared for a moment before nodding. I wasn't the only one who giggled, either.

"Okay." Mark continued. "You need to exit through the front entrance. That's the only path that's currently clear of these… *whatever* they are."

"We'll cover you," Chris assured.

"At the least, we will avenge you," Jen quipped.

She was joking. I'm pretty sure she was joking.

We didn't move in modern military fashion. There was no scout moving forward in a crouching run, using hand signals to notify us if it was safe to move forward, to stay put, or how many were around the corner. None of that.

Nope, the couple that owned the tavern strode ahead of the rest of us, akin to gunslingers with or without badges going about "cleaning up their town" while their son brought up the rear behind Sterling, the dark paladins and myself. They all walked with the same focused, predatory stride.

I caught the paladins looking at one another, smiles and nods between them. They obviously approved. Maybe they were hoping to see Mark fire the enormous revolver strapped to his hip. The trio's entry into the private dining room had been a little too busy for me to notice that he'd had it. I'd seen him wear "the big iron" on many occasions. I'd heard stories of the few occasions he'd fired it and was present for one of those times. Gotta admit, I was curious if another story was going to be made tonight.

Instead, I was afforded another bizarre sight, similar to the one we'd left.

More than fifty of the pony-like beings had been in the main dining area, along with more at the bar and raised stage. Stuffing was everywhere. Sections of partially destroyed pony beings were getting piled next to the stage by the rest of Jen and Mark's family. The two younglings were giggling and bouncing, their strawberry blond hair flopping as only children's' can.

Kyis and Oliver had made a competition of kicking the remaining pony heads, or what was left of them, towards the growing heap. The sole daughter, Ivy, was telling her younger siblings to knock it off and help gather up the stuffing.

The lads naturally doubled their efforts to see who could kick the most heads.

Most of the staff was engaged in the cleanup effort. At the entrance, Hunter, with his long hair up in a ponytail for once, was standing at the entrance door and directing the last dozen patrons to wait. They would be able to leave, he assured them, momentarily. The delay was to ensure the parking lot was clear. Lena and

Heather were at either side of the crowd, keeping a cautious watch.

Four pony beings, all bright neon colors, galloped past the open entrance doors. They seemed to be in quite a panic.

The resident Viking, Curt, charged past next. He wore his work khakis, black staff polo shirt and carried a pair of two-headed axes. His beard was split with a wide grin.

*"Run, bitches, run!"* he bellowed before letting out a maniacal laugh.

Hunter was still facing the crowd. A smirk crossed his mouth before he said in an ever so casual tone, "As I was saying, you should be able to leave momentarily."

I snorted laughter. Couldn't stop it. Don't regret it for a second.

"You think that's funny," Scott stage-whispered to me. When I looked at him, he gestured to the far corner of the dining area.

A single human male had not begun to evacuate. He was on his knees, cradling what seemed to be an eviscerated blue pony. Fragments were still strewn about him.

*"Whhyyyyyyyyyyyyyyyyyyy?"* he wailed to the heavens.

Or at least to the ceiling. I could see tears streaming past his cheeks and into the unkempt beard around his chin. He mashed the blue remains to his face and began, or perhaps continued, to sob loudly.

Scott was snickering while I shook my head.

"The best part," Chris spoke up from behind us, "is that we got hit with one of the more, eh, saner events. Just before Fellhaven got invaded, the staff members on break were reporting on posts and videos from social media."

"This was sane? What got reported?" I had to ask.

"How about a forest elemental taking a piss on a local politician's SUV before kicking it into the side of their two-million-dollar house?" he offered. "Would that qualify as stranger than this?"

"One of the 'Bigfoots' let themselves be seen?" I was shocked.

"Seen? Hell, Cat, this one walked past every security camera and upraised smartphone with both middle fingers up in salute!"

"At least they are from this realm," Sterling rejoined. "I've never seen any equestriary species like what came in here."

"Maybe Xantos has," I suggested.

Elliot's head snapped around to glare at us.

"Let's leave the dark elf out of this, okay?" he all but demanded.

"Anyways," Chris continued. "At least seven of the nine sea beings that live in Sherando Lake came up onto the land. All. At. Once. There's footage of them having what looks like a group prayer or business meeting."

"What in the hells? They keep away from each other intentionally."

"Yeah, precisely," Chris agreed. "I can't even visit two of them on the same day. They are that xenophobic of each other."

"The Staff," Sterling murmured through gritted teeth.

Curt interrupted further conversation. He re-entered the tavern. The skin of his face was a deep red and sweat poured down from his short, cropped hair. He was still grinning.

"Parking lot is currently clear," he announced to everyone. "Time to go, unless you plan on grabbing a weapon and helping if something else comes around!"

We let the other patrons disperse before us. Chris and Curt carried the weeping man to his car. He was still crying on the hood of his jeep as Sterling, the paladins, and I headed for our vehicles.

"Check out the campground," I told Elliot. "See if anyone noticed anything or anyone out of the ordinary." I paused before adding, "Talk to the gremlins, too. We'll do some research to see if there's a way to track this thing magically."

"The gremlins?" Elliot asked dubiously.

I nodded. "You'd be amazed by what they see and know. Let them know I'm involved. Apparently, I have a decent reputation with their kind."

Scott chuckled. "Lady, you've got a reputation with every kind of being from the planes of Hell. It just varies between the types of being."

"We'll be in touch," Elliot said as he headed for his car.

The other two followed his lead.

Sterling and I watched them before we got into his Stingray so we could return to my home. If there was a method to track this using a spell, I knew two beings who would know. As he maneuvered the Corvette onto the road, I began transferring the funds into the paladins' accounts.

The sooner I could check that off the to-do list, the better. Especially since I suspected they were going to earn every penny of their fee.

## Chapter Thirteen

The first thing Sterling and I did was take a long hot shower. In fact, we remained in said shower until the water turned cold. We may have also used half a bar of soap and a great deal of shampoo and conditioner, as well. Despite the events at Fellhaven, there was no forgetting what we'd encountered at Maxine's abode.

We may have enjoyed some intimate adult-time, also. So by the time we returned to the living room, I was relaxed and prepared to tackle the problem set before us.

Maekyl, as usual, was on my coffee table. Also as usual, he was talking with my baby cloud dragon who I'd acquired a year ago when the Eye of Amon had been stolen. An unexpected, and unintended gift from a former boyfriend who no longer existed on any plane, thanks to a few demonic creatures eating his spirit. My little nabrasu, a creature that devoured negative energy and produced positive, was stretched out on the back of my sofa reminding me of a content cat. Aside from the cheetah-like coloring and multiple tails, it could have easily passed as a cat. Especially since nabrasu also purred when happy.

Staff of Chaos

After Sterling and I had settled in the living room, each of us with a beverage of choice, Maekyl finished discussing the history of dragons with 'his' young charge. I found it amusing that the ancient, powerful, captured undead dragon had claimed the role of mentor and father-figure to my little cloud dragon the moment I'd brought the egg into the house. Not that I'd ever tell him that. Maekyl already had an over-inflated ego. One that did not need a boost of any sort.

"Are there any spells -and I do mean any- that can be used to track down the Staff?" I asked Maekyl when he turned his attention to me. "We can't just drive everywhere and hope we sense it being used or had been used recently."

If skulls could frown, Maekyl would've had the deepest. Instead, the glow of his eyes shifted to a darker color.

"There are spells that could lead you to a similar signature of equal power, but the source could be anything. Not just the Staff." He wiggled on the coffee table until he was closer to where I was sitting on the sofa. "Think of it as an infrared device. You can see the heat sources. Their size and shape, but there is no way of knowing if the blob on the screen is the blob you're looking for, since a lot of hot-blooded creatures have similar sizes and shapes."

"So it would be like searching for a single person in a crowd of people of the same size, shape, and weight while using an infrared device of some sort," I stated.

"Exactly," Maekyl replied grimly. "If you had enough people to canvas the area and search out the dozens, if not hundreds, of results it would be useful… otherwise-"

"Not so much," I finished for him. "Great. So, we have zero useful suspects, a missing artifact that's creating chaos already, and no way of tracking it down magickally."

"I thought the demons gave you some suspects," Maekyl intoned. "Tell me what happened."

"They gave Cat three," Sterling replied. "We know the first, Rick Barker, created a box found in another suspect's house. Barker, though, had a wand charged by the Staff. The wand, I might add, was driving the incubus insane. We left him unconscious in his home."

"Definitely not the guilty party," Maekyl mused. "What about the other two?"

"Both women," I said. "Maxine Olson and Sophie Conner. A sloth demon and envy demon, respectively. Sophie was nowhere to be found, but the Staff had been used there at some point. We have a box Barker made at Sophie's place, complete with a photo of her with Barker."

"Olson was a complete waste of time," Sterling stated. "Hoarders would probably bow before her, due to the amount of… items she's collected. Including the trash, insects, and pests that have infiltrated the home she's living in. The smell was horrendous, and her behavior was childish, immature, and pathetic."

"I never dismiss a sloth demon from suspicion," Maekyl stated, his glowing eyes moving to Sterling. "Despite their name, your dislike for such, and the believed demeanors, they're incredibly sly and cunning beings. They can surpass even the most conniving greed or envy demon. If she's got her sights set on that Staff, don't count her out because of some act she put on for you two."

"It was a pretty convincing act then," I replied before drinking some of my soda.

Maekyl snorted. "The demons that have come after you, Lady, are ones with an agenda. Those you've destroyed or sent back to Hell have been ones desiring to harm you or yours. Otherwise, you've avoided the denizens of the Lower Hells for the most part."

Tipping my soda can towards him, I gave a nod. He wasn't wrong.

"Do you have a suggestion?" I asked.

"I'll contact Trix," Maekyl replied in a smug tone. "We'll confer and place a spy on her."

"Do you have someone who has a cold? Or no sense of smell?" I asked, my lips twitching into a smile. "Remember the 'good ol' days' when the moats smelled like a latrine on a hot, humid, summer day? Triple it and you've got Maxine's abode. Only with more creepy crawlies and other varmints."

"I'm sure we can find someone," Maekyl replied. "Or bespell them. There is a spell or four that will keep them from smelling that stench."

"It still brings us back to the problem of one missing suspect and no solid leads," I said with a sigh.

The demon in my necklace took a moment to react to my growing agitation by flaring his wings before settling them against his back. He didn't feel annoyed, though, despite the fact he was brooding in his prison. Even as I stroked the gem, he didn't seem to settle into a content position.

"A pity we can't just scry for the demon," I said, trying to puzzle my way through where the missing demon could have gone.

"You know," Maekyl began. "Demons have their own hierarchy. All the ones here on this plane answer to someone 'above' them. You may not be able to discover where your missing suspect happens to be, but all the demons know when something happens to one of their kind."

"That's very true," I mused. "It seems all the demons I've encountered are aware of what happened to my little companion here."

At that, the demon seemed to flop down and curl into a very tight ball inside the precious stone. There was a definite air of sulking coming off my talisman. Rolling my eyes, I continued to stroke the gem. Slowly, the demon stopped sulking and relaxed.

"The question left is who to contact about requesting that information," I said, glancing at Sterling before turning my eyes back to Maekyl. "Dante is outcast, so I doubt he'd be much help in putting in a call to whoever is Conner's superior."

"Keisha, then," Sterling replied. "She should know who to contact, as well as know the proper channels to do so."

"We need more information. Not just on the suspects, but the Staff, as well. Sure, we can try to trail after where the damn thing has been, but that's not going to help us locate it," I said, stating the obvious as I complained.

"You're also not asking the most important question," Maekyl chimed in, this time not sounding the least bit cheerful. "Why hasn't it been used more often by whoever is in possession of it? What are they waiting for?"

"I really hate it when you point out the obvious," Sterling grumbled. "It's even more annoying when you're being logical."

"Not to mention concerning, when he isn't cheerful about it, too," I added, eyeing the skull. "Do you have any theories, oh wise and dead one?"

"Not at the moment, but I'd check a calendar to see when the next big celestial event happens to be," Maekyl replied. "Next new moon, full moon..."

Considering we were in the first weeks of February, I drew a breath and let it out slowly. There was one event I'd used often during my glory days and Maekyl knew it.

"When is it this month, Maekyl?" I asked, closing my eyes, and hoping he didn't say 'next week'.

"It begins on the twentieth, Lady," Maekyl replied.

"So, we have until then, give or take a few days, to find the Staff. I suppose that's better than a week," I stated.

"And what event are you two discussing? I know it isn't the meteor shower that occurs this month. That peaks on the seventh or eighth," Sterling stated. I could tell he was trying to not be snippy.

"When the moon moves into the Winter Circle," I replied, my tone anything but happy.

The Winter Circle was an asterism composed of five stars, each from different constellations. It was more of a hexagon shape than a circle, but it still counted with magick.

"Why not the full moon?" Sterling asked, curious. "Or even the asteroid shower?"

Maekyl's teeth began chattering in his version of laughter. I hid my smile behind the soda can.

"You of all people, asking why one event and not the other," Maekyl said, his teeth clattering together even as he spoke. Don't ask me how he did it, but he managed that feat with ease.

Sterling's eyes twinkled with mischief as he gave a shrug. "Both of the other events have power, also."

"There is more energy for that event. It's too random with the meteor shower. And the full moon, even with the thinning Veils, is not nearly as powerful," Maekyl retorted in a scholarly tone. "They have been thinning for the past year. Perhaps since the time a certain demon took possession of a certain artifact."

"A certain demon who should not have bagged as many souls as he did. Someone, or perhaps several someones, helped him up his numbers," I said, trying to figure out one of the missing puzzle pieces. Maekyl's eyes brightened, and he bounced a little on the table. Even the demon in my talisman had stilled completely. "Who do we know that can't bag souls, yet somehow makes Deals?"

"Dante didn't steal the staff," Sterling stated with complete assurance.

Maekyl snorted. "Doesn't mean he didn't help get Kevin Daniels into that position. Doesn't mean he doesn't know more than he's letting on."

Giving Maekyl a nod in agreement, I turned to Sterling.

"We need to contact Keisha. Ask her to contact whoever Sophie Conner's supervisor happens to be," I suggested. "Then, we need to search Kevin's home. I don't care how we do it, but it needs to be done. If there's a connection between Kevin and any of the suspects, it may be at his place. We should also search back over Conner's place. She's got boxes of photos. There might be something else hidden among them."

"And the chaos created by whoever has the Staff?" Sterling asked. "That being is staying somewhere in the area. We can't stop on that front, either."

"We need a hacker. Someone who can search through the computers of the local hotels, rent-a-homes, or air b&b's or whatever they're called these days, along with any of the other places someone can stay. If there's a connection, we need someone who can find it," I replied evenly. "I'll give Mark and Jen a call. They may know someone."

"Why not your cousin in Richmond?" Maekyl asked. "Piero would know someone, and you know he'd be honored to help."

I shook my head. "No. I don't want him or his family involved in this. Bad enough that if anything happens, we're going to need to contact people in the area to keep him and the rest of the family safe."

"Mundanes?" Sterling asked, drawing the word out slowly. "Mundanes are aware of you?"

"My family from my father's side. Some of which have needed training in magick," I replied easily. "It's not spoken of, and no one asks me to do parlor tricks or curse anyone."

Not that I hadn't done those things, because I had. Kids are easily entertained with magick, and when you are able to do the real thing? It works great as bribery.

Sterling grumbled under his breath but didn't say anything more. Maybe he was finally learning that sometimes it was okay for mundanes to know about our world.

"Get the right person, and they can have the gremlins help out," Maekyl suggested. "If the Veils drop, they're going to be tasty snacks for a lot of critters out there."

"Back to the task at hand," I said, suppressing a shudder at the thought of the gremlins being eaten. "We'll call in my guards, Jade, Roland, Alesio, and Trix. They all can work with the dark paladins on containing the chaos that pops up while we search for who has the Staff. Roland and his pack should be able to contain some things. Same with Alesio and his cabal of vampires. They all can contact each other, as well as us should it be needed."

I had zero doubts that Sterling and I would end up being needed for some of the things that would happen.

Sterling handed me his phone. Keisha's name and number was already pulled up. I quickly added her information to my phone.

"Take care of contacting her, then we'll call in the rest of the troops," Sterling said as I handed him back his phone. "I'll call Fellhaven to see if they're back up and running. If so, we can either pick up the order or meet there."

Glancing at Maekyl, who looked a bit glum, I smiled. "If we meet there, we'll have to take the talking skull."

"Only if he promises to behave," Sterling stated, looking down his nose at the skull.

"It's Fellhaven," Maekyl replied in a prim tone. "Everyone behaves at Fellhaven." He paused, before adding, "Well, if they know what's good for them, they do."

"Indeed," I replied as I tapped the number for Keisha the Demon. Maekyl snickered as I waited for her to answer the phone.

"Hello, Lady," Keisha said by way of greeting. "I presume you have more questions."

"I have a request, actually," I replied. "I have a question for whomever is Sophie Conner's superior. She's missing and I'd like to know if she's on this plane of existence, back in Hell, or elsewhere."

Silence was my immediate reply. A long heavy silence. The call hadn't dropped. I knew that because I double checked.

"All three suspects were under the same Duke of Hell," Keisha replied, almost reverently. "I will make the needed calls and contact you with the answers you seek. If not myself, then a minion of Crocell."

"Thank you," I said simply. "Should a meeting be required, may I suggest Fellhaven?"

"Of course," Keisha answered. "If a meeting is needed, I will speak with the owners to ensure everything is prepared without any difficulties for any party involved."

"Perfect. I will be looking forward to the reply."

"Until later, Lady," Keisha said, then the line went silent.

This time the call actually ended. I turned to Maekyl and Sterling.

"Right. One more task done. You still have a direct line to Trix?" I asked Maekyl. He nodded. "Good. You contact her. I'll call Jade, my guards, and Roland.

Alesio will still be sleeping, so I'll leave a message with him."

"I'll call Fellhaven while you do that," Sterling stated, tapping at the screen of his phone. "What time do we want to meet?"

"Five?" I suggested. Sterling nodded. "Good. That'll give us some time to kill."

Maekyl's eyes narrowed slightly as he studied me. "And what are you planning on doing between now and the meeting?"

"I plan on scrying Xantos so I can check in on my daughter," I replied. "I miss my baby girl and even if I can't visit, I can at least see her. I hope."

"Oh," was the only thing my undead dragon had to say.

Guess he hadn't expected that answer. Sterling, though, was smiling.

"Care to join me for the call to Xantos?" I asked him.

As Sterling nodded, I began tapping at my phone's screen. The sooner we got our calls done, the sooner I could contact Xantos. With luck, I'd get to at least see Lenore for a little bit and ask how she was doing.

At least I knew she was safe. Far from me but also far from the dangers we faced. Xantos was with the only person who could ensure she survived whatever the realms threw out while her father and I faced the challenges head-on.

Staff of Chaos

## Chapter Fourteen

The dark paladins hadn't found anything useful at the campground or anywhere else the previous day. I had to give it to Elliot and his team, they were thorough when they went about a task. They'd talked to the gremlins, the mundanes, and even ferreted out those from our community. I didn't ask for their methods, and they didn't volunteer details, but they were confident in the truth of the answers they received.

One of the things I'd learned long ago was you had to delegate your tasks and place some trust in the ones you employed. The better you treated your people, the better the results. You'd garner loyal followers as well as those who were only in it for what they could get from you.

You would also get traitors, spies, and thieves, but usually the threat of torture and death kept them to a minimum.

The dark paladins were hired by me. They had a reputation to uphold. Not just among the community, but with their normal employers. There was little to no concern about them possibly betraying me. I hoped.

The fact that someone either had or was going to betray me left a bitter taste in my mouth. I knew who wouldn't betray me. Those beings I could count on my fingers. Maekyl. Jade. Sterling. Xantos. My parents. Mark, Jen, and their family who weren't even close enough to really be a Judas to me.

I didn't think Trix would betray me. Shadow dragons typically didn't shift loyalties without first being betrayed. She'd had ample opportunity to betray me over the past decades but hadn't. So, I didn't think she'd do it now.

The list of beings who could and would betray me was far longer than I wanted to consider. Despite knowing there was no point in stressing over who was a traitor to me, and ultimately, the world, if they ended up using the Staff.

Sterling glanced at me as he drove through the streets of Waynesboro the morning after the evil stuffed pony attack at Fellhaven.

"What's on your mind?" he finally asked.

"I keep thinking about what Fi's gremlin said. About 'beware of the Judas'," I answered, watching the buildings pass by us. "I have a very short list of people I know who wouldn't betray me and what feels like a never-ending list of people who might turn on me."

"Welcome to living a long life," Sterling replied with only a little humor to his voice. "All of us who live for more than a century rack up a long list of enemies, 'frenemies', and beings who would turn against their sibling or parent or spouse with the right incentive."

"Or child," I added with a sigh. "You're right. I shouldn't dwell on it." Shaking my head, I turned back to what I could get answers for. "What do we know about Kevin Daniels?"

"A sloth demon who was the information technology supervisor of ShenValley Shipping," Sterling replied. "Reputation of being a jerk but was good at delegating work. He kept the department running smoothly and with few hiccups. After the company was bought out and became demon owned and operated, he gained a bigger head, according to his employees. I believe they called him a bigger asshole bordering on a dictator."

"Fi mentioned he was giving her a hard time about her wanting to take a week off," I mused. "Wonder if that attitude began after the buyout or if he was like that before?"

"No clue. He didn't appear to have a lot of hobbies. Though his work browser history showed a love for watching people racing sports cars," Sterling said.

"Nothing like having very little information to go on for these people." I complained.

"Not everyone can lead an exciting life," Sterling teased. "Despite what entertainment might have you believe, most people really do live boring lives."

"Demons, even demon-possessed, do not qualify as 'normal people', especially those who want to be in charge of an artifact like the Staff of Chaos," I retorted as Sterling pulled into Kevin's driveway. Leaning forward, I peered at the house. It was too nice. "Are you certain this is his place?"

Sterling nodded. "I'm certain."

"I'm not the only one wondering how he could afford this, am I?" I asked as we got out of the car.

"Not hardly," he replied.

The white house was a bizarre three-story building. From one angle it appeared to be a modern take on a country estate. There was certainly enough acreage surrounding the house, complete with an upscale neighborhood and nearby crop fields.

Pulling to the west side of the building to park, the illusion skewered for both of us. The steps up to the front patio were actually two-stories. The front door was on the second floor. The ground floor, clearly above soil level, had the occasional double windowpane. Then we could see the back. The rear door emptied onto a larger patio that was halfway between the ground floor and where the front door was set. This back patio allowed for a single step down into the yard.

So, a country home, part ranch, part what the hell else? At least the top floor looked structurally normal, with a peaked window facing each of the primary directions.

Together we followed the concrete walkway lined with little red bricks up to the front patio. A large planter filled with greenery sat to the side of the doorway. I took a moment to look around the front yard at the carefully trimmed hedges, the mulched flower beds, and grass that obviously hadn't needed to be mowed. Probably not since Daniels' death. Two trees sported branches of thick green needles. Mulch circled the bases and I wondered who he'd hired to tend to his lawn.

"Wonder how well he paid the lawn service?" I asked.

"Maybe there's a bill we can find so we can ask them," Sterling suggested as he unlocked the door and opened it.

He gestured for me to enter, and I stepped across the threshold and into Daniels' house.

Mundanes, and many magickal beings, can create thresholds to prevent evil from entering. Without being welcomed into a home, that same threshold can lower the power of the magick a being can do or the harm that can be caused through non-mundane methods. It certainly won't stop anyone from using a gun, sword, knife, or any other type of physical violence.

If you're an evil being, no matter what race or species, you typically cannot create an effective magickal barrier to prevent those with harmful intent or even dark energy from entering. It was the equivalent of two magnets of the same sides pushing against each other. Vampires and other similar creatures had the same problem.

Unlike many of the demons of the current day and time, Daniels did not employ a security system of any sort. At least, there were no signs stating one was in place. Nor did we notice any cameras.

A very good thing considering we were entering the house illegally. Maybe I was a bad influence on Sterling? Or maybe he wasn't in a mood to worry about social legalities, I thought, studying his grim expression. Either way, we shut the door behind us and turned to the task of figuring out where in the two-story house we could find something useful.

Unlike the homes of the other demons we'd visited, or even Dante's adobe, Daniels' house appeared more like a normal, mundane-owned abode. Photos and classic art dotted the walls. Most were photos of Kevin Daniels with his friends at sporting events like baseball or football games. Although, there were just as many at a racetrack. There were a couple of him leaning against a red sports car on a racetrack of some sort.

Sterling immediately began going through the rooms, pausing to search the furniture for something useful. I studied the photos as I moved slowly through the rooms. Someone had to have taken the pictures, since they weren't selfies, and none had a photographer's logo on them. That meant someone had a camera or phone with a really good camera. The people in the photos with Daniels changed, but none were people I recognized.

The first room I walked through was a living room. Spacious and neat, it reminded me of something I'd find in a magazine. In fact, the more I thought about it, everything in the house and outside reminded me of a professionally decorated house.

Aside from the inch of dust on everything.

I do mean everything. We moved through the living room, down a curved ramp.

The stainless-steel kitchen was big enough for two families, along with ample counter space. The round table and four chairs were set, but the dust was visible on the plates, silverware… even the fruit bowl in the middle. A hunch on the lack of flies made me look closer. Yep, the fruit was all plastic or wax. Fortunately, the back door we'd seen was in this room. It was a pair of glass sliding doors, thus plenty of sunlight illuminated the area.

The lounging area past the kitchen had a matching set, couch and loveseat, and a large, curved television- did demons all shop at the same place? - hung on the wall.

Sterling tapped my shoulder. He pointed out a note that was stuck to the side of the kitchen cabinets, against a magnetic whiteboard.

"That is the resignation letter of the cleaning service for this house. Dated two days after Daniels' death," he explained.

"I suppose the groundskeeping service took longer to figure out they weren't getting paid," was my response.

"So, this is how a sloth demon keeps a presentable residence," Sterling said, looking around. "At least until he departs this plane of existence."

I nodded.

"Lots of space, high-end decor, pay for everyone to do everything."

"Maybe I will pull some influence and have this place cleansed. I could use new quarters," Sterling joked.

"Ugh. I'd get vertigo trying to traverse the floors on a daily basis. And we haven't even checked the bottom and top floors."

"Imagine how discombobulated any would-be intruder would get, though."

"You aren't wrong," I conceded, while I continued to look for stairs that went in any direction.

I found the steps past the pantry. They lay in opposite directions with a polished wooden landing between them. The descending set went under the ramp that connected the living room and kitchen area. The ascending set traveled parallel to the wall where the lounge tv hung. Then the biggest oddity of the interior, so far, struck me.

"There's a hidden room on this floor," I told Sterling. "This platform, and the stairs? They don't come far enough towards the front entrance to fill the space to the left of the door."

Sterling looked all around and agreed. We went back to the front door.

The wall which the front door opened against seemed completely blank and complete. Now, the flat wall we saw when first walking in, just before the living room, made sense. On the other side of it was where the platform and stairs would be found.

Still, there was a dead space big enough for a small room. Like a private office. We just had to see if there was a way to get in.

Ten minutes of looking over the surface, corners, and molding like a pair of mundane sleuths did nothing but make us both impatient. I tried a reveal spell but got nothing. Sterling pulled out the "big guns" and cast one of his own, calling on centuries more experience than I had.

A section of the wall literally melted away. We walked inside.

"I only know of a few beings, in all the realms including Hell, who can cast that level of metamorphosis spell," Sterling stated at my questioning look. "The number is under five."

"That explains why it was still there despite Daniels being dead," I stated, almost afraid to move very far into the room.

Sterling nodded, standing beside me as we took in the room. "He definitely allowed his slothful ways to show in here."

It was my turn to nod.

The walls of the room reminded me of a reversed sticky note. Papers were stuck to the wall without the use of any pushpin or tape. There was a mound of gray matter resembling a rectangular block in the center of the room. What I guessed was used as a chair, made of the same material, and reminding me more of a tree stump than a chair, was positioned behind the rectangular mound. Both had an oily appearance to them, but thankfully no smell.

As Sterling moved to check out the desk, I perused the papers on the wall.

"I think I know where he got his money from," I drawled as I studied the papers. Sterling looked over at me. "Pretty sure these are blackmail receipts. Unless you can think of some other reason for there to be papers with names, dates, payments received, and details on an awful lot of naughty behavior worthy of blackmail." I paused before adding, "There's an awful lot of people who I'm sure are delighted he's dead."

No wonder Daniels said he had a lot of enemies.

"Define 'naughty behavior'," Sterling requested.

"Extramarital affairs, skin trade, running drugs, underage escort service," I said, rattling off a few of what I was reading. Following the rows and rows of papers, I lost count of the number of names mentioned. I did not lose count of how many had the same workplace. "There's more than those mentioned on these papers. Looks like he was blackmailing at least half of the ShenValley Shipping employees. Our charming Mr. Daniels kept track of not only his victims' workplaces but made a note of how they met. Any of those who he didn't work with he met at ShenValley Shipping. My bet? They're customers and clients of the company."

"He's been a busy boy," Sterling stated. "Notice any familiar names?"

"None that are connected with our suspects," I replied, glancing back at Sterling. "At least not yet."

Sterling made a noncommittal sound before saying, "You're going to want to look at the ledger."

Turning to Sterling, I stopped examining the papers to take the proffered ledger. Sterling, meanwhile, began examining the gray lump.

After two pages, I found what Sterling had noticed. Printed photographs of Sophie. Not in apparel meant for walking into church, or school, or most anywhere else. There were dates for each photograph. The ledger page with the pictures had a list of hotel expenses and receipts. The dates matched the ones of the photos.

Some of the photos had Daniels in them. Others had different beings. Or at least parts of them that I had no interest in ever seeing.

"Hmmm… was he the pimp, or did they have a more mutual relationship," I wondered aloud. I turned the page.

More hotel dates and expenses. Names next to some of the expenses. A blank page to accommodate future expenses and dates. After that, the ledger had dates, names, and payments.

Lots of names from the work people I'd seen on the walls. Mayor of this town, the occasional county official or supervisor. More than a few demons that Sterling and I had run into. I wondered what Maxine had paid for, or why the list often had Dante next to someone else's name. More payments either to or from Sophie and businesses. What did a sloth demon at a shipping company have on the local McDonalds, Wendy's, or a bee farmer?

"Any theories on this ledger?" I asked, flipping through the pages.

"Not enough facts to form a solid theory," Sterling stated as he gingerly touched the gray mound.

He poked at it with a disgusted expression on his face. Probably uncertain if he really wanted to try looking for a drawer. I shifted my weight and continued flipping through the pages, skimming over the names until my eyes landed onto a single name.

Debbie Ann Kaelin.

The proverbial light bulb went off in my head.

"This isn't his list of blackmail. Or a backup of any sort," I said with certainty. "This is how he managed to bag enough souls to throw his name into the demons' lotto to be a guardian of the Staff of Chaos."

Sterling jerked around to face me, eyes widening before narrowing. "Why do you think that? Not that I'm dismissing it, but I'd like to know your reasoning behind that theory."

"Because Debbie Ann Kaelin wanted me to convince her boyfriend to marry her. She was pregnant at the time and seemed pretty desperate to get what she wanted." I tapped the paper beside her name. "She met me at the Clocktower when I was searching for the Eye of Amon. Said she'd find someone else to do it when she didn't like my proposed terms. It appears she went to Dante. And since Dante can't bag souls and Daniels' could, there's only one reason she'd be in this book with Dante's name beside hers."

"What were your terms that she didn't like?" Sterling asked, honestly curious.

"I told her she'd have to agree to an orgy with people I chose so she and her lovers could power the magick," I replied, smirking. "She didn't like the idea of having an orgy with strangers despite the fact she and her beau weren't together at the time."

Sterling coughed. Cleared his throat. Then began snickering.

"So, instead of chasing the poor guy using mundane methods, she went to you. When you didn't snap your fingers or wiggle your nose or wave a wand, she decided to sell her soul just to get her boyfriend to marry her?" He paused, the laughter subsiding, though the smile remained. "How did she get your name?"

"Uncle Tony gave it to her. I don't know how she knows him, and I didn't ask," I replied with a shrug. "Find anything else useful?"

"No," Sterling replied. "Though, I think this is plenty."

"Should we tell Raziel about all of this?" I asked, gesturing to the walls.

Surveying the room again, Sterling nodded. "Raziel should be informed."

"Think he'll be able to get in here without a problem?" I asked as we departed the now not-so-hidden room.

"Absolutely," Sterling replied with a grin. "Especially since I'm going to remove the spell and place a simple glamor over the hole in the wall."

Chuckling, I watched as Sterling did exactly as he said. Together, we departed the house. As we headed for his car, I took a last up-close look at the strange house. Oddly enough, I thought the house suited Sterling rather well. Though maybe with more flowers and kids' toys littering the yard.

With a smile, I slid into the passenger seat of his Stingray. "Where to next?"

"Give our dear angel of mysteries a call while we head to Sophie's place," Sterling stated. "We'll give her living quarters yet another search. Make sure we didn't miss anything the first time."

"Sounds good to me," I replied, pulling out my phone.

## Chapter Fifteen

Part of me wondered how everything worked with real estate and the like when a demon died without family or relatives to take over the property. Who handled settling the bills? Selling the houses? Giving it all a mental shrug and dropping that long line of questioning, I turned back to the task at hand: searching Sophie Conner's home. Again.

Upon entering Sophie's adobe this time, we began searching every piece of furniture in each room. Despite the fact we didn't find anything, it didn't stop us from searching. As we moved through the house, looking for any clue, we found only evidence of her being an artist.

Sketches, sketch pads, markers, pens, and pencils were neatly nestled in drawers and desks. Cabinets contained various art and craft supplies in neatly detailed containers. This time, we took extra care to search for hidden rooms, but didn't find any.

Slowly we made our way back up to the second floor where we repeated the process. We didn't say anything to each other. Lost in our own thoughts, I supposed, which was fine. The silence wasn't nearly as annoying or irksome as it had been the first time around. I paused in my search to consider that, then I realized an interesting fact.

"The influence left by the Staff is gone," I stated aloud. "We've been through the entire first floor, and the energy left by the Staff is gone. Do you think Raziel and his crew removed it?"

Sterling shrugged. "That's feasible but rarely done. A cleansing also tends to have an overall effect, not just 'one element is gone' from a place. Doesn't matter the size of the place, either. Does the house feel different to you in any other way?"

"Not that I can tell," I replied, considering his question. "The energy from the Staff has a distinct feel to it. That feeling is no longer here."

"Did you notice it when you were around Fi?" Sterling asked as he began going through a wardrobe in the guest bedroom.

"No, I didn't," I replied thoughtfully. Opening the top drawer of the nightstand beside the bed I found it empty, aside from a phone cable and wall charger. "Maybe the energy dissipates after a time?"

"Possible," Sterling said, closing the doors. "The wardrobe is pretty empty. Some hangers, a set of bed linens. Nothing remotely close to being called 'evidence' or useful."

Or maybe this was part of my being 'tainted' by the Staff, I thought silently. Not wanting to voice it.

"Back to the master bedroom?" I asked as we finished searching through the empty closet.

Sterling nodded and we left the guest room. There wasn't any change to the master bedroom that I could tell. Hopefully if there was a clue, it was something Raziel had overlooked. Though, I didn't think he was looking for something that would point towards the Staff or who might have taken it. He'd been looking for evidence of who killed Kevin Daniels.

If we could find the answer to that, we'd know who had the Staff. Or at the very least, who was involved with Daniels' death. That person could then be used to locate the Staff. Like with everything else in life, it wasn't that simple. I didn't think anything was ever that simple.

Sophie Conner had been an envy demon. She and Kevin had some sort of business arrangement, as well as a personal attachment. An artist with low self-esteem and even lower self-confidence. She coveted the Staff.

Had she wanted to possess it? Or use it?

Crossing to the dresser in the room, I opened all the drawers until I found the one filled with her lingerie. There, I found lace garments, silk garments, and a neatly folded stack of 'granny panties'. That particular stack was most definitely out of place, not just in type but in how neatly they were folded and stacked.

A smile curled my lips as I moved them to the side where I found a little black book embossed with an owl on the front. A tiny little lock dangled from an equally tiny clasp.

There are a few things that a possessed person doesn't let go of, and keeping a diary seems to be a typical thing for certain types of people. Hopefully the little black book held something more than sketches and wishes of power, wealth, unicorns, and ponies. Of times long gone and impossible goals.

Unlocking took less than a breath of magic. Flipping to the last few entries took only a couple seconds. Reading backwards took more time. Fanning the pages, I decided I did not want to spend hours reading through everything she'd written in her little book. So, I did the next best thing: I cast a spell seeking familiar names.

As Sterling turned to see what I was doing, a few names rose into the air above the book. One name in particular stood out.

Dante.

"It seems he's becoming an interesting party in this not-so-little investigation," I stated, closing the book with a snap. Brushing a hand through the names, they blew apart as though I'd waved away smoke.

"Indeed," Sterling replied. He had two handfuls of photos. "Care to help search through these?"

"Absolutely," I said, crossing to the bed and the box of photos. "Which box is this?"

"The most current, from what I can tell," he stated, nodding towards the label. He held up a photo, the back facing me. "These have the most recent dates on them. At the very least, they have current tech in them."

"Not to mention the company. That one has only been around for two decades," I stated, nodding to the photo. He flipped the photo over and I chuckled. "That phone, though, hasn't been around for two decades."

Sterling smiled and resumed going through the photos in his hand. I reached into the box and withdrew a stack. Sitting on the edge of the bed, I began flipping through them. The discarded ones went into an ever-growing pile on the opposite side of the box. After fifteen minutes and probably a couple hundred photos, we finally found something useful.

The photos were taken at different places. One was a photo of her and Dante dressed to the nines for a night out. She had a smug smile and Dante appeared pleased, as well. Another photo showed Sophie with Kevin at a baseball game. I recognized a logo as one of the local teams. Sophie had a huge grin on her face while Kevin didn't seem thrilled to be there. A third photo was one of her and Ricky in a position no one needed to see. The last photo was the most damning of them all.

It resembled one of the old Polaroid photos. Since I'd seen the newer versions in the house, and the photo hadn't yellowed from age, I figured it had to be from the newer models. Considering the content of the photo, I wasn't surprised it hadn't been taken by a phone or digital camera.

Not when the chance of a demon seeing Sophie sitting in what I guessed was Kevin's office holding the Staff of Chaos could be high. She was wearing a long, flowing dress and holding the Staff as though it were a scepter. I presumed she believed she was pretending to be some queen of Hell. All she lacked was a tiara to complete her fantasy.

"I think I'll give Raziel a call. Find out if he's heard anything about the knife we discovered," I said, looking through the photos. Minus the one of Ricky and Sophie. That one I didn't need to see again. Ever.

"Do you think he'll tell you?" Sterling asked.

"He owes me," I replied. In honesty, he would be owing me for a long time, but Sterling didn't need to know that. Or why. "Should we continue going through the box?"

"Let's be completely thorough this time around," Sterling suggested. "I don't think we need to go through all the other boxes."

Nodding, I grabbed another stack of photos as Sterling tucked the photos into a pocket. "Might as well make yourself comfortable. This is going to take a while."

Chuckling, Sterling shoved the photos on the bed over and sat before diving into the box.

## Chapter Sixteen

y the time we finished going through the entire box of photos, my eyes were blurring and I'm pretty sure I'd lost a few IQ points. It was past noon and both of us were starving. Since Sophie's abode was in Staunton, we debated on where to go: one of the many restaurants in town or our favorite eatery in the 'boro, as most people referred to Waynesboro.

"Let me give Raziel a call and see if he's available," I suggested after ten minutes had crept by. "If he is, he can decide where we meet for food and a chat."

Sterling nodded and I rang the Angel of Mysteries.

Twenty minutes later we were enjoying sandwiches, fries, and beverages in my office. We were waiting for Raz to show, but since he wasn't eating, we had started.

Since I was there, I booted up my laptop and logged on. Scrolling through my emails, I found one from the Order of the Scepter. Reading over it, I pursed my lips. It was dated the day before the demons wanted to meet me. Curious.

"What *is* the Order of the Scepter?" I asked Sterling. He started, the sandwich half-way to his mouth stopping in mid-journey. I continued "Obviously they aren't the ones who punish miscreants and such. Nor are they the ones who create the laws that govern our society. The Council does that."

"The Order of the Scepter is a group of archangels and dukes of hell. Members are the ones that can come to this plane of existence. Through their paladins -dark, light, and anti-paladins- they are the ultimate watchdogs of magickal artifacts." He set the sandwich on my desk. "Why?"

"They sent me an email prior to the demons meeting me," I replied. "From the way this reads, I think they were wanting to either meet with me or hire me."

"Have there been any other messages?" he asked. I shook my head. "Then they are aware you're searching for the Staff. Ask Raziel when we see him. He's not part of the Order, but he knows the members. He would know more about the angels' side of this business."

Sterling returned to eating his sandwich. I munched on fries while I went through my emails. Then I turned to the messages left on my desk.

Roland, the alpha of the local werewolves, had taken over my day-to-day tasks. He'd brought in his second to help. The workload had been growing over the past year as my name became more prevalent in both the magickal antiquities market as well as being known as the Speaker of the Council.

Roland was efficient, as was his second. The two of them had figured out a filing system and a way of prioritizing everything. My business was going to need to expand, and I was definitely going to need to hire more people if my life didn't settle down. The more I thought about it, the more I liked the idea of expanding my business.

Before I could broach the subject with my beau, there was a knock on my office door. Sterling and I both looked towards the door's frosted window to see Raziel's silhouette on the other side.

Sterling made a slight gesture, and the door opened. Raziel frowned slightly before stepping through the threshold and shutting the door. He still wore what I now considered his trademark leather jacket, jeans, and polo shirt. At least this time he didn't appear frazzled or quite as weary.

A small part of me wondered how long it would take me to anger him this time. The thought brought a slight smile to my lips. To keep either male from asking what I was smiling for, I gestured towards the other chair in front of my desk.

"Thank you for coming, Raz," I said pleasantly. "We have a few questions that I hope you can help answer."

"I will help as much as I can," he replied warily.

"To begin with, have you been able to learn anything about the knife?" I asked, folding my hands on the desk.

Raziel sighed and leaned back in the chair. "It's an active murder investigation."

The smile on my face darkened, as my eyes narrowed. "Yes, and you owe me." At his glower, I held up a hand. "I'm not asking for every detail you and your team have uncovered. We just need to know who owned the knife."

"Very well," Raziel grumbled. "The outcast demon, Dante, owned the knife. It's an antique and is several centuries old. It's been in his possession since it was forged."

"How do you know that?" Sterling asked. The look he gave me said there would be questions later about why an angel would owe me.

"This isn't the first time it's been used in a murder," Raziel stated simply. "It *is* the first time the knife hasn't been found in Dante's bloody hand."

"You haven't questioned him," I said. It wasn't a question.

The Angel of Mysteries shifted. His shoulders rose and fell. I suspected if we could have seen his wings, they'd be ruffled in agitation.

"There is no possible way for an angel to interrogate a demon, even one that is outcast. The rivalries between us would be too strong. To say a fight would begin would be a vast understatement," Raziel said, irritation coloring every word. "Having a mundane person conduct the interrogation would be pointless, because he could easily manipulate them or lie better than any human."

"So, you need someone to question him who he can't lie to or manipulate," I stated, my mind whirling with possibilities.

Raziel nodded. "That regards any investigation involving Dante." His eyes drifted to Sterling before returning to me. "Unfortunately, neither of you qualify as a 'someone' I can utilize."

"We'll worry about that part. In the meantime, we need you to give us your opinion on what we've found," I said, nodding to Sterling. "Dante's name and likeness is showing up a good bit in our investigation."

Sterling slid the photos we found in Conner's box to him. I slid the ledger over.

"The photos were found in a box at Conner's place. The ledger was inside Daniels' hidden office," I explained. "We suspect the ledger contains documentation of all the souls Daniels' bagged. Where the contracts were signed, and what demon assisted in him bagging them." I paused as Raziel opened the ledger and began flipping through the pages. "As you can see, Dante's name appears a great deal."

"When a demon is sloppy, that is what occurs. I have a large file on cases I suspect he had a hand in, or more. But more often than not, he has covered his tracks efficiently," Raz said, looking up from the ledger. After a few moments, Raziel handed the ledger back to me and looked over the photos. As he handed those back to Sterling, he said, "Tell me what you know."

Taking turns, Sterling and I gave Raziel a rundown on everything we knew about the suspects, what we'd found, and what we'd been told.

"There are a lot of questions, most surrounding Dante, his involvement, and a motive," I said. "Keisha said Dante wouldn't be able to handle the Staff. Dante brushed it off as though it were no big deal. Until we have further evidence to the contrary, I'm not going to doubt Dante's inability to hold, or use, the Staff of Chaos."

"That doesn't mean he didn't conspire with Conner, though," Sterling added. "Considering Dante is a demon, it's not out of the realm of possibility that he's appearing to be helpful just to divert suspicion."

"There are many possibilities that fit the evidence," Raziel began, leaning back in his chair. He dropped his illusion and gave what sounded like a sigh of relief. "Dante has been banished from Hell for several centuries. Ever since he sent Khatep to kill you, Catherine, and you captured Khatep within your talisman. From all reports, Dante hoped to rise in power. I suspect he didn't anticipate his fellow demons turning against him and being banished for his actions."

"He's had a long time to plot vengeance," I mused.

Raziel nodded. "Demons are rarely short-sighted creatures. They will bide their time and plan for the future. Decades to centuries into the future. It's very possible Dante has been waiting for a chance to find someone gullible enough to be used so he can have revenge against the very ones who banished him."

"You believe Dante searched for a demon who would 'bag souls' for him. Just so that demon could be manipulated into putting his name in the lottery and hope to become one of the guardians of the Staff." Sterling shook his head slightly. "The first two parts would work, but there was no guarantee the demon, in this case Daniels, would become one of the guardians."

Feathered wings rustled as they furled before settling against the angel's back. "As long as Daniels continued to work with Dante, he could continue to put his name into the lottery. Odds alone say he would eventually be named one of the guardians."

"Let's continue this line of thinking," I interjected. "Dante supposedly loves not having the restrictions of being a full-fledged demon of Hell. He can't bag souls, but he can do everything else. He's able to gain wealth and power. He can manipulate mundanes, and probably even a lot of those in the magickal world without them realizing it. He's sly, cunning, and completely untrustworthy. So why would he want to destroy the Veils and bring about the End of All?"

"Where did you hear that phrase?" Raziel asked, his eyes narrowed on me.

I smiled sweetly. The angel frowned, and I could see his irritation growing. "Xantos, actually. We're on good terms."

"Speaking of untrustworthy," Raziel grumbled. I shrugged. It was pointless to argue with the angel. He continued when I remained silent. "Chaos of any sort preys upon the mundanes. It makes them reckless, illogical, and willing to do things they wouldn't otherwise consider."

"Perhaps the goal originally wasn't to use the Staff until everything is destroyed and all Hell breaks loose," Sterling suggested. "Perhaps he knew Daniels would pull out the Staff to show it off and flaunt it, knowing the chaos it caused would encourage that behavior from mundanes. He'd be able to claim more souls with less work."

"That's certainly possible," Raziel conceded. "But what changed?"

Sterling said, "We'd only be guessing at that. I'm sure we could all conceive theories that fit the facts, but the only one who truly knows is Dante. For all we know, it may have been a matter of the demon not anticipating this turn of events. Daniels' elimination by violence, let alone the Staff being 'out in the wind', to use an old military phrase? If Dante has no true motive for the worst end result, perhaps he's just improvising to try and keep his position without losing face."

"Or perhaps he wants the ultimate revenge," I suggested. "By stealing the Staff, or having it stolen depending on how it was done, he can bring about the ultimate downfall of Heaven and Hell. He, in turn, would reap the benefits. Daniels can't be the only demon he works with in bagging souls. By destroying the Balance both sides work hard to keep, he can reap the rewards. People will be willing to 'do anything' to gain what they want."

"The only way to know for certain of his involvement, and the extent of it, is by questioning him," Raziel stated. "And it has to be by someone he can't lie to."

"What about contacting the Order of the Scepter?" I asked. "Shouldn't someone from the Order be able to question him?"

Raziel gave me a slight smile. "I could contact one of the archangels. Gabriel, Michael, Uriel. Any of the others. They would then have to contact their paladins, who would have to contact an intermediary, who would then have to contact one of the anti-paladins. One of them would then have to contact their duke. Who would then have to question Dante. The answers would then have to be sent back by sealed letter through the same channels."

"In other words, we might get answers eventually," I said with a sigh. "But the time would be difficult without having someone as a go-between that can get it done faster."

"Indeed," Raziel said, staring intently at me.

"In other words," Sterling said, echoing me. "Catherine."

"It's so lovely to be wanted," I grumbled. "Perhaps eventually someone else can be wanted as much as I am."

Both men snorted, but there was amusement in their eyes.

"Fine," I said with a sigh. "I've already requested answers from Keisha, one of the demons involved with this whole mess. Once I know how her superior wants to contact me, I'll investigate how to contact one of the dukes of Hell. Hopefully they won't hold a grudge for my, ahem, past actions."

"Have the meeting at Fellhaven," Raziel suggested. "Even the princes of Hell obey the rules set forth by the owners. In fact, they've used it to their advantage a few times. Both sides enjoy having a place of neutrality."

"Good to know," I said. "Before we conclude this meeting, do you think Dante is the one behind all of this?"

Raziel met my eyes and held them. "I honestly do not know, Catherine. The facts are there. It's not out of his capabilities, but I don't know. It wouldn't be the first time a demon tried to plot the downfall of the world. But it also wouldn't be the first time one was framed to take the fall."

With those troubling words to ponder, Raziel stood, his usual glamor returning to hide his wings and celestial self. He gave me and Sterling a nod before departing the office.

Sterling and I shared a troubled look before returning to our meal, which we finished in silence.

If someone had framed Dante, we were really in a lot of trouble, I thought as I continued going through the notes and other items left by Roland.

To keep myself from worrying too much on the 'what ifs', I turned to my previous question about my business.

"To change topics a bit, what do you think of my hiring more workers?" I asked Sterling.

His eyes brightened as our conversation shifted to the pros and cons of expanding my business. Who to have in charge, how to expand, and what types of beings would be most helpful to have as employees.

Despite the discussion, in the back of my mind, I couldn't help but wonder about Dante, the Staff, and if he was guilty.

## Chapter Seventeen

The days were crawling by with no results. The hacker that Lena knew, and who had agreed to assist in searching for the Staff of Chaos, hadn't found anything useful. At least we had people willing to help in locating it. There had been no more bouts of chaotic magick, either. Which did nothing but raise the unease and tension everyone seemed to be feeling.

Generally speaking, most agreed that having something to track, even if it was pockets of insanity that the mundanes encountered, was better than nothing. All Sterling and I seemed to be able to manage was visiting all the local hotels and bribing people in the hopes of hitting pay dirt. So far, all we'd accomplished was finding one person who'd seen someone who'd looked like Sophie. Said person had left the day before the stuffed ponies attacked Fellhaven.

No one at the local hotels had seen her. Either that, or we hadn't been bribing the right people.

We were discussing how far out we should investigate when I received a text from Keisha, asking us to meet at Fellhaven. Since neither Sterling nor I were one to turn down the possibility of gaining answers, we hopped in his Stingray and headed for our favorite eatery.

Jen met us at the door wearing the perfect poker face. No emotions shone in her eyes or on her features. Even her body language was neutral and void of a tell of any sort.

"Is everything okay?" Sterling asked, studying the lady proprietor.

"A meeting has been requested between you, Sterling, Keisha Cole, and the one known as Robin Daves." She paused before asking, "Do you agree to this meeting?"

Sterling and I looked at each other before looking back at her.

"We agree," I answered. "We swear to abide by the rules of this establishment and the Code of Visiting."

A smile flashed across Jen's face before her stoic expression returned. This time it was a smidge softer.

"Well spoken," she stated. "Follow me, please."

Sterling and I nodded again and did as requested.

Jen led us to the second of the two dining rooms. The main one we used for the last meeting was maybe a third larger than this one. The phrase 'larger on the inside' definitely applied to Fellhaven, because you'd never expect to find so much space just by looking at the building from the outside. That is, if you took the time to compare the exterior to the interior.

Maybe thieves, grifters, and masterminds would notice. But none would dare do anything about it. Not if they wanted to continue to breathe.

I was not expecting to see Mark and Chris standing on either side of the dining room doors. Both had rigid body language and grim expressions. The frowns were nearly identical.

Ifrit and dragon. Father and son. Ready for the worst. Mark even wore the large antique revolver on his hip for this occasion.

The sole occupants of the room were sitting at the center table. Wine glasses sat at their places, and they were talking quietly to each other. When they noticed Jen, Sterling, and myself, both stood.

Stepping to the side, Jen allowed Sterling and me to move forward to the table.

"You all know the rules. The appetizers will be in momentarily," she said before turning to me and Sterling. "Do you have any preferences for beverages?"

"No," Sterling and I said together. We looked at each other and smiled.

"Your beverages will be brought in with the appetizers," she stated and gave us a nod. Without another word, she turned and departed the room.

Robin Daves studied me as I studied him. The name could have been either male or female. I suspected the demon before me shifted his appearance to fit whomever he was meeting. His straight black hair fell to his shoulders without a single wave to the strands. Dark eyes met mine and there was definite amusement glittering in their depths. He wore a white button-up tucked into dark blue khakis with a matching dark blue blazer.

Despite the business casual appearance, the power oozing from this demon told me more than anything else. This wasn't just any demon. Robin Daves was higher in the echelon of this realm's Hell than Keisha Cole or the others I'd met. Including the demon in my necklace who was kneeling with his head bowed.

"So. You are the Lady of Death," Robin said, his eyes drifting to my talisman before rising back to mine.

"That was my title," I replied easily.

Keisha spoke up, her eyes darting between us. "Lady, Consigliere. May I present Crocell, Duke of Hell. Also known as Robin Daves."

Robin aka Crocell smiled. It wasn't a pleasant smile, either. He gestured to the chairs opposite of him and Keisha. "Why don't we all sit?" Once we were all seated, he continued. "You had questions for me concerning the missing Staff of Chaos."

"We appreciate you meeting us," I began. "Unfortunately, it seems our list of questions have grown since we last spoke to Keisha."

"The opportunity to meet you on equal terms was vastly appealing," Robin replied, the smile not fading. "It isn't often a being who captures a powerful demon survives as long as you have managed."

"That sounds a bit like a threat," Sterling said evenly, giving voice to my thoughts.

"Not a threat," Robin corrected. "Most beings powerful enough to do as she has done end up making foolish mistakes. Usually, they want more power. More wealth. A higher position in life. The Lady of Death did none of those things. She's an enigma among my people. Those of my position and higher."

"How did you know I captured the demon and didn't kill him?" I asked. "Or is that a recent discovery?"

"Khatep was not one of mine. He was beneath Abigor. When Abigor no longer felt his presence upon this plane or in Hell, he knew something had occurred. Though he suspected Khatep hadn't been killed, for that would have sent Khatep back to Hell, Abigor did not know what had happened. And so, when Khatep's faithful approached Abigor, telling a story of Dante trying to usurp his throne by having you kill Khatep, he accepted it as truth."

Robin paused in his narration to sip his wine. Keisha picked up the tale.

"The dukes and princes all questioned your intentions, Lady," she explained. "Most believed you sided with Dante. Whether you were his unknowing pawn or an active participant, none knew. And so after punishing Dante, a trifecta of dukes went to observe your kingdom."

"We were… surprised by what we found," Robin stated, turning the wine glass in his fingers. "A half-fae necromancer holding elaborate parties, ruling in a way no mundane would ever have considered. Your people were loyal and wary of outsiders. Happy. Few wanted for anything. Fewer were interested in Deals." He shuddered. "We were delighted when your reign ended. It allowed our people a smorgasbord of possibilities and contracts."

"That brings us to our first question," I said, before Sterling could say anything. "Can you tell if the demon possessing Sophie Conner is alive on this plane of existence? Or if she has died and returned to Hell?"

"We cannot verify anything other than that she has not returned to any plane of Hell. Even those I prefer not to frequent," Robin replied, before taking another sip of wine.

"Meaning she was either destroyed, captured in a way similar to what the Lady did, or on a plane that you cannot reach," Sterling stated. He gave a slight smile. "At least we all can rule out the possibility of her being in Heaven."

Robin barked a laugh.

"No," he conceded. "She has not managed that. Wherever she is? When she returns, there had best be the penultimate reason for her absence."

"That should be an interesting conversation," said Sterling. "But we also have ample evidence that Dante is involved, somehow, with this unfortunate set of circumstances."

Keisha and Robin became very still. Their eyes were locked on Sterling.

"The outcast is involved either with the Staff's abduction or those responsible?" demanded Keisha.

I brought out the ledger, turned to the pages where his name was prominently listed.

"This was Kevin's ledger, found in his private office at his material residence," I explained in a slow, deliberate manner. "I saw several of those listed in this ledger at his abode, during one of his little parties."

"Dirk Cain," Keisha said quietly to Robin. "I remember that one."

Robin gave a curt nod but didn't say anything while he turned the pages. His eyes were riveted to the ledger, and I wondered if he was memorizing the names or looking for familiar ones.

Probably both, I decided as we sat in silence.

Fortunately, the silence was broken by a knock on the door. Once it opened, Mark and Jen entered with trays of appetizers and drinks. They moved with swift efficiency and in tandem. Neither got in the other's way as they placed the trays and glasses before moving back.

"Would you like to place orders for your entrees or wait?" Mark asked, his eyes not leaving Robin. I noticed that the male co-owner's right hand was in close proximity to the revolver he wore.

Robin finally looked up, startled. "Come back in ten minutes?" He paused before looking at both me and Sterling. "If that's acceptable to you both?"

Sterling and I exchanged glances before nodding.

"Ten minutes, then," Jen stated, placing menus between Sterling and Keisha.

The owners left once again, Mark following Jen out.

"Do you have anything aside from this?" Robin asked, his eyes darting from the ledger to me.

"Raziel informed me that the knife used to kill Kevin Daniels belonged to Dante," I stated, keeping my gaze even with Robin's eyes.

Robin's glamor shifted momentarily, and I caught the briefest glimpse of the demon behind the human guise. Gray mottled skin over a protruding nose and mouth. Holes where ears would normally be. No hair, black on black eyes. The true appearance vanished as his human guise reformed, but I wasn't about to forget what I'd seen.

His jaw clenched as he drummed his fingers on the table. There was a sharp tap-tap-tapping that went with each finger as it hit the tabletop. It reminded me of a woman's very sharp fingernails or claws tapping a wooden floor. I suspected the latter more than the former.

"The illustrious Angel of Mysteries would not be able to question Dante," Robin stated. There was no maliciousness or snideness to the comment. "Being outcast, that means any of the dukes or princes can demand answers."

Giving a slight nod, I said, "You would know far better than I."

A smirk flashed across Robin's features. "Are you attempting to manipulate me, Lady?"

"No," I replied honestly. "I believe that both Heaven and Hell want the Staff of Chaos reclaimed before it can be used. I hope that would mean all those interested in maintaining the Balance would be willing to work together in any way needed to find the answers."

"And finding the answers will hopefully help locate the artifact," Robin concluded. "You would make a fine demon, Lady." He paused, tipping his head thoughtfully to the side as his eyes narrowed slightly. "Or not. You do seem to lack the ambition that drives my kin."

"Perhaps my ambition is simply different from that of you and your kin," I replied evenly. "We can't all be the same. That would be terribly boring."

Keisha coughed lightly, ducked her head, and lifted her glass to her lips. Robin's eyes narrowed until they were mere slits. They remained that way for several long seconds before he burst into laughter.

"You're neither demon nor angel," Robin said, once his laughter faded. The smile didn't fade, and it finally showed in his eyes. "Once we have placed our orders, we can work out the details on when and where we shall question Dante. Until then, let us enjoy the fine food provided by our esteemed host and hostess."

Sterling and I waited until he and Keisha had filled their plates before taking our share. The conversation shifted to idle topics of no importance to anyone. As the four of us ate and conversed, the tension in the air lessened.

We would never be friends, or even close comrades. Admittedly, it was nice to know I didn't have to go searching for someone who could demand honest answers from Dante. Perhaps, with luck, he would get punished for his hand in this mess.

## Chapter Eighteen

Sterling, Keisha, Robin, and I all agreed it would be best if I confronted Dante. Robin would appear only after I was in his presence. That way, the lesser demon would not realize he had no advantage.

I didn't mind. Dante did not scare me. He wasn't even very amusing. He *was* annoying.

While we were enjoying coffee and dessert, I called Dante and arranged to meet him. He requested his place, which was fine with me. For one, that meant I wouldn't be tempted to overindulge in Fellhaven's delicious food. For another, that meant our confrontation would be out of the public's eyes. It also meant Robin could dish out any punishment without concern of any mundane noticing.

The last time I'd visited Dante's abode, he'd been hosting one of his 'parties'. If there had been better music, better food and beverages, and less smoke from legal and not so legal substances, I would have felt at home. But, alas, all it did was make me disgusted at how easily mundanes could be duped by various vices, easily offered by those with the time, money, and contacts.

I had fonder memories of the exterior of his home. It resembled a miniature version of a grand Mexican hacienda on the corner of a street filled with ranch, colonial, and 1950s house designs. A small hedge path surrounded the place. At night everything was lit up like it was fiesta time.

Since the sun hadn't set yet, the lights hadn't been turned on for the full 'the party is here!' effect. That's not to say the place didn't already look like "good times central" without the light show. I counted at least twenty vehicles cramped onto the street at and across from the hacienda. Plenty of noise leaked around the thumping sound of a subwoofer cranked to the max on a catchy tune. Beings laughing, screeching, yelling in festive tones, like something out of graduation night on a campus.

Certainly, I could have knocked. Somehow no matter how much racket was being produced inside, someone always answered the door. Usually that someone was Dante, but not always. However, I was in the mood to make an entrance.

While I walked the carefully maintained concrete walkway to the front door, I reached out with my senses. They found, and then identified the spells used to protect the threshold. Sterling had been teaching me new ways to approach magick anywhere I encountered it. Using the methods he had tutored, I dissected each layer of energy being used, redirected all of it to somewhere else.

In my first years as The Lady of Death, I'd just hit any defenses with all the power I could muster until they cracked or broke. This new method deliciously proved to be not only faster but more satisfying. Knowing that Dante's wards were now powering the alarm systems of every car within three blocks of his place gave me an evil little thrill. The cacophony of ringing sirens was a modern little twist on the old blare of trumpets announcing the approach of a significant dignitary.

Manipulating a bit of that power, I used it to blow his front door open. The instant I walked through the entrance? My body became ignited with green and blue fire.

This was of my own doing, actually. I wanted to make an entrance and I succeeded in doing so.

Between the car alarms blaring and my very not-human appearance, any mundane beings made quick work of getting out of the house. Some of the magickal beings hung around for a moment or two. Many recognized me and then found somewhere else they needed to be.

Dante had that damned smirk on his face when I found him. He was leaning against the grand piano in his large living room. A pair of goblins were around him, looking a bit anxious. Their black eyes darted between Dante and me.

"You scared off my patrons for the evening," he observed.

"Don't you mean witnesses?"

"Even if you are correct, two will work almost as efficiently as fifty. The mundanes wouldn't be able to comprehend what we are saying, regardless. These two will, and they are law keepers for their race."

"Oooo, goblin lawyers. The stuff nightmares are made of."

Dante waved my snarky reply away. "So, you've been a bit saucy and flashy for this visit. I hope you don't expect me to be impressed." He continued. "Your manners were lacking when you demanded this meeting and have not improved upon your arrival."

"Up until today, I thought you deserved some civility," I countered. "That time has passed."

The briefest frown came over Dante's features. He recovered before a full second had elapsed, but oh yes, it was there.

"Perhaps I should have invited three law keepers to this," said Dante, "to make sure every word you say is duly noted for later."

I smiled. Not my friendly smile.

"That would have been delicious. Every. Single. Word. Because that would mean the same would apply to everything you say, Dante. Goblin lawyers are such sticklers for facts and rules. They make the mundane look like children at play. However, two should be adequate for this. Shall we begin?"

All frivolity flew from Dante's appearance. When he spoke again, his voice was lower, more predatory. Definitely pissed.

"Make your case, witch. I tire of your arrogance. Unseemly manners do not become you," he said with disdain, even hate.

"Oh, I'm just waiting for my plus one," I teased. "Then we can really party."

Right on cue, energy spiked a few yards to my right. Ah, brimstone and sulfur. A demon who really appreciated the old troupes. Red and yellow flames to disguise the portal he was walking through. And his actual form, all eight feet high and ten-foot wingspan of it, making the scene.

I still thought my entrance was at least on par, if not a bit more shiny. But I had to admire how he made Dante and the goblins look like they wanted to shrink into nothing. Admire, hell, I admit I envied it.

*"Crocell,"* Dante whispered.

"Speak my name again, *outcast*, so it may be the last words coming from your mouth."

Okay, I really hadn't expected Crocell aka Robin's voice to be so different without his human shell. *This* voice was so much deeper, forceful, and projected. The windows and floor literally shook with each syllable the demon spoke. Pretty sure the strings inside the piano were snapping as well.

"Oh, good, you *do* know each other!" I exclaimed in what I hope was a confident- if impish- voice. "No need for introductions! That's lovely! So, about the questions I have?"

"You will speak Truth, outcast," Crocell demanded.

Yep, there went another half dozen piano strings and pretty sure a window cracked. I wondered if this demon gave vocal lessons.

Dante just nodded. The slightest tremble was visible in his body.

Maybe it's just my vicious streak being hopeful, but I swear the goblins looked to me like they wanted to hug each other and sob.

Removing the ledger from, well, nowhere, I held it up for Dante to see. "You may or may not recognize this darling little ledger. It's what the former living Kevin Daniels used to keep track of all his Deals. Names. Places." I paused, my smile not leaving my lips. "The demons who helped set up the Deals. Your name appears rather frequently. Care to explain?"

Dante's eyes darted to the Duke of Hell beside me, his jaw clenching. "I used Kevin to make Deals for those who wanted my... particular type of help. They were willing to pay anything to get what they wanted." He tried to smirk but failed. "Kevin had the power. I had the clients. It was a mutually beneficial arrangement."

"Except you garnered more wealth and he got… what? A larger number of souls? I'm sure that didn't bother him at all."

I caught Crocell glancing at me, but I couldn't decipher the gleam in his eyes. I probably didn't want to know what the high duke was thinking, either.

"He was happy with the arrangement," Dante snapped.

"Or so you claim," I said slowly. "Your little arrangement allowed a demon to place his name in the lottery for guarding the Staff of Chaos. A demon completely unworthy of the task. One who was known to flaunt what little power he did possess." My tone grew softer, smoother, and silky. "Tell me, Dante. Did you encourage the little toad to put his name into the lottery? How much goading did it take? I'm certain he claimed it was all his idea afterward, since I doubt he would want anyone to know he was so easily manipulated by an outcast."

"I didn't discourage him. How was I to know the whelp would go and get himself killed?" Dante replied.

"You didn't arrange for his death," I countered. "Or point any other demon in his direction? Put a little suggestion in their minds that he might be easy prey? That he was currently in possession of the Staff, perhaps? After all, you'd know who was eager to shift their position on this plane of existence, as well as any level of Hell."

Dante hesitated.

"Answer the Lady. Speak your confession."

Two little sentences, spoken by a rather irritated Crocell.

The piano collapsed under its own weight. The goblins were depending on the instrument to keep them upright, because they fell to the ground right along with it. The floor cracked beneath Dante. I doubted there was an intact window, at least in this room of the house.

A small part of my mind wondered what anyone outside would be hearing or seeing.

"No!" Dante shrieked.

His guise was fading. Tattered wings fluttered over his slumped shoulders. His face was sunken and sharper. The eyes were no longer human. His hands came up in supplication. Scrawny digits with ragged nails instead of the immaculate, manicured hands I was familiar with.

"No," he continued. "I only agreed to Kezth's arrangement! Kevin, that is! I collected enough souls for him to petition for a knighthood in the deepest realm of Hell! He used them for what he wanted, idiot that he was. Spent too much time letting the petty humans interest him! I took the arrangement because it allowed me only what I can amass on this toilet of a realm!"

I looked to Crocell. Fortunately, he nodded once, quickly. Looking at an unglamored demon is not a pleasant experience, no matter what else you've seen.

"Kezth was his true name. Dante would only know it if he was told personally."

Crocell spoke those words, but the effect was significantly less than anything he'd said prior. The room barely shook, and no further damage ensued.

"To be clear, so there can be zero questions about all of this: you had no part of the Staff being stolen. Either through manipulation of another, a plot of your own, or any other possible method," I said, hoping there was no wiggle room for Dante to get out of it by way of omission or truth or even a half truth.

Crocell spoke again, in that less epic manner, as if he'd read my mind. Maybe he did.

Ugh.

"Your involvement in all of Kezth's affairs and end, outcast. Did it begin and conclude with the simple arrangement you described to us, here, in this room, moments ago?"

"Yes," Dante mewled. "I had no further interests or involvement with anything in Kezth's existence or demise. The Staff of Chaos is not of interest to me. Its abduction does not serve me in any manner."

Dante sank to the floor. Maybe speaking that much truth was exhausting to demons. Gods know, it wears out more than a few humans that try to make a living from lies and deceit.

"*Punishment,*" Crocell declared. "For your lack of foresight. For your part in making the Staff available to the enemies of the Balance. Hated the Balance may be, but it may only be tilted in our favor if it *exists.*"

I'd seen demons like the ones that seemed to bleed upwards out of the floor at that moment. Similar ones had been summoned to devour my old ex-boyfriend, Nick Wright. I must have taken a step back when they came, because I was suddenly further away from Crocell, Dante, and everything else. The demons wrapped around Dante's arms and legs like constricting snakes. The sound of sizzling meat mingled with Dante's cries of anguish. It couldn't have lasted long but tell my brain that because it felt like hours.

When the devourers melted back into the floor, Dante kept phasing between his true appearance and the human guise. Both had deep, burned grooves in the skin where the demons had coiled over him. I doubted those wounds could ever heal.

Crocell must have felt his work was done. I felt the surge of energy, and the tearing of matter a moment before the fiery illusion around his summoned portal returned. He slipped through without sound or hesitation.

Which left me there with a mewling demon and two goblins that had soiled themselves. In the middle of a well-furnished room that was now a trash bin by comparison. I could hear a few car alarms still going off outside. No voices, thankfully.

So, I left. There wasn't anything to say, really. No need to make a spectacular exit. A simple spell made me undetectable by anyone mundane. Nothing impeded my exit.

## Chapter Nineteen

Back at my house, I sat at the kitchen table with Jade and Maekyl. Sterling hadn't returned from wherever he'd gone, and I didn't feel like more company. Having my best friend to talk to while gorging on junk food was exactly what I needed. Arylla was curled around Maekyl's skull and Kharzsa was perched on Jade's shoulder. Okay, draped over her shoulder might have been a more accurate description.

"So, we're back to square one?" Jade asked, munching on the chips in front of her.

There were bags of chips, candy bars, and a couple empty bowls that had held ice cream near us. Bottles of hard cider from a local brewery sat on the other side in a bucket filled with ice. Yeah, it should have been used for wine or champagne, but this called for something stronger than wine.

"Yup," I said with a sigh. "I really need to learn that spell. Those demons are kinda handy to have around."

Jade snorted. "Did you say that to Crocell?"

"Are you kidding? They may owe me for bringing Dante's actions to light and the fact they need to do better checks on whoever's name gets dropped into their hat. But that doesn't equal teaching a spell of *that* caliber." I shook my head. "I kept silent and didn't even think of it. Crocell would use that as a trap, and I have no desire to owe him. Better to keep everything equal."

"Why not just ask Xantos?" Maekyl chirped up. "If he doesn't teach you personally, he has plenty of beings in his employ who could do so." His tone grew sly as he added, "I doubt he would… tell a lady 'no'."

Warmth flooded my face, and I scowled at the skull. Xantos had said similar when I'd suggested a few nights of debauchery with no strings attached while I'd been in his realm. I hadn't had the crystal skull used for contacting Maekyl out at the time, yet somehow Maekyl knew what had been said. Or maybe it was a common phrase used by the ancient docelfar?

"I'll ask, when I have some free time," I muttered.

Maekyl's teeth clacked as he laughed. Arylla gave him a disgusted look but didn't move.

"Okay, before the skull gets used for handball, let's get back to the subject," Jade intervened. "There's a pattern we haven't realized in all this. Possibly an unknown player."

"Both," I agreed, grateful for the chance to regain composure.

"Cat, I think it's time to expand and use all available resources," Jade confided. "Someone that can see with a fresh set of eyes."

"Just whom do you recommend?" Maekyl demanded. "Shall we bring her parents into this? Ooh... Perhaps

Cat can hire the gremlins to make this entire quandary into an online puzzle game and let the mundane gamers figure out answers for us! No, no… too far out of character for all of you. I know, you can all gather and eat the entire menu at that tavern you treat like the only eatery in the state. No doubt the answers will reveal themselves just before the inevitable food coma."

"What's your quarrel?" Jade snapped back, even as she stood to loom over us. "Have you been huffing on the Staff and lost your usually considerable mind?"

Kharzsa had hopped down when Jade stood. She now seemed to be sizing up Arylla. In return, Arylla took a defensive posture while still perched on Maekyl's skull.

I wanted to interject. Try to de-escalate the growing tension between my two oldest advisors. My mind searched for answers, or distractions, something to get Jade and Maekyl or even the two creatures to calm down just a little.

My mouth said, "With help like this, we're all fucked."

When those words were spoken, they rang above everything else. Four pairs of eyes snapped toward me. None of them were human. And they were all filled with rage.

The demon purred in its cage that hung around my neck. My mind knew this was all going to go badly.

And I still couldn't make myself do anything to the contrary. I felt energy gathering at my hands, about to be formed with malicious intent.

That's when Kharzsa shrieked and toppled over.

A thick, palpable silence engulfed the room. I glanced at Jade and Arylla, who were in turn looking back and forth between each other, me, and the limp Kharzsa. Who took that moment to explode.

Literally.

We were all blown back from the energy released. None of us landed with any amount of grace or style. But as we all crept to upright positions, I realized that I could think clearly. Jade looked as if she'd come to full awareness as well. Arylla looked indigent even as she flew over to the pile of soot where Kharzsa had been.

"Kharzsa feeds on negative energy," I began.

"We just force-fed her a buffet of that," Maekyl continued from somewhere. His voice sounded muffled and distant. "Her body must have tried to produce enough positive energy to keep up, and it got to be too much."

Jade looked mortified. "I'm sorry, Cat. I don't know what got in my head, but everything made me angry."

"It wasn't just you. Arylla, Maekyl, myself, even Kharzsa were acting the same."

"Yes, but... Cat, we just killed Kharzsa by the emotional equivalent of explosive diarrhea."

"Considering that we've all come to our senses, or as much as you bipeds can come to your senses," scolded Maekyl. "Could someone get me out of this predicament?"

Jade and I began looking around. Arylla continued to peer curiously at the pile of ash. I joined my little dragon's gaze, somberly. Kharzsa had been a gift, a blessing, and I never wanted any harm to come to-

The pile of ash quivered, interrupting my thoughts.

Arylla pecked at the pile once, then twice. Kharzsa's head popped out of the soot. She stood and shook most of the ash off of her body. Her coloring had become more vivid and brighter. She also seemed bigger.

Arylla stepped forward and nuzzled her. Kharzsa gave the dragon hatchling a lick on her muzzle.

"Huh," I wondered aloud. "Kharzsa seems okay. Her kind and phoenix must have some commonality in their DNA. She was 'reborn' from the ashes."

"How delightful!" grumbled Maekyl. "Will you bother to locate me now? I can see almost nothing, and I believe I'm upside down!"

"I have been looking, oh grumpish one," Jade cheerfully retorted. She had made her way to the other side of the room. She hurried over to the couch and crouched. A moment later she stood, holding the skull upside down.

"He was under the couch, like this," Jade explained.

"Due to the massive wave of positive energy pushed out by the nabrasu, I'm completely trapped in this vessel!" Maekyl complained. "I cannot project my astral self at all!"

"Meaning as long as I keep the skull upside down, he remains disoriented. Or at least inconvenienced." Jade chuckled as she looked at the skull she held.

She did set him right side up on the couch cushions. Eventually.

"His current situation does lend to your theory that he lives off of perpetual snarkiness," I observed. "If a big slap of happy vibes traps him in the skull completely..."

"No! Don't you two start making plans!" Maekyl chided.

"I've often wondered if this skull would fit properly in a bowling bag. I'm sure I can find an old one for sale online. Preferably one with lots of room and in poor condition." Jade mused.

I laughed, just before I realized the bigger issue at play. My "ah hah" moment occurred the same time Jade's did.

"The Staff!" we said in chorus.

"It must have just been used!" I blurted immediately after. Looking at Maekyl, I asked "Did that happen closer to us than in previous events? Is that why we were so affected?"

"Possibly," Maekyl allowed.

But it was his tone that concerned me. He sounded cautious, even wary. Was he scared? Surely not.

"The greater probability," he continued, and there was definite hesitation in his voice, "is that in your pursuit of the Staff? You've repeatedly been exposed to its energy. Even in small amounts, such is having a cumulative effect. Akin to radiation poisoning. The more you get, the worse the effects become. Now, you've absorbed so much that it's spreading to the rest of us. At least while in close proximity."

"Gods… she's reflecting or refracting the energy whenever the Staff gets fired up?" Jade exclaimed. The horror in her expression matched what I felt in my gut.

"I'm afraid so. Her body has become used to the energy signature of the Staff. So, when that energy becomes available?"

"They connect to each other," I concluded Maekyl's trail of logic. "Sterling is likely having a similar problem. No wonder everyone even slightly sane wants this thing put away."

Arylla and Kharzsa took that moment to settle on Jade's broad shoulders. I didn't blame them.

My entire being felt soiled. Used.

The idea of becoming a greater and greater risk to those around me while the Staff was uncontained was horrific. My mind was racing in ways it hadn't since I was less than a century old. When I didn't know how to harness or control most of my ability. My biggest mistakes had been made, then. They could be surpassed by this current situation.

No. I could not let that happen.

"Isn't there some way we can use this?" I desperately asked.

There was unwelcomed silence for a minute.

"I suppose," Maekyl suggested, "that since you've experienced this sensation, you'll be more apt to recognize it. Perhaps traveling around the area, making note on a map of where you feel the same or similar? Hopefully not as strongly, since that would mean the Staff has been brought out again. Or used."

"Not a bad idea, at all," Jade said. "We can call up maps of the county, towns, and cities. Print them up, do a 'crawl' of the area. Will have to work fast, because we don't know when- *Aw, shit! The staff might have just been used!*"

"Just remembering that, are we?" Maekyl rejoined.

The realization struck harder the second time. I pinched the bridge of my nose.

"I wonder what mayhem is out there, now."

The communication crystal I used to keep in touch with the dark paladins lit up.

"Aw, hells. Guess we will find out, now," Jade groaned.

Five minutes and one transportation spell later, we found ourselves in the county, just outside the town of Stuarts Draft. We were in the parking lot of a snack cake manufacturer's factory and distribution center. Considering what we saw all around us, there was no need to worry about suddenly appearing out of a portal in front of dozens and dozens of mundanes.

Kobolds. A fuckton of kobolds.

Looking like short statured goblins that take the height difference very personally, or house elves that outgrew their rags before their twelfth birthdays. Lots of anger issues, cornered-rat mentalities, and greed. Oh, and definitely of the German variety. Right out of *Das Buch der Kindermärchen*. Well, verdammt. Won't this be fun.

At least one for each mundane in visible sight. And the kobolds were armed. Because of course they were.

Swords and spears and clubs, oh my.

The dark paladins darted and wove death in the thick of this mess. No wasted gestures among the trio as they went from cluster to cluster, protecting the mundanes while whittling down the kobold numbers.

Scott was the first of the three to move near us. Two of the larger kobolds had noticed our arrival and made their way to see if we were easier prey. We didn't need saving. But when a professional warrior jumps over a crowd and executes a perfect kidney-level slash, dual-handed, versus a pair of unsuspecting attackers? I will let that person work and be grateful for the show.

"Are you-" I began, as the pair of kobolds crumpled to the blacktop.

"Up to our knees in kobolds, really wanting some tacos and tequila, but otherwise fine." Scott blurted, drawing out the last word. The braids in his red hair and beard whipped around as he glanced from us to the various kobolds. "Thanks for askin'!"

And with that, he charged back into the fray.

Despite the overwhelming numbers of adversaries and frightened people around them, the trio was making some headway. I made out at least twenty corpses of the non-human variety, with only a pair of mundanes and a wounded half-elf for the other casualties.

Elliot threw a quintet of hard punches at one of the largest kobolds before finishing it with a brain-crushing blow from the steel baton he carried in a holster. His white smile beamed out between the goatee and mustache before he took on another foe.

Michael Black just mowed through any kobold that came within arms-length of his Gladiator-styled short swords. He seemed to glide from crowded section to crowded section.

Scott Williams went back and forth to where the most immediate danger to the mundanes was happening. Either splitting muscle or sinew and bone with his axe or slicing body parts with the bastard cross hilt sword in his other hand.

Each of the paladins carried firearms; I could see them on their web-belts. But in such close quarters, they had decided to get, well, medieval on these kobolds.

But the numbers still made me a little nervous. Too much chance of someone getting hurt or worse, still.

"I'm thinking you need to keep these fighters around. Add them to your bodyguard payroll," Maekyl declared. "Perhaps give them a vacation in Xantos's realm. I surmise they would do well."

Hearing my undead dragon companion's voice startled me. I looked around, finding the ornately carved skull sitting comfortably in Jade's hand.

"I didn't say you could leave the house?" I said out of shock.

"Nor did I expect to fly through your summoned portal and be brought here." Maekyl confessed, "I am quite thankful that Jade has such splendid reflexes."

"The Staff's effect?" suggested Jade. "Perhaps its influence runs on myriad levels?"

"I suppose," was my uneasy reply.

Glancing back to the battle royale before us, I said, "What can I do about this, then? Without risking greater harm?"

"Let me try," Maekyl interjected.

I gave consent with a single nod. Jade stepped past me, holding Maekyl's vessel ahead of her.

Light erupted from the skull's eye sockets. The dark paladins wavered and swayed as if they had been struck with fearsome blows to the head. All other humans collapsed to the parking lot surface.

One second later, the skull let loose with another flash, this time with a different hue. All the kobolds, dead or alive, were gone.

I stepped beside my best friend, asking, "What did you do?"

"I cast a pair of very broad-based spells," Maekyl replied, "to lessen the chance of the Staff or its effects changing the parameters of my intent. The first was a memory wipe to affect any non-kobold beings within one hundred yards of my casting. The second was a mass transport spell against any kobolds in the same area."

"Where did you send the kobolds?" asked Jade.

"As far out into the Atlantic Ocean as the spell would allow." he explained with glee. "I can promise they are not within one hundred miles of any shore on this coast."

This is one of the many reasons why I didn't let him out of the house.

The paladins staggered up towards us.

"We were fighting something just a little bit ago, weren't we?" asked Elliot.

Michael held up his short swords with the blood dripping off of them. "We just stopped, according to this mess," he observed.

"We need to get out of here before the mundanes start to wake up. Come on, you've all earned tacos and tequila, on me," I said.

Scott gave out a war whoop while I opened a portal back to my place.

When we stepped into the kitchen, nothing unexpected came through that time.

"You've got tacos and tequila, here?" Elliot asked, before observing, "I need to learn your kitchen secrets, since I can't smell either. Or is the Lady of Death just as skilled a chef as she is a sorceress? Going to whip up some street level tacos before our very eyes?"

"I'm fair in the kitchen, but we are here to drop off Maekyl," I explained. "Then we feast at Fellhaven or Puertos, your choice."

"Fellhaven," the trio said in perfect chorus. I cocked an eyebrow.

Scott explained. "More authentic Mexican food at Puertos, sure, but Fellhaven stocks more top shelf tequila. Also, we don't have to watch our words or change gear."

"And why can I not attend the festivities at the beloved Elf and Demon Tavern?" Maekyl demanded. "Have I not proven my worth out of your basement only minutes ago?"

I started to give a rebuttal but realized I had little in the way of argument. I looked around at the rest of the living beings in my place. Everyone had a similar confused and perhaps shocked expression. Lots of silence.

"Oh, what the hells," I said, just before opening the Door to Fellhaven.

We walked into the hallway that stretched between the private rooms at the tavern. I glanced behind us to see the wide opening that capped the hall. It showed my living room area just before closing behind Michael. Then it was just a pair of doors that would fit in any restaurant or service area. Wider than most, with the sign declaring it the exit to only be used in case of emergencies. Looking back towards the restaurant proper, I realized Jen and Chris were walking towards us.

"Private room for five?" Jen began, her usual hostess smile wider than usual. "I see you left the dragon and nabrasu at home. What prompted-"

Jen noticed Maekyl in Jade's hand. Her expression instantly darkened.

"Oh. You brought him. No wonder they didn't come," she said flatly.

Chris looked like he was ready to punt the skull out of Jade's grip. And then do gods knew what to it.

Instead of speaking further, Jen turned smartly to her right and opened the closest door. Chris stepped back and gestured for us to follow. His skin began to look a bit, well, scaly and blue. The paladin trio didn't seem to care. They happily made their way into the room.

"Hello, youngling," Maekyl said as Jade walked past Chris.

"Greetings, wyrm," Chris said back in a common tongue used by dragons.

Confused and growing a bit concerned, I realized my feet had carried me into the private room regardless. After a moment, I recognized this room as the same I'd met the group of demons in. Those who wanted to aid in finding the Staff.

"What will it be?" Jen asked in a professional tone.

I couldn't remember the last time either of the owners hadn't had something to suggest, or had ready, when I'd arrived. Alone or with others.

"Tacos and tequila, if you would, good lady!" Scott chimed in. "I don't know what our compatriots would like, but that's what the tres amigos are here for!"

Jen smiled, but it didn't quite meet her large blue eyes. Which now were a very dark blue, I noticed. Were her ear tips sharper than usual?

Then the door flew open. In the hallway loomed a thing of black smoke and ichor. Green and blue flame licked around black eyes, horns, and massive wings. Light was obscured around the creature. It made a single, long step into the room.

But it was Mark, Jen's mate and fellow tavern owner, that walked in. His cold black glare focused on Maekyl's host skull sitting on the table next to Jade. I hadn't managed to sit, yet.

"Oh, it's him." Mark grunted. As his gaze swept towards everyone else, the more human brown eyes became visible. He didn't look pleased or jovial, but at least he appeared calm. "Have a seat, Cat, everything is cool. Hey, love, I will take this one."

Jen blinked twice. She glanced at Mark, back at Maekyl, then at me. After a single nod, she began striding out of the room.

"I'll be nearby, sharpening my dagger," she said by way of goodbye.

"I'd heard there was better service at this humble bar," Maekyl declared.

Jen stopped at the doorway. Suddenly, somehow, Maekyl was in Mark's left hand. A hand that was now much larger, taloned, and turning blacker by the second. Jen glided up next to her partner. Both had smiling faces that were just, well, evil.

"Rip him out of his safe little box, love," Mark growled. "I'll eat what's left. Catch the screams to play on the crystals when we're bored. I'll give the dry bones to Chris to add to his nest."

"You can't." Maekyl challenged.

Jen's left hand shot out, hovering above the skull's eye sockets.

"Ohhh, skull boy done fucked uuuuuup," Scott commented.

"Is it too late to order popcorn?" asked Michael.

Green light oozed from Jen's fingertips, crawling into Maekyl's sockets.

"I just want my damned tacos," grumbled Elliot.

"Ummm, guys?" I tried to interject. Jade's hand unexpectedly tightened on my shoulder. When I looked back at her, she gave me a single, sober shake of her head.

The onyx black hand gripping Maekyl's vessel squeezed. Cracks formed where the fingertips pressed in. A loud, peeling cry filled the room.

"He's not coming, old wyrm." Jen purred at the skull. "Our fealty and tribute to him was paid. Did he not tell you that? Pity. Perhaps you aren't as favored as you think. Or maybe he's just amused right now, watching as he does."

"*Misericordia!*" Maekyl shrieked.

There hasn't been much that unsettled me as much as the low, throaty chuckle coming from the demon, mingled with the high cackle of the elf. Not a sound I'm looking forward to ever hearing again.

The knock on the door startled all of the guest occupants in the room.

"Dad? Mom? The lights are flickering out here. Maybe another night, okay?" Chris's calm but firm voice came from the door.

Jen's lip curled as she closed her hand into a fist. The green light was replaced by a sickly yellow. The cracks in the skull vanished. Mark unceremoniously dropped Maekyl on the floor between them.

"Food and drink are on the house," Mark declared. He looked pointedly at me before saying, "Find that bedamned Staff, soon."

He turned, urging Jen to follow him. They walked out of the room together. Chris entered with Curt, Ivy, and Kyis. I think. Each of them had trays. There was a possibility the young strawberry blonde carrying the covered hot dish was Oliver. I didn't see the two youngest boys of the family often, and they looked very similar.

"Wow, who pissed off the parental units?" Ivy asked in her droll tone as she set down a tray of tacos and sides before the paladins.

The youngest in the room put his covered tray in front of me and Jade. At some point I had sat down, it seemed. Then his brilliant purple eyes noticed something on the floor, and he smiled.

"Ooooooo! Neat!" he squealed before dropping out of sight.

Definitely Kyis. Oliver had milk-chocolate-colored eyes.

"Hey, Ky, give that to Ms. Cat, okay?" Chris instructed. "It's hers. More or less."

"Awww!" Kyis protested before he popped back up, handling Maekyl like a pre-teen might handle a sports ball. He placed the skull next to the tray with a loud THUNK.

"Thanks, Kyis." I said, giving him the best smile I could muster.

"Okay? You're welcome!" he cheerfully said and looked to his sister for confirmation.

"Good job, little man," Ivy told him without making eye contact. Then she did a double take at Maekyl. Her eyes widened.

"Is that?" Ivy asked, looking between Jade and me.

Jade replied, "Yep, and he got snarky."

The only daughter smirked and looked down at Maekyl.

"You aren't family. That's how *I* get away with it," she announced. Ivy then took Ky's hand and led him to the door. He looked back to smile brilliantly and say "Bye!" to us.

"Your drinks, ladies," interrupted Curt. He placed a tall glass of sweet tea before me and a mug of dark ale near Jade. I saw three tall shot glasses and two bottles of top shelf, celebrity sponsored tequila between the paladins. They were already inhaling the tacos.

"How is the search coming?" Curt asked. He looked at me with deep intent.

"Not very well. It's as if we are only putting out fires. Not gaining any ground on what's starting them," Jade confessed.

"I've been keeping track of all the, er, 'fires' since this started… don't know if that will help?" Curt replied. "But I can show you the map I've made if you want to check out the pattern I'm seeing."

Squeezing the bridge of my nose between finger and thumb, I nodded, then said, "We might take you up on that, Curt. Thanks."

"No problem! You know where to find me." he said with a wide smile.

Curt stepped back and headed for the door. Chris, the last staff member left, walked up. He had a small tray in his left hand.

Chris pulled the cover off of the tray in front of Jade and me. A pair of large plates each housed a two-inch-thick steak. These were complemented by grilled onion petals, broccoli, and cauliflower. I didn't realize how much I'd wanted something simple, even primitive, until the sight and smell hit my senses.

Holding the large cover in his right fist, Chris put the small tray next to Maekyl. A tiny candle was on it. The eldest offspring held his left forefinger over the wick. A spark jumped from his finger and the candle was ignited. The smoke trailing from the burning wick was blue. The smoke drifted directly into the nose and eye sockets of the skull. There was an audible sigh.

He leaned in towards Maekyl.

"You owe this youngling now, old Wyrm." said Chris. "Disrespect breaks every law here, and you knew it. They stopped because I asked. The energy renewing you now is some that I have personally stored."

At that, Chris straightened up and smiled at us. I glanced over at the paladins. They'd already worked through half their tacos and almost a full bottle of tequila. Seemingly oblivious to all else. Looking back at Chris, I thanked him.

He nodded and suggested we let him know if we needed anything else before making his way out the door.

Staff of Chaos

## Chapter Twenty

The meal was rather subdued for the first ten minutes. After that, conversations began and soon there was laughter and mockery. Mostly towards Maekyl, who remained sullen and silent.

Excusing myself halfway through the entree, Jade gave me a quizzical look. I glanced at Maekyl then towards the door. Understanding flashed through her eyes.

I'd forgotten how nice it was to have her at my side. Without using words, she understood my intentions.

Departing the room, I headed for the bar where I found Jen laughing with a patron. The lady was perhaps in her early forties with chestnut hair that brushed her shoulders. Her exact age was difficult to pin down. She carried herself with the confidence of someone conquering middle age, but her lightly tanned and svelte figure suggested late twenties. I knew a fae when I met one and this lady was definitely fae. Her laugh was infectious, and Jen knew the woman well.

Keeping back, hopefully out of Jen's sight, I noticed Mark come out with a tray of odd-shaped meat that appeared to be barbecued. Under the sauce, I could see shades of red, green, and black skin that was not from any bird I knew of. At least, not from this realm.

"As promised," Mark said cheerfully. "A platter of dragon wings for the lady." He gestured to the three different types. "The reds are extra spicy, the green is mild, and the black are Cajun style."

"Oh, my!" the woman said, the smile growing brighter on her face. Her words had a touch of an English accent, so I wondered which fae realm she called home. "You've certainly outdone yourselves with this treat!" She shook her head. "You really did not have to do this."

Jen touched the woman's hand. "Candy, you've been the best teacher our kids ever had. Certainly, one of the best in the entire county. I can only imagine the insanity you've been dealing with lately. Believe me when I say this is as much a pleasure for us as it is for you."

"Children are all the same, no matter what they are," she said slyly. "We all miss Oliver and will be looking forward to his return from his visit with his godfather."

Mark and Jen laughed.

"The last we heard, he was enjoying running around his godfather's home like the cub he is," Mark replied. "Thankfully, he hasn't figured out how to open the doors at his godfather's home."

"Yet," Jen added with a wink. "I think that's only because of all the mischief he can get into without leaving the house."

Candy laughed merrily. "I can only imagine! Your children are absolutely dears, but they are definitely mischievous. And Oliver is not only fast, but clever."

"It'll keep the old man on his toes," Chris muttered as he passed behind his parents, but there was a smirk on his face. "Hi, Candy. Good to see you."

"Hello, Chris," Candy replied. "I suspect your brother would keep anyone on their toes. When they aren't trying to catch him!"

There was a round of laughter before Jen noticed me. Her smile faltered slightly but didn't vanish completely.

"Excuse us, please," Jen said warmly to Candy. "Enjoy your meal!"

"Of course," she replied, turning to the tray before her as Jen turned towards me.

Moving from behind the bar, with Mark close behind, Jen said, "Let's talk in the office."

I gave a nod and followed the elf and her ifrit to their office. As usual the door to the office appeared as part of the wall until Jen touched the wall in an intricate pattern. Then, it opened into a large office eerily similar to Xantos' office.

"I wanted to apologize for Maekyl's behavior," I said without preamble. "I don't know why he did it, but I want to apologize for it."

Mark and Jen exchanged looks before turning to me.

Jen spoke first. "Your apology is accepted, even if it wasn't required."

"Maekyl knew the rules of our establishment. He knew well that being rude to any of us would result in punishment," Mark added. The smile on his face grew fiendish and his true demonic form peeked through his human guise. "Maekyl is no stranger to either of us. He knew exactly what buttons to push, and he pushed them. If he thought Xantos was going to save him, then he never understood my lady's relationship to Xantos. Maekyl doesn't have the connection Jen does."

"Wait… you knew Maekyl before my father trapped him?" I asked. As tempting as it was to ask exactly what relationship Jen had with Xantos, now was not the time.

"Oh, yes, we met long ago when he still had a body. An actual body," Jen said, running her fingers through her hair. "He was an egotistical asshole then. His death and subsequent undeath didn't change anything. Even when Simon stuck him in that pretty little skull, he had the same personality. Believing he was better than everyone else. Our rules have never changed over the centuries. We've always followed the proper guesting laws of our realm and this one. Want to guess his opinion of those laws?"

I didn't have to guess. I knew what his opinion of the guesting laws were, and they weren't nice.

"So, he insulted you, in your own establishment, foolishly thinking he'd be safe from retribution," I surmised. Mark and Jen nodded. "What an idiot."

The pair snorted, then Jen began laughing. As the tension in the room dwindled, I gave a silent sigh of relief.

"That wasn't the only reason you wanted to talk to us," Mark said thoughtfully. "There's something else. About the Staff, I'm guessing?"

"Actually, the main reason was to apologize. But there is something else," I admitted. "Crocell has stated that the demon who was known as Sophie Conner is not in Hell, which means she wasn't killed and sent back. They cannot find her on the material plane, either, as far as we know."

I paused, allowing the pair to digest what I'd said. Mark had an unreadable expression on his face, and Jen appeared thoughtful.

"Were they aware you captured your little playmate?" Jen asked, her eyes darting briefly to my talisman. I shook my head. "Then the question is if she was captured or destroyed."

"That's the question of the day, yes," I replied. "Dante's knife was found at her place, along with a lot of photos and there was a signature left by the Staff. But no one can find Sophie Conner."

Jen turned to her husband. "This isn't something I can do. If we were in our home realm, it wouldn't be a problem. But even we have to follow the rules regarding the Balance here."

Mark gave Jen a smirk before kissing her temple. He turned to me. "I can determine if she was killed by a violent method. If she was murdered, it would leave a trace that I can detect. If whoever it was has been in Fellhaven, I'll know."

"I doubt we would be that lucky," I said with a heavy sigh. "But at least this way we will know if we should continue to search for her."

"Do you want to wait at the bar or go finish the meal with your friends?" he asked. "It shouldn't take very long for me to pop into her home. If there's anything there, I'll find it quickly."

Watching the pair, I took a few heartbeats to think about my answer. "I'll wait in the room with the others. Thank you. Both of you."

"Anytime you want to be done with the obnoxious jerk, let us know," Jen said, winking.

"I'm fairly certain I now have a better threat than dropping him into an active volcano."

"That's a good one. I suppose we are a bit closer than Hawaii," Jen commented thoughtfully.

"Maybe we can make it a trip for both our families," I joked. "Could be fun. Visit the beaches, the jungles.

Throw Maekyl into one of the active volcanoes. Would be a great science lesson for all the kids."

Jen and Mark burst out laughing.

"Okay, I have to admit, that would be very tempting," Mark admitted. He turned to his wife. "Why don't you walk Cat back to the private room while I visit Sophie's place."

"Happy hunting, love," Jen said, giving him a brief kiss. She opened the office door. "After you, Lady."

I took the hint and left, leaving Mark to his methods. Jen fell into step beside me as we headed back to the room. With luck, Mark would have some sort of news about Sophie's fate. Otherwise, that was one more mystery we'd have to solve in order to locate the damned Staff.

## Chapter Twenty-One

Maekyl kept quiet even after we returned home, and I placed the skull in its usual place in my basement. Guess he'd had enough adventure time and humiliation for the day. A small part of my mind wondered how long he was going to sulk.

Too much else to worry about, the rest of my mind insisted. Because I knew his ego wouldn't let him sulk for too long.

According to Mark, whom I didn't doubt, Sophie had been killed. His suspicion was that the Staff of Chaos had been used to kill her, and her body had been completely destroyed. Either that, or the Staff had completely absorbed her. If the latter had occurred, we were really fucked, because it meant it had been fed a body and soul to power a spell. Or it was being boosted to power one really big spell.

I suspected the latter. In fact, I think all of us suspected it was the latter.

Giving the skull a pat on the head, which I knew he hated, I headed back upstairs.

Once I returned to the ground floor of my home, I found Jade texting on her phone. She had one of those that was the size of a small tablet. The sight made me smile, since I rarely got to witness her using computer technology. Her face had a pinched look to go with the scowl on her lips.

"Problem?" I asked.

"Oh, I've been fornicating with a couple for a while now, and they want me to come hook up with them," Jade replied casually. "Apparently, the insanity around us all or halting the cause of such is not nearly as important as them trying to impress me with sexual escapades."

I must have been struck speechless for longer than I realized. Jade glanced over at some point and snickered. "What?"

"I guess I never figured you out for hooking up with humans on a regular basis," I admitted. "I know you don't go for the demonic types, and I can't think of another race who ignores everything going on around them for the sake of some nookie."

A full burst of laughter erupted from Jade. When she could speak again, she said, "You've got me there, but only the female is human. The male is a wood elf. But he's definitely embraced the attitude of 'what we want is more important because we can't affect anything else' that the demon kind have been whispering to humans for eons. So, they're two of a kind in that regard. But, hey, they are fun, if clueless."

A human and a wood elf? Why did that strike a small gong in the halls of my memory? More stuff for later. Either way, the current annoyance didn't change that my friend was enjoying something other than our adventures.

"Hey, if what they give makes you happy without bringing you problems, the arrangement has my blessing!" I replied with a genuine smile on my face.

"Yay for supportive friends," Jade said with her signature droll tone. "But I don't need their distractions while the Veils get thinner, and everything rushes into this realm. I'll show them the best time that their little minds will comprehend when it's all done. Presuming we come out on top of this. Which, between us, I'm still worried about."

"Right there with you," I admitted. After a moment's consideration, I added, "Mostly I'm concerned with the possibility of the Veils being irreparably damaged right now. That finding the Staff and stopping its recent use won't be enough."

"I'm not qualified to speculate on that, not like your two favorite spell slingers are, but have to admit, that's crossed my mind as well." Jade put her phone in a Kevlar sleeve before tucking it away. "Think we'll get a chance to quiz Maekyl about that, anytime soon?"

The communication crystal hummed in my pocket. I pulled it out and braced myself for what I was going to hear.

"Hey, boss," came the voice of Elliot. "We've met up with your babysitters. It's all clear where they are. What do you suggest, next?"

When we'd departed Fellhaven, I had asked the paladins to find my contingent of bodyguards and help them patrol the largest park in the area. There was a concert and carnival style fundraiser happening there to benefit the volunteer fire and rescue units. The open space, lively atmosphere, and large number of beings seemed like too easy a target for this mayhem and chaos to pass up.

Fortunately, my elven bodyguards, who look like a biker gang in their twenties and thirties, agreed with my summation. They willingly forwent the job of watching over me to go watchdog the community we lived in.

"How much longer is the event supposed to go on, there?" I asked the paladin.

"Maybe another hour," came the response.

I said, "If something pops up elsewhere before the party wraps up, especially if you hear about it before I do, let me know how many of the group are going. If we have no further disturbances, reconnoiter back to my abode."

"Understood." Elliot answered before the crystal went silent.

For a long moment I just stared at the crystal before putting it away.

"Want to join me in the armory?" I finally asked Jade.

Her face lit up in a grin. Together we headed for my basement and the room where I kept all my weapons. We'd reorganized the room during the last year. I'd started while pregnant with Lenore and Jade had joined me in changing it around to suit us both.

Nesting is a thing no matter what race you happened to be. Magickal or mundane, every woman went through it.

Unlike most, though, we'd created a wall for our little cache of uber-powerful weapons I'd been crafting since Lenore had been born. If Sterling knew, which I was confident he did, he hadn't said anything. Maekyl had merely crowed with delight and watched with glittering eyes.

This time, he had a more solemn demeanor about him.

Speaking the words to the spell that created uber-powerful weapons, I added the extra phrase that allowed the spell to continue for more than just one item. From a box of items, I grabbed a hefty butcher's knife and spoke the keyword. The knife shifted into a two-handed bastard sword.

The demon within my talisman purred as I used the magick to create the weapons.

Handing the newly created weapon to Jade, I pulled out another knife and spoke the word. Another sword grew within my hand. I handed it to Jade, who hung it on the wall.

We continued the process, creating swords, bows, arrows, daggers, and more. Weapons that could be used by anyone.

"This just sucks." I sighed after I handed her the tenth weapon. Jade gave me a quizzical look. "Not having any leads. Only fire after fire to put out."

"What really sucks is that the gremlin you questioned didn't have any real answers," Jade observed as she leaned a hip against one of the counters. "Same with that demon who was lazily guarding the Staff. If either had any substantial clue about the snatcher? All of this would have been avoided. You, Sterling, hells, the whole Council would be able to concentrate on the Veils' instability and how to possibly reverse it."

"Gaston wasn't trying to be useless or difficult. At least, it didn't seem that way. It was almost as if he was bound to..." I trailed off.

"You just had what the mundanes call a 'lightbulb moment', Cat. What did you just think through?" Jade coaxed.

My pulse started to race as I explained. "Gaston might not have been able to give details, but he's not the only gremlin there at ShenValley Shipping. Hells, he isn't even the only gremlin I'm on a first-name basis with!"

Jade's green eyes flared with realization. She gave me a wolfish grin and asked, "Circle or call? What do I need to grab?"

"I'm going to call. No need to do the whole summoning circle. Viriato is in my debt and will come. Let's fill a bowl with the vanilla and bourbon ice cream I've got in the deep freezer," I said as we left the room.

We never bothered to lock it. Who was going to break into my house with Maekyl guarding it? Once we were on the upper level, I went into the den and knocked on the antique coffee table.

A French provincial coffee table, it was an antique that had been made around 1910. It had inlaid floral designs carved into the walnut wood. A gift from my father, it had also been something of a joke due to my love for the animated furniture in the Beauty and the Beast fairy tale. He'd bespelled the table to become animated with a key phrase.

Then, like every magickal item, it grew to have its own personality. Magick was weird in that way.

"Wakey, wakey, Ahndray!" I said. The table shifted and came to life, the corners seeming to perk up as it awaited instructions. "I need you by the bar."

My enchanted coffee table trotted with me to the bar. I placed three shot glasses and the best bourbon I had atop a silver tray sitting on the antique surface. I knelt down to look level with Ahndray.

"I'm going to have a gremlin arrive on your top, and he will probably remain on you for his visit. Best manners, Ahndray." I instructed in a soft, affectionate voice.

My father's gift stood steady.

Five minutes later, I spoke the words that summoned Viriato.

"Viriato the Gremlin, I request thee,

To greet me in mine presence,

For a speaking of things that need bespoke,

And favor that is owed."

Within five seconds, there was a popping sound, the smell of fried ozone, and the former head gremlin of the late Nicholai Wright's estate appeared in the middle of the silver tray. I didn't know what he looked like to Jade, but Viriato still looked like a gnome-sized Portuguese native to me. Although his attire was more formal than the last time we palavered. He wore a grey sweater over a white button up shirt with a black necktie, tan khakis, and tiny Italian loafers.

"Hey, Cat, what's up?" the gremlin said with what seemed to be genuine interest. He noticed the bourbon, shot glasses, and ice cream. "Whoa, is this all for me? You know I can't kill anyone for you, right?" he joked while trying to casually stroll over to the bowl of ice cream. "Oh, man, that smells the good kind of divine! What is that?"

I said, "Glace fantaisie au bourbon et vanille."

Viriato's eyes widened even as his crooked teeth shone out in a wide smile.

"Oh, baby, I love it when you speak French!" He squealed before grabbing two fistfuls of the frozen dessert and gobbled it all down.

Jade poured a shot of the bourbon. Once Viriato licked his hands clean, he pounded back the shot.

"Right, so maybe I was a little hasty when I said I couldn't kill anyone for you," he said before smacking his lips and moving back to the ice cream. "What did you need from me, again?"

"I need you to get into a specific computer at ShenValley shipping. The one used by the former lead IT demon there, who went by the mundane name of Kevin Daniels." I paused a moment before continuing. "If you aren't acquainted with Gaston, whom I think is the gremlin leader there, I could arrange introductions."

"No need, and sure, I can do that. What dirt do you need from the deceased dumbass's hard drive?" the gremlin replied cheerfully while scooping another fistful of ice cream. "Internet history, how much he skimmed off the company, souls collected, what?"

"Actually… I'm hoping there will be some clue that helps me learn who killed him," I confessed.

Viriato squeezed the mound of ice cream he'd gotten into his open mouth. As he chewed, a thoughtful expression came over his face. His tiny eyes narrowed.

"Hey, Cat," he said once the ice cream was gone. "I have no problem scouring that fool's work comp, right down to tracking every single click he ever did on keyboard or mouse. But I gotta tell you-" he paused and looked over his shoulder as if listening to someone else, "You won't find anything that tells you who killed him and snatched the Staff."

I looked at Jade, and then him.

"Yeah, I figure the Staff of Chaos is what you really need to find. Ain't no other reason to give two farts in a martini glass over Kevin Daniels," Viriato declared, looking again over his shoulder. "Alive or dead. He didn't do anything worth your interest, or the Council's. Congrats, by the way, on taking the role of Speaker. And reclaiming your title."

"I wasn't aware that gremlins were so well informed of current events," said Jade.

"Electronic communications, internet, everything going through some manner of electronic device?"

Viriato laughed. "We hear and see it all, when we pay attention. Who do you think makes most of the trouble on said equipment, after all?"

"That *is* where they live," I added.

Jade nodded.

"Point taken," she conceded.

"Anyways, I don't want you wasting your time pursuing a course that won't get the results you need," continued Viriato. "You want that Rubenesque beauty that killed Kevin and took the staff."

He said the last part in a casual tone and manner. However, just as he was smiling after, there was a smell of burning ozone, and he contorted backwards in a way that could not have been pleasant.

Jade stepped forward and poured another shot of bourbon while asking, "That was a curse, wasn't it?"

"Yes," Viriato wheezed, as he stumbled over to the shot glass. "All of the gremlins at ShenVal were put under the same silence curse. Young imps get to play with our skin if we reveal details."

The gremlin bent drastically at the waist and buried his entire head into the poured bourbon. We waited patiently for him to resurface.

"They can sense the imps nearby, but don't see them," I surmised. "That explains Gaston's behavior, and why we aren't seeing what's attacking Viriato."

"You could just throw a wide angle reveal spell so we can see them," Jade suggested.

"To what end? If there's more than one, we won't know which one is going to torture our gremlin, here. Also, neither of us knows how to fully kill or banish imps tied to a curse. I need to ask Sterling if he knows of any methods," I replied.

"It's not something that happens often enough to remember during casual conversation," Jade allowed. She peered at the still submerged head of Viriato and asked, "Do I need to pull him out? Want to call down Arylla to give him some kind of CPR in case he's drowned?"

A loud snort of laughter burst from me. I couldn't help it. When I could speak, I said, "The level of bourbon is slowly dropping. He's just an impressive drinker."

"You told me about your conversation with Gaston. So why did he never get back to you?" Jade pondered.

Viriato's head burst out of the remaining bourbon, and he took a deep, gasping breath. Then he sank slowly down to the silver tray and sat with his back against the shot glass, which was two-thirds empty.

"There was nothing more he could tell you. And he wouldn't send any of his gang to try and tell you what was known. He avoided telling you anything directly about the being responsible for the murder and theft." Viriato explained.

He grimaced immediately after but seemed to be better.

"I'm part of his crew now. Have been since shortly after Nicholai died. But I have deep ties and debts to you, Cat. By good fortune, you called for me instead of Gaston again, or another gremlin. While I cannot name anyone directly, our history and this fine bourbon will manage for some answers. I *can* acknowledge when you have identified the culprit, for example. But I cannot speak ill of the being. The compliment I gave as a hint was enough for punishment to come. I can manage a bit more, now."

I nodded to Jade. She refilled the shot glass while I pushed the ice cream next to the gremlin.

"Okay, so… a Rubenesque beauty is who we are looking for," I ventured.

Viriato smiled.

"So, a woman, and one whose figure is round, curvy," Jade surmised. "That's something."

"As the beauties of old," Viriato almost sang. "Far longer than the last decades or even centuries. Ah, I miss when humans equated 'quite well-fed' with 'gorgeous'. Although there was less for I and my kind to do. Only so much havoc to wreak upon chariots and iron stoves."

He gave a little chuckle. Neither Jade nor I spoke. Honestly, I know I wasn't sure where he was going with his end of the conversation.

"To be honest, and no offense meant, ladies," he said, pulling himself up to the rim of the glass. "When it comes to human and human-style women, I've never been fond of blondes or brunettes."

"No… offense… taken?" I managed to say. Looking over at Jade, I discovered she looked as lost as I felt.

"You have to watch out for redheads, though," Viriato continued. He dug out a handful of ice cream before continuing. "They can be surprising devils. They also hold a grudge."

Viriato suddenly yelped and jumped. He landed on his feet awkwardly and hopped from one foot to the other. He shook his head. The ice cream in his hand was untouched, so it wasn't an acute case of brain freeze. And I was getting the impression he wasn't speaking in a drunken ramble.

After a few more agonizing moments, he stuffed the ice cream into his face. He began to laugh while his mouth worked to ingest the treat. Even before he'd managed to get half of it down, he dunked his head back into the bourbon.

"Redhead," Jade mused aloud. "A big girl. Who has a grudge. A devil? Devilish? Devil-like?"

Realization hit me like the rancid aroma in that filthy mobile home.

"*Her.*" I spat. "Not the one who envies. The one that 'does nothing' did it all."

"Thank you," croaked Viriato. "But never think such a being works alone or is in charge. That truly is beyond the ability of… that kind."

He held still, braced for another unseen onslaught.

Nothing came.

I took the bourbon from Jade. After refilling Viriato's glass, I filled the other two.

"Viriato, thank you. Don't leave until you've finished that ice cream and your shot."

Jade snatched up one of the shots, I took the other. We clinked glasses over the gremlin.

"Cheers," he said pleasantly.

She and I tossed back our drinks.

"Might I suggest calling together the Council?" a familiar voice said. The tone was more subdued than I was used to, but that didn't make me less glad to hear it.

I turned around to find Maekyl's vessel behind us. The skull was on the kitchen counter, next to my coffee machine.

"So that's where you appear from the basement? Glad you joined us, Maekyl," I said.

"I miss coffee more than treasure," the dragon leiche admitted.

"Fair enough," I replied. "And yes, I think that your suggestion is the best course. Thank you for your wisdom."

"You can thank me by brewing a cup of coffee with that excellent bourbon. I can still enjoy the smell, after all." He sounded more like his usual self.

"Coming right up."

As I began brewing the coffee, he spoke again. "You are aware there is no spell in this realm that can restore the Veils or repair them. Nor do you have enough power here."

"I do have an idea for that," I replied, knowing exactly what needed to be done.

## Chapter Twenty-Two

Nothing ever goes as planned. Especially when Chaos is reigning supreme.

Just as I was about to dial my father's number, my crystal hummed again.

Jade, Viriato, and I all looked at the crystal. Even Maekyl seemed to be eyeing it warily.

"What's up?" I asked uneasily.

"We're going to need your help." Scott's voice said and I could hear a bull-like roar in the background.

"Oh, hells, now what?" I asked aloud.

"Remember that purple cow sign?" Scott asked.

"Yeah."

"Seems whoever used the Staff was near it. It's turned into a large, pissed-off minotaur." He paused and I could definitely hear the sounds of a battle more clearly now. "Some of Roland's wolves are here, but… we need help."

"I'll be right there with Jade," I replied.

Ending the call, I summoned a portal, using Scott and the crystal he held as a locator.

"Happy hunting, Cat," Viriato said. Then, a little more softly, he added, "Be safe, Lady."

I gave the gremlin a smile, topped off his shot glass, and stepped through the portal with Jade right behind me.

The area we entered was a very small clearing in a large, wooded area. I suspected it was near the intersection of Route 340 and Purple Cow Road, where the Purple Cow sign had originally stood.

And now that art piece of wire, paint and gods knew what else had grown into a large, nine-foot-tall purple cow-headed minotaur.

Staring at the purple-headed beast, I decided that whoever was using the stolen Staff of Chaos needed to be torn apart bone-by-bone. Considering the human body had two hundred and six bones, it would be a very painful process.

Drawing a deep breath, I squared my shoulders and cleared my mind of all doubts and worries. It was time to shed the humanity I'd clung to since my reign as the Lady of Death had ended.

The minotaur had been created from the head of the purple cow statue that was a landmark for Dooms. The business had changed over the years and was currently closed, but that purple cow head still towered over the buildings and trees.

Now, it was the head of a pissed-off minotaur.

Thankfully, the Chaos-created monster had been contained in the forested area between the various roads, a Baptist church, and the campground.

Not that the paladins were having much luck with it. Some of Roland's wolves had jumped into the foray and whatever glee they might have had fighting the creature had vanished. Now they looked just as angry as the minotaur.

Jade and I exchanged grim expressions. My hand touched my talisman and her eyes narrowed slightly.

"Same as the days of old?" she asked.

I gave a nod and we separated. She went left while I went right. As I moved, I snatched up a stick from the ground. The demon with my talisman came alert, like a hound scenting its prey. I didn't have time to bother with the demon's excitement at my using the talisman.

Time to be the Lady of Death. To live up to my moniker and remind people what I could do. What I *would* do.

The stick was easily the length of my forearm and at least three inches thick. My lips moved as I pulled upon the talisman, forming the magick and power and feeding it into the stick I held within my hand.

The wood lengthened, growing heavier and sturdier as it transformed into a spear. The tip was four-sided and at least six inches in length. I tossed the spear to Jade who caught it with ease, even as I snatched a second stick. The demon within my talisman unfurled his wings and crouched low.

Using the talisman felt good. Maybe too good, but I'd been down this road before, and I knew the trap. I hadn't fallen into it when I was a century old, and I wasn't going to fall into it now. Despite what the demon might want.

Turning the sticks into weapons was easy. Tossing them to Jade? Also easy.

Figuring out what spell to use on a Chaos-created pissed-off purple minotaur? Not so much.

As I moved, the purple cow-headed minotaur watched me, a large tree gripped in his hands. It appeared that the only difference between this minotaur and every other was the fact that this one had a different colored head.

The minotaur pawed the ground with a cloven-hoofed foot, mist blowing from his nose as he snorted.

How were cows slaughtered?

The thought came in a flash, followed by a second thought.

Spotting Scott, I yelled, "Throw me a knife!"

Without questioning me, the dark paladin pulled one from somewhere and threw it at me. I caught it in the air and within moments, I'd transformed it into a wicked two-handed sword. Spinning, I threw the heavy weapon to Jade, who caught it with far more ease than I had with throwing it. As I completed the spin, my arms were outstretched, fingers splayed.

The demon within the talisman grinned fiendishly as I pulled upon the power it offered. The magick used so far was typical for the talisman. It gifted me the ability to create powerful weapons from harmless items. That was common knowledge. Legend, even. But what I did now was not known by many.

As the air heated around the minotaur, the ground began to smolder. Leaves curled and the distinct smell of smoke wafted into the air around all of us. My eyes narrowed as I watched the hide of the minotaur pinken. Small blisters formed as I turned the heat up on the minotaur.

His hide blistered, even as he howled in pain. It was an unearthly sound. From the corner of my eyes, I noticed Roland's wolves moving back cautiously and I could feel their gazes on me. The paladins remained firmly in their positions. They'd probably seen worse by their masters.

I didn't take my eyes away from the minotaur, though.

A spear flew into the minotaur's chest. Blood seeped from around the weapon. The minotaur pulled the bladed weapon free, and blood poured from the wound.

Jade hadn't missed her target: the weapon had pierced the monster's heart. With each beat of his heart, blood pumped forth, spilling down its chest. What didn't go out, went into the body, flowing into other vital organs, including the lungs.

The minotaur stumbled before falling to his knees. He slapped his hands over the mortal wound, his eyes rolling, even as he cried out in disbelief. The sounds grew more and more garbled and strangled. Blisters bubbled up on his hide before popping. Smoke rose from the body, even as the smell of hot, boiling blood filled the air, adding a distinct aroma to the area.

The wolves growled hungrily. I broke the spell and turned to find them all watching as Jade darted in. She sliced the minotaur's neck. Blood poured out, watering the ground around the monster. She spun the sword easily, giving it an approving nod.

Plucking the discarded spear from the ground, she crossed to Scott.

"Your… knife," she said, mischief dancing in her eyes. "The Lady does make good weapons."

Scott took the transformed weapon. He looked it over, hefted it a couple of times, stepped back and did a hard swing through air. He nodded before giving his observation.

"I can live with this change. Will it wear off, y'know, turn back into its original shape at some point?"

"Ever since I've used the talisman, no altered item has reverted. Jade still has the battle axe I made for her back in my early days," I replied.

"It started out as a small rusty hatchet," Jade added, having retrieved the other spear.

"Would love to hear the story of that sometime," Scott said. "And you picked up the knack for making these again, right now?"

The smile on my lips came first, as I replied, "I've gotten a little practice in, recently."

Scott grunted. "I bet you have. Thanks for the new toy. I'll make a sheath for it sometime."

Nodding, I took a look around and wondered aloud, "How long do you think it's going to take to clean this mess?"

## Chapter Twenty-Three

The clean-up for the minotaur took less time than expected.

Apparently, the werewolves had zero problems with having beef for dinner. I was fairly certain the head was going to end up stuffed, mounted, and hanging in someone's home.

I opened a portal near Fellhaven. With all the crazy shit going on, I decided people walking through a magical doorway wouldn't be so crazy. Yes, I was the Speaker of the Council. The council of magickal beings who were in charge of keeping magick hidden from the mundanes.

So, I was breaking a few laws by doing that, but there was worse stuff happening. Not like the Council was going to punish me. Not when I was basically the only way for Sterling to get his daughter back.

Maybe I wasn't playing fair.

But I had never believed in playing fair.

At the moment, I didn't even care about breaking any of our laws. Until the Staff of Chaos was retrieved, nothing was going to be anywhere close to normal. And gods forbid the Staff was used even more than previously. If that happened, things were going to get even hairier than they had been.

When we entered Fellhaven, Jen noticed and intercepted us at the hostess station.

"Any luck?" she asked without preamble. We shook our heads. "Damn. Come on, I'll show you to the private room."

"Please forgive me as I make a few calls," I said, tapping the screen of my phone. As I waited for my father to answer, I asked Jade, "Could you give Sterling a call?"

Jade nodded and whipped out her own phone.

"It's good to hear your voice, Cat. Are you okay?" Dad's voice was calm and warm, though there was no mistaking the concern.

"I'm fine, Dad. I can't say the same for what was once the Purple Cow sign," I said as we followed Jen. "Can you meet Jade and me at Fellhaven? We need to have a Council meeting."

"It's about the Staff, isn't it?"

"Yup," I replied.

Dad sighed. "I'll contact your mother. We'll be there in five minutes or less." He paused before asking softly, "Lenore?"

"She's safe, Dad. Xantos is protecting her," I replied quietly. "He swore to keep her safe. I trust him."

"Your mother is not going to be pleased," Dad stated. "But she'll be thankful she's in a realm where she'll be protected from the Staff's influence. She might not like the old codger, but even she admits Xantos won't allow harm to come to an innocent. Especially if that innocent is a baby."

"She doesn't have to like it," I replied. "I don't like any of this, to be honest."

My father made a noise that I thought was agreement, but it was hard to tell.

"Sterling can contact the other members. Although I think Dyrmith has been all but camping out in Fellhaven since all of this began."

Huh. Wasn't that interesting?

"Okay, Dad. We'll see you and Mom here soon. Love you," I replied, wondering how long it would take for the rest of the Council to appear.

"Love you, too, sweetheart," Dad replied.

We ended the call and I finally noticed where Jen had led us. We'd entered the larger private dining room. The table was large enough to hold every member of the Council plus Jade. The group of paladins and my guards were at tables nearest the doors. One group sat at each table, but no one looked unhappy. Jen was laying menus down at each place setting at the larger table.

"Mark and I figured you'd be calling for a meeting at some point," Jen explained. "Figured when you were calling your father and Jade was telling Sterling to get his buttocks here, it was that time."

"I honestly don't think anything ever gets by you or him," I said with a smile. "As usual, you nailed it. We have one part of the guilty party, but not the other." I paused, before asking, "Is Curt working?"

"Yeah, he is," she replied, setting the last menu down. "You want to talk to him about his map?"

"At some point, yes. I want to get the Council business done before I dive into that part of this mess."

I didn't feel like sitting. Probably because I was anxious about everything. Or maybe it was because I finally had something I could use and yet I knew I couldn't really do anything with the information.

Jen studied me for a moment before giving me a nod. "I'll send drinks in for everyone. Including a double for you."

With that, she turned and strode out, pausing only long enough to laugh at something one of my guards said to her. Which caused one of the paladins to make a comment. She shook her head, held her hands up towards both tables, and continued through the doors.

"When will Sterling get here?" I asked.

"He said within a few minutes. How long until your parents and the rest of the members show up?" Jade answered.

I didn't even have a chance to reply before Dyrmith entered the room. An ancient dragon, he'd been a tutor, advisor, and friend ever since I was a young child just learning magick. Tall, slender, with an unusual combination of honey gold hair, caramel colored skin, and twinkling green eyes, he wore a polo shirt and khakis comfortably.

He paused just on the inside of the doorway and bowed first to my guards, then to the dark paladins. After he stood straight once again, he moved towards Jade and me.

"Catherine, it is good to see you safe and well," the dragon said smoothly.

He held his hands out, and I grasped them. He squeezed my fingers briefly before giving me a hug.

"Dad said you've been here a lot since everything started," I replied. "It's good to see you, also."

"I felt it might be best if I remained close at hand. In case something else happened that I could assist with," he said. Though he smiled, there was a seriousness to his eyes that I'd rarely ever seen.

"Do you think it will take long for the rest of the Council to show up?" I asked as we all sat down at the table.

Dyrmith shook his head. "No. We have all been keeping in contact because of the chaos. There is only so much we can do while you seek out the cause of it."

"The Staff, you mean," Jade stated. "Just how much chaos has been going on?"

"Aside from the giant chicken that thought the brand-new shiny cars at the sales lots were insects? And the ensuing chase along Greenville Avenue? Or the tailgating at the mall? I believe that chicken ended up being the biggest game to be bagged in the area. Plenty of the hunters and general good ol' boys were out in full force for that one."

"Tailgating? And hunting in the city? I didn't think that was even legal for the mundanes?" I couldn't keep the surprise and confusion from my voice.

"It's not legal to use a firearm," Jade explained. "But bows? Yeah, that would be okay. So, did they barbecue it after they bagged it?"

The dragon-in-human-form laughed. His emerald green eyes twinkled. "I believe the biggest problem they had was plucking the thing. Though, considering how many were happy to pluck feathers as keepsakes, I don't think it took too long to pluck, butcher, then cook the thing."

Jade chuckled. "I hope they didn't get stomach aches, or worse, from eating it."

"From all accords, it resembled a chicken in every way, shape, and form. Even if it was a fifty-five-foot-tall clucking menace."

"Did you try some?" I asked, curious.

The only reply we received was a sly smile.

"So, anything else interesting happen?" Jade asked. "And who kept a watch on the Great Chicken Escapade?"

"Oh, that was Finn," Dyrmith replied. "He had a grand old time watching the entire thing and laughing his ass off as the chicken made its way from one car lot to the other."

Jade and I looked at each other and then burst out laughing.

Finn had led the Wild Hunt for a few centuries, including during my early Lady of Death days. I'd met him even before I became Speaker of the Council, and we'd always gotten along. As fae as my mother, he'd always been charming and polite.

I'd never been certain if it had been because of my mother, my being a crowned princess of a fae realm, or something else. Whatever the reason, we'd always been friendly towards each other.

The door opened to reveal Hunter and Ivy entering with trays of beverages. The younger brother, Kyis, was with them. He wasn't carrying anything this time.

Elliot said something to Kyis, who grinned and bounced over to him. Ivy's shoulders rose, then dropped as she tilted her head back and shook it slightly in apparent exasperation.

Hunter just chuckled as he brought his tray of drinks to us. "We've been keeping Ky close. What with all the insanity going on," Hunter explained as he divvied up the drinks. "He tries to help. But sometimes he's just too… energetic."

"He's a sweetie," I said. "Where's the youngest?"

Hunter studied me for a few moments, then shrugged. "Xantos is babysitting him. The thing with all this chaos energy is ramping up his mischievousness. So, Mom said Xantos can keep him out of trouble better than anyone else. Dad didn't argue, so Ollie is now keeping everyone at the old docelfar's place on their toes."

"Have you ever visited Xantos?" I asked, curious.

A grin flashed across his face. "Yeah. So has Ivy and Ky. I think Chris is the only one who doesn't visit him much anymore. Before you ask, they aren't exactly best buds."

I snorted. "Not surprised. Thanks for the drinks." I paused, before finally asking, "Which name do you prefer, anyway? Hunter or Alfred?"

"Either works," he said with a shrug. "I use Alfred in school because there's a bunch of others with the name Hunter. Thought it would be easier to go with just one name, but nah."

With a nod and smile, he turned and left, empty tray in hand. Ivy was trying to pry Kyis away from the dark paladins who were teasing and playing with him. All of them wore easy smiles and were comfortable with him.

Turning to the drinks before us, I lifted the tumbler of blue liquid and gave it a sniff before sipping it. There was the tang of alcohol and raspberry. Sweet, strong, and tasty. Exactly what I needed. I took a pull and enjoyed the burn it left behind after I swallowed.

"As for other fun things," Dyrmith said before taking a long pull of his locally brewed beer. "There was the problem with the garden statuary and such coming to life. Gnomes, toads, fairy statues. You name it, it came to life. If they weren't fighting each other, they were causing other mischief." He chuckled deeply. "Someone had a bunch of those little raccoon decorations. Those things came alive and began stealing anything not tied down. Took it back to their 'home' and piled it all up in a doghouse."

"You sound as though you've been enjoying this," I said slowly. Narrowing my eyes, I studied the dragon who had often tutored me as a child in my mother's realm. "That wouldn't be true, would it?"

"Maybe a little," he admitted with a wide grin. "Humans no longer remember what it was like when magick was strong and plentiful. They don't fear the monsters lurking in the shadows. Or the creatures that cause things to go bump in the night. It's been enjoyable to this old dragon to watch all their little securities and false beliefs vanish before their eyes."

I glanced at Jade who gave a slight shrug before looking back at the dragon. His eyes were full of mischief and delight as he took another pull of his drink. I shrugged and took another pull of my own.

Who was I to complain if he was enjoying himself? I knew dragons got bored, so this was probably the most interesting thing to happen in the past several centuries.

Hells, if I weren't tasked with finding the item that could literally cause the people I loved and cared for to die, I'd probably be enjoying myself a lot more.

Which said even more about why Dyrmith and I got along so well. It was probably why he'd set me on the path to being a necromancer as a child.

It hadn't simply been because I'd possessed a knack for it.

Lifting my glass, I clinked it with his and Jade's. The three of us drank from our glasses. As we lowered them, the door opened, and the two teens entered again. This time with trays of appetizers.

They were followed by Kyis who was beaming widely as he led Sterling and my parents.

I guess it wouldn't be long before the rest of the Council members arrived. That was fine. I'd at least have time to talk with my parents, Sterling, and Dyrmith before they did.

Smiling, I stood and embraced Sterling, before turning to my parents. Giving first my father, then mother hugs, I turned to Kyis and bowed at him from the waist.

"Thank you, Kyis," I said with a grin.

"Welcome, Cat!" he said brightly. He looked at Hunter, then to Ivy.

"Good job, kiddo," Ivy said. "Go on back to Mom and Dad. I'll bet Dad has some chips ready for you."

Kyis grinned again before turning and racing from the room. Ivy sighed and rolled her eyes. She finished putting the food on the tables of the paladins and my guards before following her younger sibling.

Hunter put the contents of his tray on the table as his mom walked in with a collection of drinks.

"We'll get your orders, then leave everyone to chat in private," Jen said brightly. "As the members arrive, Mark or I will bring them in."

"Thanks, Jen," I replied. "It's appreciated."

"No problem. Let me know when you want to talk to Curt."

With that, she turned and left, leaving me with my family and closest friends. And a set of dark paladins and my personal guards.

But who was I to quibble?

## Chapter Twenty-Four

Not even twenty minutes later the Council had convened. Although the atmosphere of Fellhaven was normally relaxed, it wasn't today. A wide spread of appetizers and entrees lay before us on the table, along with drinks. There was a palpable tension in the air that wasn't going to fade any time soon.

That wasn't because of the paladins or elves guarding the doors and room, either. If anything, they seemed to comfort several of the council members.

As for Jade, they'd all come to accept her as my Right Hand. She wasn't going anywhere. Since Sterling and my parents backed me, they didn't argue.

Or maybe it was because of my reputation? Who knew?

"What did you wish to speak about, Lady?" Dyrmith asked, after everyone had begun eating.

"It's about the Staff, isn't it?" Mother added. When silence filled the room, she pursed her lips. "We all know it was stolen and the current waves of unexplained magick has been because of it. I'm certain we all know it's Catherine and Sterling who are searching for the missing artifact."

She didn't add "like always" but it hung in the air like a floating hippo wearing a pink tutu. Unavoidable and not ignorable.

I shrugged. "Someone has to locate it and it seems I'm the best person for the job." Glancing at Sterling I added, "Sorry, darling."

"No, no. That has been the general consensus since day one of this mess," he replied, touching my hand with his. "You've found something and that's why you need all of us here."

"You're both correct. I was finally able to figure out, with help, who stole the Staff, but the problem is: she doesn't have it," I stated bluntly. "Before anyone asks questions, let me start at the beginning. Maybe one of you will have an idea of the identity of who we are looking for. Though I think I know how to locate him or her."

Everyone had similar grim expressions on their faces, but they all nodded. And so I began, with Jade and Sterling adding in details and comments. Gave a few theories we'd cooked up along the way. By the time I'd finished, I wasn't the only one with a plate of uneaten food. I didn't know if it was because the story was so interesting, or they'd lost their appetites because it was so worrisome.

Either way, I was starving, so I began delving back into my plate of food. Besides, this was not the time to insult the host and hostess by not eating the delicious meal.

"So, this sloth demon, Maxine Olson. She killed Kevin Daniels and then, what? Possibly gave the Staff to someone you know and possibly trust?" Sabine asked, echoing the worst of my suspicions. The brunette woman gestured as she spoke, the fork held tightly in her fingers. "You aren't known to trust a lot of people. Not when you were under a century of age and certain ones feared your reign. I suspect you trust even fewer now. So, your list of suspects must be short."

The sorceress was only a couple centuries older than me, but one would never know it by the way she spoke, the clothes she wore, or her appearance. She wore her hair loose and unstyled. Her clothes were the latest fashion you'd buy at the local boutique. Sabine wore makeup flawlessly and used it to highlight her bright blue eyes.

"She's not wrong, Cat," Jade said slowly. "We can rule out Maekyl, Trix, Roland, and Alesio. None of them would cross you. You might have bargained for the guards, but they're still loyal to Xantos."

"Are you certain Xantos would not betray you?" Mother asked, her eyes on the food before her.

Finn scoffed. "Really, Viviane?" He shook his head. "You sound like a young maiden scorned by the handsome noble."

When she slapped her hand on the table and glowered at him, he laughed merrily.

Somewhere I could hear the faintest sound of baying hounds. Maybe he still had connections to the Wild Hunt, after all. I glanced at Jade, and she had a thoughtful expression on her face, so I suspected she heard the baying, also.

"Xantos is as sly as the most cunning creature known to any living being. I doubt there isn't a being here who hasn't encountered him in one way or another." He gave my mom a sly grin. "Even he wouldn't do something as foolish as use that Staff. Not to mention, if he had it? He'd be bragging about how he snatched it away from the demons of this realm."

"He's not wrong, Viv," Dad said gently. He placed his hand upon hers and squeezed her fingers. "Besides, we all know the Staff is still in this realm, and few beings would be able to hold the damned thing. Let alone use it."

"So, who does it leave?" she demanded. "You never had many friends."

"It would have to be someone who knows her well. Someone who would know her movements," Dad added.

My mother started before turning to Sterling. "Someone she trusts. Someone who knows her movements. That means… Oh, gods. He hasn't been in my realm, Myrddin."

Sterling stared at my mother, and I was confused as hell. Something should be clicking, but it wasn't, and I was hating it.

"Are you certain, Viviane?" Sterling asked.

She nodded once. I saw realization showing on my father's face, along with deep sadness.

Sterling turned to me. "It's Cildur, Catherine. Cildur Laedragryl was your childhood friend. You trusted him as a child and now as an adult." He paused before adding quietly, "You placed him in charge of your spy network."

Closing my eyes, I leaned back in my chair. Drawing in a deep breath, I let it out slowly. I didn't want anyone to see it felt like a punch to my gut. I'd been warned there was a Judas. I'd known someone I trusted was going to betray me. There was silence in the room while my mind warred with denial and the facts we had. Damn my practical mind, it won. The piece fit too well in the hole of the mystery.

No warning can ever prepare you for the feeling you get when you put a name to the fact. Especially when you had so many memories of fun, laughter, and good times. When it was someone you'd cared about your entire life.

It really sucks when you're betrayed by someone you trust. Even worse when it's someone you considered family.

"Are you okay, sweetheart?" my dad asked.

Opening my eyes, I nodded once. "Now we know who the Judas is, we can start searching for him."

My eyes drifted around the table. I knew I sounded cool and collected. A queen preparing for war. I'd heard my mother use the same cool, calm tone. The understanding I found shining in her eyes brought a slight smile to my lips.

Funny how I now understood my mother a little more because of literal chaos that meant utter disaster for everyone and everything.

Maybe that's how my mother felt when she had to defend her realm on the rare instance it was needed.

"This is not something any of you can handle," I stated in that same calm tone. "What Sterling and I need from all of you is to be prepared for what might happen. If Cildur uses the Staff, as we fear he will, then the Veils will be torn asunder. There will be nothing to prevent anything from entering our world." I looked directly at my mother. "Or the fae realm."

"If the Staff is used, how will we repair the Veils?" Sabine asked. There was no challenge to her voice, but there was a coolness to her features that hadn't been there a few minutes ago.

"Sterling and I will travel to Xantos' realm. My power is strongest there. We will seek his counsel and find a method to repair the Veils from that realm."

"If the Veils fall, and you leave this realm, who will be upholding our Laws?" Eldrid Helvig asked. "The Council has never been a group of enforcers, only jury and judges. Word will spread of your absence.

The man could have easily been an extra from the TV show about Vikings. His blonde hair was cut short, and his skin had a tan. His hazel eyes were hardened, and he wore clothes in Earth tones. I suspected somewhere he had a sword or two hidden by illusion. Part of me wondered how many women drooled when he walked into the restaurant.

I laughed. I couldn't help it.

"If the Veils fall, there will be no need to concern ourselves about most of the rules. Aside from the very basic ones of 'do no harm', 'kill none', and the such? You'll be too concerned with doing what you must to protect house and home to worry about the Laws."

Sterling gave a nod. "The rules to hide magick will not be useful and concealing ourselves from the mundanes will be pointless. It will be up to the magickal community to protect the mundanes who cannot or will not fight what enters our world."

"I don't think there would be many who would think twice about breaking our laws if it was life or death,"

Sabine mused. "There are always those who will do what is needed, regardless of the consequences."

"It sounds as though you have witnessed such," I said thoughtfully.

Sabine gave me a sly smile before taking a sip of her water. I chuckled.

"If the Veils fall, it will be up to each of you to let our members know they no longer have to fear the Council for stepping into the light and using magick openly," I added, leaning back in the chair as though it were a throne. "We will need all the assistance we can get should the Veils fall."

"What if you are capable of stopping it?" Finn asked, tossing back half his glass of hard cider.

"Then it will be up to the Council to keep things from falling apart while Sterling and I go to Xantos' realm to repair the Veils," I said with a shrug. "So, basically, life as usual. More or less."

"Let's hope you can stop Cildur in time," my father said. "Otherwise, we'll need to bring out our weapons of old and hope they will be enough."

"Actually, if the Veils fall, come find me," Jade said, after glancing at me.

Dad lifted a brow, though I could tell he was trying to not smile. "And why is that?"

"I'm in charge of Cat's armory," Jade replied easily.

Mother groaned, dropping her head into her hand as she propped her arm on the table.

Dyrmith laughed. "Seems you've won another bet, Simon."

As the rest of the council members laughed and raised glasses to salute my father, my mom just shook her head. Though I could see her lips twitching in an effort to not join in the laughing.

"So, it's settled?" I asked once the jesting died down.

Everyone looked to each other then to me and nodded.

"Wonderful! Then let's not let this delicious food go to waste. Otherwise, Mark and Jen may not allow us back!" I said.

"What about Maxine?" Sabine finally asked after several moments had passed. "What do we do about her?"

"We keep her involvement in this quiet," I stated, pausing with a forkful of food halfway to my mouth. "Sterling and I will handle her punishment once we're certain she won't need to be questioned later."

"Good plan," Mom said. "Otherwise, our charming host may decide to just take care of her before you can say otherwise."

There was a lot of snickering and nods from the other council members.

"Speaking of our hosts, I'm going to request some refills," Finn said, pushing his chair back.

Another round of agreement went up before silence filled the air again for a few moments before conversations began once more. Laughter and warm voices filled the room. By the time Finn returned with our hosts and refills, even the paladins and my guards had moved to tables closer to us. Conversation flowed, and I savored every second of it.

It wouldn't be long before the weight of saving the world came crashing down on my shoulders again. And I wasn't certain how events were going to play out this time. If everyone survived, I suspected it would be only because of a lot of luck and skill from every person sitting in the room.

## Chapter Twenty-Five

I watched as the last of the council members left the room. My parents were enjoying coffee while chatting amiably with Sterling and Jade.

Standing, I headed to the table where the paladins were chatting with my guards. At some point, they'd all moved to a table closer to the doors and were enjoying each other's companionship.

"Since Scott has a new toy, would anyone else like a new one?" I asked.

Best to get arming my allies out of the way before searching for the enemy.

Elliot, Michael, and Scott looked at each other, then back to me.

"That would be appreciated, Lady," Elliot said, a grin on his face.

He pulled a ballpoint pen from his pocket and handed it to me, mischief in his eyes.

Snickering, I murmured the words to the spell that would alter the mundane into powerful weapons. The pen shifted shape and material until I held a broad-bladed dagger.

Disappointment flashed across his face, but he didn't say anything.

From the corner of my eyes, I noticed my parents and Sterling turning to watch me. My father wore an amused smile while there were frowns on Mother's and Sterling's faces.

Ignoring them, I winked at the dark paladin and took two steps back, so I was clear of the tables.

I snapped my hand down, my thumb touching a knob on the handle near the guard. The handle expanded suddenly and became a six-foot spear with a broad-bladed tip. I tested the balance and gave a slight nod of approval.

Holding the weapon up in front of me, I offered the collapsible spear to the paladin.

The look of delight on Elliot's face reminded me of a child who'd just been told Santa was real and his every wish was being granted.

Accepting the spear, wide grin still on his face, he hefted it. Finding the knob on the dagger, he pushed it and the spear collapsed back into the broad-bladed dagger.

"Heh, mightier than the sword," he said, still grinning. "Nice."

Returning to the table, he sat again, examining every inch of his new weapon.

Looking towards my parents and Sterling, I discovered they'd turned back around in their seats and were talking again. Huh. Guess they weren't concerned about me making weapons for the paladins, after all.

Turning back to the table, I waited for Michael to decide what he wanted me to weaponize.

"I've been pondering," he admitted. "And want to see what you and that talisman can do with something a bit more… dangerous."

Intrigued, I waited patiently. What he did next was not what I'd imagined. He pulled a disposable lighter out of one breast pocket and placed it before me.

The lighter was the inexpensive kind that one would buy at the counter of a convenience store. Plastic shaft which also contained the fuel reservoir, metal cap at the top, with the steel wheel to spark the flint and ignite the butane gas. The plastic on this particular lighter was a festive red.

"Alright, this should be interesting," I said as my right-hand fingers touched the item, and my left grasped the talisman.

Speaking the required words again, I also poured energy and will of my own into the lighter, until the talisman took the bait and flooded its own into the item.

The lighter bubbled, grew, and shifted until what was left resembled a large water pistol. It even retained the festive red color throughout most of its final form. The plastic was now a thick polymer or ceramic. Even the fuel tank, now a thick cylinder that hung beneath the barrel, was the bright hue from the original plastic.

"Ummm… what in the Hells is that?" Michael asked, peering down at the weapon with trepidation and doubt etched on his whole body. His hesitation only lasted for a few seconds. He picked up the faux gun with both hands and examined it. He looked at me.

"I'm going to go find our hosts and see if there's somewhere I can test this, safely." Michael announced. Once he made his way out the door, my parents approached.

"I'm not using the talisman as a parlor trick," I told my parents. "Nor am I just weaponizing anything for anyone."

"Not here to ask or scold you about that, dearheart. We were wondering if you'd heard anything about Lenore, how she's holding up during this." Dad explained.

"I haven't checked in today. Let's do it together."

Pushing my hand into a pocket, I grasped the crystal that Xantos had given me to communicate with him. I kept it separate from the other crystal used to communicate with the paladins, or anyone else. They weren't as convenient as a mobile phone, but I never needed to worry about being out of service.

"Hold that thought," Dad interjected. He darted out the door.

Mom didn't watch Dad go out the door. I did, but found her eyes locked on me once I looked away from his exit.

"I don't disapprove of your choice of babysitter, Catherine. We are understandably anxious about her safety, just as you are," Mom said in her calm, more personable tone. "You've shown remarkable restraint and instinct during this disastrous event. I wanted to let you know, I am proud of you."

My jaw dropped. I couldn't help it. Her words caught me completely off guard.

"Thank you, Mom," I said as I hugged her.

She returned the hug, kissing me on the cheek after the embrace ended.

"This doesn't mean I will treat either of your male companions with anything less than the royal disdain they've been given so far," she whispered.

"I'd expect no less," I replied.

We shared a laugh that lasted even when Dad returned, followed by Hunter and Michael. Hunter was carrying a stone basin but had the widest smile on his face I'd ever seen. He placed the basin on my table.

"That pistol you made is a freakin' *plasma gun!*" Hunter practically shouted. "It's soooo awesome! Mike burned a circle the size of my fist-" he held up his closed hand to demonstrate, "through one of the concrete barricades we keep in the back field for events.

Clean through it! It only had enough energy left to singe the grass behind, but wow! Can I ask for one for my birthday? Or Samhain? Or any holiday you want?"

"New Year's Eve."

My dad stepped up next to Hunter and said the three words again.

"New Year's Eve. Remember that one a few years back, Hunter? After you wanted a wand to see if you had the same gifts that your mother has?"

Hunter began to say something, stopped, and then seemed to deflate slightly.

"Let me know if you need anything else," the teen said in a somber voice as he went to leave.

I cocked an eyebrow at my father. He chuckled.

"That year, Hunter asked his parents if he could have a wand. Probably got caught up in the hoopla of that series of books," said Dad. "So, they asked me to craft him a simple one as a Christmas gift. I did. As often happens with anyone at that age, he listened to maybe one fourth of the instructions and warnings given to him by any of us. He wound up exploding Chris's first car in the parking lot, here. Chris shed his human form and came quite close to eating Hunter's head right off his shoulders."

I burst out laughing. I couldn't help it.

"Why did you make a wand for Hunter that would channel that much power?" I finally asked. "I would've thought you'd use materials that would only allow for very minor magicks."

"That's the best part," Mom interjected. "Your father did exactly what you thought he'd do. And yet, Hunter managed to conjure a fireball the size of a car door. The wand withered in his hand, which he didn't notice until later. He was so taken with what he'd accomplished! Until, that is, he heard his father and elder brother stepping out of the kitchen to see what was 'taking him so long with the garbage'. Hunter panicked, flung the fireball away, right into the back of Chris's automobile. The young dragon was, as your father implied, very angry."

"May I see the crystal, Cat?" Dad rejoined.

Surprised, I fished the crystal out of my pocket and handed it over.

"Excuse me, Lady, but may I ask a question?" Michael had come back over to my table.

Once I gestured for him to continue, he said, "Any idea how much, uh, ammo I've got in that thing? Is it magically replenished when the-whatever is in that tank- runs out?"

"I have no idea at all," I admitted. "I doubt it could be replenished. You gave me a disposable tool. One that is used and then discarded. But to be honest, that's mostly a guess on my part. I've only made the more modern style weapons a handful of times."

"What do I do when the military or governments come after the, uh, weapon? I mean, I'm not going to use it around civies, or mundanes, if at all possible, but you know how camera tech is everywhere in this realm?"

My parents and I gave a short laugh.

"They won't," stated my father.

"Magick scares them," added my mother.

"The moment they discover any measure of magick is used, they go away and make excuses. It's been that way since the 1800s," I said.

"That's reassuring," Michael observed. "We haven't had any interference, Hells, we've done jobs for all of them, but never with tech they didn't have."

"No worries," I replied.

Michael nodded and went back to his comrades-in-arms, who were giving the plasma weapon a good looking-over.

"Now then," Dad said.

I looked back towards him. He held the calling crystal I'd given him earlier. He carefully placed it into the center of the stone bowl. I hadn't realized it was two thirds full of clear water before he did that. While his fingers were still in the bowl, Dad said a single word.

"Aspectum."

The water shimmered with a bluish light. Dad looked back at me.

"Okay, stand over the bowl, Cat, and activate the crystal," he instructed.

I did as I was bid. The crystal illuminated from within, as it usually did while in use. The glow spread to the water's surface, obscuring any view of the crystal or the inside of the bowl. Looking over at my parents, I noticed that they were looking into the bowl, leaning closer to it and me.

The glow was replaced with a view. My eyes and mind interpreted what we saw as what could be seen on a screen when a video camera had been placed on a seat or similarly sized piece of furniture.

Lenore filled half of the view in the bowl. She was being changed by someone who was outside the angle. Only the being's dark hands and arms were visible. My child was at a horizontal slant from my and my parents' view. She cooed at whomever was standing above her.

"Speak," came Xantos's voice from the water. It was as clear as if I were holding it.

"Hello, Xantos. I'm checking on Lenore. My parents are present."

Lenore began turning her head, looking for the source of the voice.

"Understood," said Xantos. "Hello, Cat, and her esteemed parents, Vivian and Simon."

"Greetings, Xantos. I have added the sight enchantment for our conversation," my father replied.

He looked at my mother, who continued to look into the bowl. Gently, he nudged her.

"Well met, Lord of the Great Forest," she managed to say.

'Lord of the Great Forest?' my thoughts declared. I hate everyone knowing more than me. Too many questions about everyone and everything in my life.

"Gracious of the queen to observe the formalities, and of her king to provide his intent," said Xantos. "One moment, and I shall provide you a better view of the lovely child."

Lenore had a fresh cloth diaper. The purple silk dress she wore was replaced to fall down to her knees. The hands picked her up and she was lifted out of view. We heard her coo again, followed by a squeal of joy. The view in the bowl abruptly shifted to the right. Lenore was closer, and her upper half was completely visible. She was sitting on the lap of someone who wore the black robes favored by Xantos. This person was sitting in a throne-like chair. Lenore looked at the person holding her and made another happy squeal.

"As you may witness, the child is in good health and spirit."

"She is eating well?" my mother asked. Lenore looked around more intently.

"Indeed. Lady Lenore seems to have found the milk here to be a revelation. I may have to send supplies upon her return to you." Xantos replied. He even sounded to be a jovial kind of amused.

Dad spoke up. "Have there been any disturbances along the scale that this realm is experiencing?"

"If so, such is occurring on another landmass than this one. And I do mean all the way to Faedale, and the opposite coast." A more serious tone came with that declaration.

The name "Faedale" meant nothing to me, nor did I have any idea of the size he was trying to convey. My father, however, seemed at least content with what had been said. I decided to take my turn at speaking.

"At the rate the veils are thinning, it seems you would need to expect me at your praedium, soon. I doubt I will be coming alone." While I spoke, Lenore squealed and held her hands to the air. Xantos gave a light laugh.

His voice went back to the familiar silken tone as he replied, "All would be welcome. I would prefer that you and yours have survived the events in your realm. No matter what you need to accomplish in mine."

"Thank you for your hospitality," my mother said.

"Graciousness and mercy are traits we share, Queen. Be assured, the charge of your granddaughter's well-being and safety is taken in the most grave manner."

"Of course," she said in a relieved response.

Xantos spoke up again. "Catherine, have you discovered who the 'Judas' is? Your betrayer, as I think the reference is used?"

I felt my eyes rolling. Of course, he knew about that. Why would I think he didn't?

"Yes. The betrayer is my childhood friend from my mother's realm," I bitterly replied.

At my tone, Lenore's face became sad. Xantos began bouncing his leg to engage her.

"Ah. Perhaps you should send the demon of our mutual acquaintance after this person."

"Something I need to handle personally, thanks."

There was a pause before the dark elf said, "As you wish. Speak something cheerful to your child, Lady. My jostling her will only accomplish so much."

"I love you, Lenore. We will be together again, soon!" I offered.

As the image in the bowl faded, we all saw Lenore brighten once again.

Silence hung in the air.

The door opened, letting Jen into the room. "Mark suggested you might want to talk to Curt, now? Should I send him in? Or do you need more time?"

"Now would be fine, thank you."

## Chapter Twenty-Six

"You could send him after Cildur," Dad said quietly as we waited for Curt. "He could find him and retrieve the Staff faster than anyone else."

Apparently, everyone knew Mark's identity as an ifrit. A vengeance demon.

"But what if he uses the Staff against him?" I countered, meeting my father's gaze. "Even if he does succeed, he wouldn't be able to take the Staff without harm coming to himself or his family." Shaking my head, I added, "No. I can't ask him to go after Cildur."

No one had the chance to argue because Curt strode in, a stack of papers in his hand. The smile beneath his well-groomed mustache and beard wasn't as large as usual, but it was there. His dark eyes were serious yet shone.

There was no argument of his Viking heritage, between his coloring and his build.

"Hey, Cat. Jen said you wanted to see my maps," he said, moving around us to the table. He meticulously arranged the papers on the table until the pieces formed a map of the area.

The printouts showed Staunton, Waynesboro, and most of Augusta County up to the borders of the other counties. Some of the pages went further out before being cut off.

Those pages had small yellow dots on them. Just as the other pages had yellow dots on them in specific places. There were other colors on the pages, too.

Meticulous. Neat. And organized. I expected no less from him.

"Right. So. When all this started, I got with Chris and Lena, and we began keeping track of all the hell going on around here. Not just the weird stuff, either." He moved back until he could lean against the chairs. "The police, rescue, fire fighters… all emergency personnel come in. Even doctors and nurses. We've been keeping tabs on the uptick in fights, disorderly conducts, accidents. Anything out of the usual. Or, more than the usual."

Everyone, I realized, had gathered around the table, and subsequently, the map. One of the sheets had a legend. The yellow circles were the literal circles of influence where violence or fires had occurred. Green dots were places of intense chaos. Such as the kobolds, the chicken, the purple cow minotaur.

The dots followed roads.

The circles were scattered about, and I couldn't see the connection between them.

After a few minutes, Curt spoke again. "Anyone recognize the location of the yellow circles?"

He was all but bouncing on his feet.

We all looked at each other then to the map. There was a unanimous shaking of heads.

"I didn't think so," he replied, obviously trying to hide his excitement. "Those are the campgrounds. Those are the ones that people can rent year-round. A lot of people live there in those big campers. Some even have little buildings or what's basically 'tiny homes'."

"How do you know so much about the campgrounds?" I asked, trying to get my brain to wrap around everything he was telling us.

"I like my women a little on the trashy side," he replied, his cheeks turning pink.

Biting my lip to keep from laughing or teasing him, I turned my eyes back to the maps. "Right. So, what are you suggesting, Curt?"

"I think whoever it is has some sort of camper or something. He, or she, is traveling from one campground to the other. Not sure why, though,' Curt replied, nodding at the map.

"To keep the chaos from growing too strong and tipping off everyone," Sterling suggested. "He doesn't have the Staff in anything that will keep the chaos contained. Gods only know what he's been using it for."

"To bring the Veils down," I stated. Clenching my jaw, I kept my voice calm. Not that I felt calm. Quite the opposite.

"Do you know where the last place of chaos happened?" I asked Curt.

His excitement drained slightly. "The last thing was around Purple Cow Road." He paused, before adding with a shrug. "At least, that's the last thing we've heard about. Shift change isn't for a few more hours."

"You've been keeping up with all of this," Dad said thoughtfully. He tapped the map. "Do you have a pattern of travel?"

Curt's eyes grew large and round. Until we could see the whites all around his irises. "Oh. Yeah. Yeah, I think so!"

Leaning forward, he found a yellow circle near Purple Cow Road and the former minotaur. His finger trailed a path from the location in Waynesboro to Staunton.

"There are only two RV parks in Staunton with more on the west side of the county. One in Churchville, a couple in Mount Solon, and further to the west," Curtis stated, pointing to the circles as he spoke. "Not sure how much ya'll know about that side of the area, but it's pretty rural. Sure, there's subdivisions and little towns. Most of it, though? Is rural. Lots of farmland, forested areas. That kind of thing."

"Which means the chaos would have less chance to hit people as it would inside the city," Dad stated. "Makes sense. And even if it did, I doubt it would even have the same effect."

"Why is there only one circle in Staunton if there are two RV parks?" I asked, pointing to the general area of Staunton.

"One closes to vacationers during the winter months. Only long-term stays are allowed there during the winter," Curt explained. "The one you see with the circle? That one is open year-round for long or short stays."

"So, you think he would be at that one." Curt nodded. I sighed heavily. "Well, since we can't use a spell to locate him or the Staff, I guess we arm up and go after him."

"Do you think that is wise?" Mom asked. "What is to prevent him from using the Staff against you? Or whomever approaches with you?"

"Because he isn't aware we know it's him," I replied quietly. "We've spent time looking for the guilty party at hotels and inns. We never once thought about checking the campgrounds and RV parks."

Sterling wrapped an arm around my shoulders and pulled me towards him. I went willingly, leaning against him. He rubbed my upper arm before kissing the top of my head.

"Perhaps we could approach from multiple sides," Sterling suggested as he held me. "If we get close enough, we can approach from various sides of the camp. Should the Judas not be friendly towards us, we will have multiple avenues of attack."

"Even the Staff's magick cannot affect obsidian. No magick can affect that material," I stated. They may not be shields, but my scythes will at least allow protection of some degree."

Everyone nodded, but it didn't make me feel any better.

"Shall we all have one last drink before we go in search of the bastard?" I asked, turning to my friends, family, and allies.

There was another round of nods and murmurs of agreement.

"Thank you, Curt, for helping. I don't think we could have figured this out without you and the rest of your cohorts," I said. At Curt's blushing, beaming face, I couldn't help but share the smile. "It is greatly appreciated."

"No problem, Cat," Curt replied, still grinning ear-to-ear. "I'll go let Mark and Jen know you need a round of drinks in here."

"Be sure to bring them in and join us." At his puzzled expression, I explained. "You should be a part, since you helped us with the final piece of the puzzle."

"Yes, ma'am!" he exclaimed, before turning and striding to the door.

Looking around at the grim expressions on the faces in the room, I decided I wanted Cildur's head on a platter.

The question of the day was: would I get to have that desire fulfilled? Or did Cildur have something else planned to prevent it from happening?

Staff of Chaos

## Chapter Twenty-Seven

For once, Sterling didn't argue about opening portals in front of mundanes. Everyone agreed time was of the essence, so we broke the rules.

Not that the rules were doing anyone much good. Not where the Staff was concerned. We needed to find a way to reverse the damage done if we wanted to continue in peace with the mundanes. Otherwise, every fictional portrayal of catastrophic results that could happen when the magickal and mundane face each other could come true.

Except I suspected it would end up with more bloodshed. Possibly with even more deaths than what occurred during the witch hunts of centuries past. And those days were bad enough.

Or maybe it would be more peaceful. One never knew how mundanes would react to knowing the 'monsters' of myth and legend were your neighbors, teachers, and the person who saved your ass when shit hit the fan.

My parents, the dark paladins, and personal guards chose to join in the excursion. Jade accompanied me and Sterling, since she and I were once Cildur's friends. Despite the fact my mother came, she promised to relinquish punishment to me and Sterling. Mostly me, though.

Not because I was her heir or the Speaker of the Council, but because he'd betrayed me.

This was personal, and there wasn't a single being among the magickal community who didn't understand what that meant.

When Sterling, Jade, and I stepped through our magickal gateway at the front of the park, we heard yelling and shouting coming from all sides. The three of us stopped and looked around, taking in the scene.

On every side of us people were arguing. Some were starting to square off to throw punches while more were up in each other's faces yelling.

"This is bad," I said, probably winning the understatement of the year.

Closing my eyes, I drew a deep breath and reached for my talisman. If we didn't stop this, more people were going to die. The taste of chaos was all around us.

I felt a hand on mine, and I opened my eyes to find Sterling staring at me, his eyes glittering.

"I'll take this one," he said quietly. "Conserve your power for Cildur."

Giving him a nod, I kept my hand on my talisman. The demon was pacing, his wings curled over his shoulders. I stroked the talisman. Not just in an attempt to comfort my captured companion, but also because the movement was one of old and brought me comfort.

Sterling moved a few steps away and held his hands slightly apart, pulling energy into a tight ball between his palms. His lips moved as he whispered words in a harsh tongue. His hands moved apart as the ball of energy grew until it encompassed his entire chest.

With a word, he flung his hands out, allowing the energy to explode around us.

People jerked as though they were puppets on strings. Shock swept across their faces before they collapsed to the ground, their eyes closed and faces slack. They almost looked peaceful.

"For now, they will sleep. With luck, they will awake and not begin fighting again," Sterling stated. "Let's find the bastard that did this."

Jade and I exchanged grim expressions. We followed Sterling into the campground. Knowing the specific taste the Staff gave off, I was able to follow it much like a hound followed the scent of a fox.

We started finding evidence of the power the Staff gave off within ten yards of leaving the entrance. Small creatures, such as squirrels and birds, littered the ground. Their eyes glazed over in death. When we noticed the first human body, I held my hand up. From a pocket, I pulled a crystal.

Scrying my parents, guards, and dark paladins, I said, "Stay on the edge of the campground. Secure the area.

Dad, I need you to call Raziel. He's going to need a large crew."

"*Mekkăm bigĭch*," Mother's voice snarled. "Kill that *bigaj imboch*."

I heard my father clear his throat and Sterling was looking down, a smirk on his face.

"That's the plan, Mom," I said, trying to figure out when I'd heard my mother swear like that before.

My mother was a lady. A woman who wore the title of queen as a badge of honor and duty. She never swore! She must be really pissed at Cildur. Either that, or the chaos was starting to affect her, too.

"I'll get on it, Cat. Be careful," Dad said.

"We will secure the perimeter with the assistance of the paladins," Zarkull stated and there was an affirmative from the other guards.

"I'll be in contact," I said, before ending the communication. The words "I hope" hung in the air around all of us.

The three of us continued forward towards the RV. More bodies could be seen, and I could hear the crying of young children. There were some voices, so at least not everyone was dead or crazy. Which left me a little hope.

Death didn't bother me. I'd lived through plagues and wars. I've seen battlefields littered with dead bodies. But the crying of children? Yeah, that bothered me. It bothered my companions, too, because they kept looking towards the sounds.

"This is it," I said, nodding towards the RV parked at the very back of the campground. It was white with black swishy stripes on it. It had Aspen Trail painted on the side. White against the black flourishes. There was a Ford pickup attached to the pull-along camper.

"Doesn't look like anyone's home," Jade commented as we drew closer to the camper.

Shaking my head, I tried the passenger door to the truck. It opened without any alarms going off. Picking up a stack of laminated tags, I flipped through them.

"He's definitely been to the campgrounds," I stated, holding the tags up for the others to see. "They're all for this year."

"Shall we check the camper?" Sterling asked as he gestured towards the camper door.

I gave a nod as I drew my scythes. One black obsidian weapon in each hand, I crossed them in front of me, to better shield myself from an attack. Sterling opened the door and I braced myself.

But no attack came.

What did come was a wave of chaos that billowed out and around me. What touched the blades dissipated into nothing.

Cautiously, I stepped up into the camper. It wasn't very big. Certainly not a luxury item that I knew he could have afforded. In fact, most of the campers we'd seen in this park were the larger types, close to the size of a smaller single-wide mobile home.

This one was small with a single large bed directly to the right once you entered the camper. Directly across from the door was a dinette area. The table and benches were attached to the floor. They reminded me of something you'd find in a diner. The cushions to the benches were black and the tabletop looked like black and white marble.

To the left was a single small sink and equally tiny stove. I could also see a pantry and two other doors at the end of the narrow hallway.

Despite the camper being small and no luxury item, compared to other campers and Cildur's estate in my mother's realm, the bed had silk sheets and a plush comforter.

Everything was neat and clean. In fact, the camper looked as though it had just come off the showroom floor, despite the aged designs and styles used to decorate it. I was no expert on the things, but even I could tell it was an older model.

When I didn't hear or see anyone, I sheathed the scythes and called down to Sterling and Jade, giving an all clear.

Jade beat Sterling into the camper. She brushed by me to check out the other areas.

"Definitely Cildur," she called after looking into the room at the end of the hall and to the right. She held up some of his clothes. "These are from your mom's realm, and they have his initials embroidered on the neckline."

"He's not here and we have no clue where he went," Sterling said as he turned to me. "Cildur is from your realm, Catherine. You know his name."

Nodding, I met my lover's gaze evenly before turning to Jade. "You know what I need."

Jade nodded. She checked the rest of the room before opening the other door. Bending down, she reached for something. When she rose, she had a fiendish grin on her face.

"He's not bald," she stated, her hand outstretched.

Laughing, I accepted the strands of hair from her. "Good thing, huh?"

"Indeed, Lady," she replied, folding the robes meticulously.

Just like old times, I couldn't help but think. Jade was helping to prepare for my spellcraft. Except this time, it was for something far more dangerous and important than fighting over land. Well, it had never just been about land.

The battles and spellcraft had been about people's lives. Instead of a country this time, it was a world. Multiple worlds, to be exact.

Nothing like a little pressure for encouragement, right?

Jade placed the folded garment on the table. I placed the hair atop the clothes. Sterling and Jade moved back until we formed something resembling a triangle with myself as the main point.

"Cildur Laedragryl. *Qa sawmapi meku*," I commanded.

For a second, nothing happened in the chaos energy-filled camper. Then, the hair began smoldering. Smoke drifted up into the air above the folded robes before taking the rough form of a sphere.

I had no clue what Sterling saw in the sphere, but I recognized the images flashing within it. Without looking at Jade, I asked, "Recognize it?"

"Yep," Jade replied. "Not that far from here, either."

Sterling cleared his throat, and we looked at him.

"He's at the waterfall," I explained.

Sterling's eyes widened.

"Let's hope we can get there before he uses it," Sterling stated.

"Agreed." I turned to Jade. "Do you think you can handle the area a little longer?" She thought for a moment before nodding slowly. I continued. "Good. Recon. Locate the babies and get them out if you can. Worst case scenario, use Maekyl."

"Are you certain, my Lady?" Jade asked, eyes wide.

"You'll need him. We will be in Xantos' realm, and you have to admit, he and Trix are probably the most powerful and knowledgeable right now."

Jade had a doubtful look on her face, but she still nodded. "Good luck. Both of you."

We gave a nod and Sterling took my hand.

The last thing I saw before we vanished from the camper was my friend's grim expression.

Gods be with all of them, I thought as Sterling teleported us to the waterfall just past the motor mile in Staunton.

The waterfall had been an open secret for a long time. Then, someone decided to take some photos and share the location with the local television station. Suddenly, it became a popular gathering place for everyone. Far too many people who didn't know what it meant to not leave their mark behind visited the location. They left their trash everywhere. There were carvings on the trees, as well as spray paint.

Since it was technically owned by someone in New York, the locales didn't care if they trespassed or not. Those within the magickal community despised the mundanes for trashing a place with strong leyline ties.

Maybe with the Veils down, someone could do something about it. Though, I probably shouldn't wish such things on the very population I was trying to help. But I hated assholes who destroyed nature simply because they thought it was their right as an air breather.

# Chapter Twenty-Eight

To get to the waterfall in Staunton, one would park at a little pull off beside the road. You would have to climb up a bank that's just shy of being a ninety-degree angle, then walk along what was basically a deer path. Barely wide enough for a person, there was a bank going up a hill on one side and a sharp drop off on the other side. Trees and brush lined the edges.

After you managed to pull yourself up the sharp angled bank, and continued a few hundred feet, there was another steep climb down. At least you had a few foot-wide barely-there steps made of tree branches and hardened red clay mud. Unless you came when it was wet, then you had squishy red clay mud. From that climb, the path continued to the waterfall and small creek that ran through the area.

The waterfall was short enough that you could jump off and not kill yourself, especially since there was a pretty deep basin at the bottom. The rest of the creek was barely two feet deep. If that. Along the far side was a bank, with algae and vine-covered rocks, near the waterfall itself. Behind the waterfall was a tiny cave and the rocks on the far side formed large platforms you could climb, if you were nimble and daring enough to try it.

Beautiful. Serene. A place of power and energy.

And the home of a now-dead water elemental.

There was no mistaking the familiar tang of death in the air. Sweet and rich, yet at the same time, cold and sharp.

Sterling had teleported us to the clearing near the basin of the waterfall. Probably in the hopes of being able to stop Cildur from doing anything really stupid. But it was obvious we were too late.

Every life form has a distinct taste and texture. Humans, fae, werewolves, vampires, even elementals. Everything is unique from plants to intelligent creatures. If it could be counted as "alive" in any way, shape, or form, the death left a unique taste. Or, maybe it was because I'd been taught to tell the differences as part of my necromancy studies.

I was pretty certain Sterling also knew there was no stopping what was happening, but maybe I was wrong. I hoped I was wrong.

Jumping down to the main path, I slid to a stop on the smooth rocks that led to the edge of the pool at the bottom of the waterfall. At the top of the waterfall, in the middle of the water, stood Cildur.

He wore a crazed grin, and his eyes were wide and blood shot. The fact I could tell they were bloodshot was more than a little disconcerting.

Smoldering wood, burnt ozone, and brimstone filled the air, making it thick and heavy. The water flowing around the fae, over the rocks, and past us boiled and churned. Dead fish lay upon the top, along with any other creature that once called the water home. The mud near the water had dried and was cracking. Even the rock beneath my feet was hot enough I could feel it through the soles of my shoes.

"Cildur!" I cried out. "What have you done?"

"You're too late, Catherine! You and Myrddin are too late! The spell has already begun! There is no turning back, now!" he shouted down to us. He held the Staff of Chaos up for us to see. "Now you will understand what it's like to be powerless!"

I'd never seen the Staff of Chaos before, only in photos or sketches. Drawings and paintings. The real thing was far more impressive.

Even from where we stood, I could see the fissures from lightning running the length of the wood. The shining golden-brown hue had blackened areas that only enhanced the beauty of the staff that held amethyst gems. They were not tumbled and smooth, but rather left in their raw form. Though I had to admit, they did appear smooth. And they were glittering and shining with purple and white light.

A beautiful and deadly weapon in the hands of a crazed maniac. Because, of course, it was always a crazed maniac.

"If we kill him now, will it end the spell?" Sterling asked me quietly.

My demon shrieked, unfurling his wings as he stood seemingly uncertain as to what to do. He kept shaking his head, his hands in fists. Every muscle in his body tense.

"No," I said slowly, taking my cue from my captured demon. "If we kill him now, I think we would take his place."

The demon nodded his head before kneeling, his head bowed.

Shit. It's never good when any demon does that, let alone one who still felt as though he were in charge of his little prison.

"Damn it." Sterling sighed. "So much for that idea."

"Tell me about it," I muttered before turning to Cildur. "What do you mean 'powerless'? You've never been without power!"

It was difficult to not keep staring at the Staff and the power pouring forth from the crystals. No one mentioned the damned thing had what was basically a type of quartz crystals embedded into it. Would've been nice to know what was powering the thing.

Cildur threw his head back and laughed for several moments before looking back at us. "You idiot. You don't know what it's like to be a man in a world run by women. You were born with strong magick to powerful parents. You don't know what it's like to have to scrape and claw your way up to a position of any power! It's always been handed to you!"

Okay, so he wasn't wrong. I glanced at Sterling and shrugged slightly. It wasn't like I could argue that point.

"It isn't like I was born knowing everything, Cildur. You grew up with me. You had more freedom to do things I was never allowed," I countered.

"You were protected, yes, but have you ever once thought about those beneath you?" he argued. "Even when you came to this realm, you were always worried about protecting your equals!"

"Okay, that's nowhere near the truth," I countered hotly. "I cared for every single person I ruled over. I ensured none went hungry; be they peasant, servant, or noble. I ensured the fields were fertile, the water clean. Harvests were always plentiful because I cared about those less powerful than me. From the weak and defenseless to the armies. How do you think I ended up with people begging me to rule them? They wanted the protection and prosperity I provided my subjects!"

"And yet you've never once been one of those! When you 'need' protection, you bat your pretty eyes and the volunteers come running! You couldn't even choose a fellow fae! You had to choose Merlin!"

"Is that what this is all about? Petty jealousy?" I demanded, with disgust in every word. "Jealous that I was born a woman? That I chose Sterling as my lover?"

"What was the Deal you made with Maxine?" Sterling asked, finally speaking up.

"So, the mighty 'consigliere' finally speaks!" Cildur cackled. "Maxine and I shared similar opinions about our stations in life. She hated all the foolish rules demons were forced to follow. Yet that whelp, Dante, was able to do as he wanted. An outcast demon was able to do more than those who were still welcomed and part of Hell. He was even able to make Deals through that pathetic waste, Kevin. She wanted to see all of them fall. To see their world crumble down around them, just as hers did around her!"

"Who killed Sophie?" I demanded to know. Might as well get all the answers we could while we were able.

"I killed that tart in the hopes of throwing all of you off," Cildur replied proudly. "I planted Dante's knife, hoping that stupid angel would fall for it. But you had to come and ruin it all!"

The air around us was growing thicker and heavier, even as I saw energy pulsing around us. Static electricity crackled and popped. My hair was swaying on an unseen wind, growing frizzier with every passing moment. Even Sterling's hair was starting to stand on end from all the electricity and power growing around us.

It really sucked when everything made sense.

"You made a Deal with Maxine. She got the Staff, and you would use it to strip away the Veils," Sterling stated, his hands clenched into fists at his sides. "Killing Sophie and planting the knife in an attempt to frame Dante was icing on the proverbial cake."

"Yes! That's exactly what I did!" Cildur shouted exuberantly. "I agreed to use the Staff and when the Veils had thinned enough, I'd use the Staff to bring them down. Then everyone would realize how powerless they truly are!"

"But why kill Sophie? Was she just an innocent bystander in all this?" I asked.

Cildur sneered. "She threatened to tell Robin what Maxine did. She gave that idiot the wand I'd charged for her. She was supposed to be an ally. Instead, she got greedy. When I refused to give her another, she threatened to tell Crocell. So, instead of allowing that to happen, I killed her with the Staff."

Staff of Chaos

For someone who had once been one of the brightest fae I knew, he was turning out to be a complete and utter idiot.

"You're willing to die just so you can tear the Veils down. Putting everyone you love in danger. Including your parents," I stated simply. "Did Maxine tell you the Staff will consume you once the spell peaks?"

The stunned expression on his face said everything. Apparently, Maxine hadn't told him everything. Sly to the very end, it seemed.

"What?" he asked.

"The apex is near, and the Staff will demand a sacrifice," I replied. "The sacrifice of the user."

Cildur held the glowing staff in front of him, his eyes staring at the pulsing amethysts. He turned his head to look at Sterling and me.

"My parents care nothing about me," he said in a frighteningly calm voice. "My cousin just gave birth to a daughter. I heard my parents discussing who will get the duchy. After all the years I put into running the lands, that is the thanks I get! No better than the humans." He spat over the waterfall in disgust. "Let them pay. Let them all pay. I shall not be here to witness the downfall of all those who could have once been great!"

Holding the Staff of Chaos above his head, he closed his eyes. As light flared out from the crystals, I turned my face to the side, covering my eyes and talisman as I did so. Once the light faded, I looked back to the top of the waterfall.

The only thing I saw was steam coming off the water. Two seconds later, the last vestiges of the Veils vanished. It felt as though I'd been hit by a Grand Piano. I couldn't stop myself from collapsing to a knee, much like a man proposing to his beloved. Sterling staggered until he was leaning against a tree trunk.

"Oh, that hurt," I grumbled. "If he weren't already dead, I'd want to kill him." I paused before asking, "I wonder if we could summon his ghost and kill it, instead?"

Sterling chuckled a little before groaning. "If only. The Staff absorbed him completely, soul and all. So, no ghost to kill." He gave me a tiny smile. "Though I don't think I'd argue had it been a possibility."

Slowly picking myself up, I looked up to where my former childhood friend had stood. "You okay? We need to go fetch the Staff."

Pushing away from the tree, Sterling crossed to me, reminding me of someone whose every bone was aching. Not that I could say anything, I felt that way myself.

"Let's go. We can hold each other up," he joked.

Laughing a little, I wrapped an arm around his waist and together we trudged up the hill. The Staff lay beneath the flowing water where it had fallen. Despite the steam rising, the water was surprisingly frigid as I stepped into it to retrieve the Staff.

Picking it up, I wanted to vomit from the taste of power still wafting from it. It was worse than boiling a demon's blood for spellcraft. And believe me, that was bad enough. Boiling demon's blood was something akin to cooking three-week-old rotting meat.

Sterling held out my bigger-on-the-inside bag and I dropped the Staff into it, thankful to not be holding it anymore. I slid the strap of the bag around my wrist, thankful it weighed barely more than an empty gift bag.

"What now? Everyone with even a slight propensity for magick felt the Veils vanish," I said, no longer certain of anything. "How long do you think it'll be before our realm starts being invaded?"

"Maybe a few hours, if we're lucky," he replied. His jaw clenched briefly. "Jade and Maekyl have their standing orders, as do your parents, guards, and the dark paladins. There's only one place we can go to restore the Veils."

"Despite what everyone may think, there is no way I can do that even with my talisman. It's not enough power," I replied quietly.

"I know," he said.

From a pocket he pulled a necklace I'd seen and held for a brief time. The Eye of Amon hung from a chain.

He slid the necklace over my head, tucking the amulet beneath my blouse, then beneath my talisman.

"You now have three artifacts within your possession," he said, lifting my chin tenderly. "Within Xantos' realm, your power is strongest. We will go there, find the spell needed to restore the Veils, reclaim our daughter… and do it together."

"We don't have time to regroup or prepare within this realm," I replied, meeting his gaze.

Sterling frowned. "Do you believe Xantos would arm and armor us?"

"If you behave, yes," I replied evenly. "If for no other reason than to have us in his debt."

At that, Sterling laughed and nodded. I could feel him pulling on the magick that flowed within the ley lines around us. With a slight gesture, a portal opened before us.

On the opposite side I could see a very familiar elegant office. And I could sense the presence of the ancient docelfar whom I knew well.

Leading the way through the portal, I knew we were entering his estate unannounced. I hoped he wouldn't be too grumpy about it.

Staff of Chaos

# Chapter Twenty-Nine

Xantos' office was luxurious and nothing short of enormous. Soft, thick carpet covered the floor, silencing our steps. Paintings of elves lined one wall. Bookshelves lined the other. The walls were not stone, as one would expect in a medieval-style society, but a dark rich wood. Between the paintings and bookshelves were weapons of all types. Swords, daggers, double-bladed axes, even crossed halberds filled the spaces.

I was torn between duty and rushing across the room to the elaborately carved bassinet positioned beside the desk that would put the most expensive executive desk to shame. Tearing my eyes away from my daughter and the ancient elf who held her, I turned towards the mirror filling the wall directly opposite the pair.

The influx of power wrapped around me like a lover's embrace, which for once did not have me contemplating all sorts of debaucherous things. Drawing a deep breath, I let it out slowly.

Speaking the words to scry to my realm, I contacted the two people I knew Xantos would complain about the least: Mark and Jen.

The reflective surface of the mirror rippled. Almost as though someone were dropping pebbles into a puddle every three seconds. Or, as though it were keeping time with the ring of a phone.

Within two minutes, Mark and Jen stood before a mirror. Jen wore an expression of pure confusion, which quickly became one of amusement.

"You look like a Disney fairy," she said between giggles.

I held a hand up and shook it. Sparkles of actual magick fell to the floor, most of it vanishing before it hit the carpet. Shrugging, I couldn't help but grin.

"Yeah, but I still can't fly," I joked. Jen laughed even more.

"The Veils are gone," Sterling interjected, bringing an end to the laughter. "We were too late to stop Cildur."

"We know," Mark replied, his eyes on me. "Raziel is doing cleanup at that campground. Your mother returned to her realm to prepare. Your father is currently here, but he said he may cross over to her realm, should it be needed. Everyone else is preparing for Hell on Earth."

"Vengeance is yours to have," I said formally.

As I spoke the words, Mark's lips split into a wide smile that could only be described as evil. His eyes gleamed as wings sprang into view and unfurled. He grew taller, while smoke billowed around him.

Without shifting my gaze from the dark slits that could not be called eyes, I continued. "The demon

Maxine Olson is who planned all of this. Cildur made a Deal with her. She killed Kevin Daniels and gave the Staff to Cildur. He was the Judas, but she was the whispering in his ear."

"Finally." Mark all but breathed.

The large demonic form became the dark viscus smoke that had been rising around him. That smoke flew up the large vent in the ceiling and was gone.

"Happy hunting, lover." Jen sighed. The gleam in her eyes suggested there would be a very warm welcome for him when he returned. She turned back to us. "Anything else we should know?"

"We, Sterling and I, will work on restoring the Veils from this realm," I said. "We'll keep in contact as much as possible."

"I'll spread the word. Safe journeys, Lady," Jen said before the mirror rippled and shifted back to reflecting the room and its occupants.

From the reflection, I met Xantos' gaze and held it. Though his expression was bland, I couldn't miss the gleam in his eyes.

The docelfar had been expecting us, which meant he'd been watching.

I turned around to face him. "We need your help." I paused before adding, "I'm afraid you may need to watch Lenore for a while longer."

Staff of Chaos


To Be Continued in Book Four of the Lady of Death:
Tome of Evocation